After years of thinking he was dead, Adele, a Native American Witch, opened the door to her long-lost best friend, Jake. She gazed into his eyes and saw that the boy she had fallen in love with over a decade ago had grown into a handsome man. She wanted to wrap her arms around him and tell him she'd never stopped thinking about him, but the pain in her heart stopped her. He'd abandoned her when her dad was brutally murdered in front of them, and for years she'd looked for him, but it was like he had just disappeared.

Now, after all these years, he's back. Why?

Jake, a Lycan, knocked on the door to the old cabin, looking for the girl he fell in love with so long ago. He wanted to see her one last time before he disappeared again for good.

Victor, an evil Witch, is lurking in the darkness, waiting for the right time to take back what he believed was rightfully his. *Power.*

Adele must learn to control the magic inside her and embrace the powerful Witch she was born to be, fighting back against Victor before he kills the only man she ever loved.

Adele Wolf
Copyright © 2023 Jennifer D Torseth
ISBN: 978-1-4874-3658-2
Cover art by Martine Jardin

Published by eXtasy Books Inc

Look for us online at:
www.eXtasybooks.com

ADELE WOLF

BY

JENNIFER D TORSETH

DEDICATION

With love and gratitude to my husband, daughters, and grandpa. Without their support, I would never have gotten the chance to fulfill my dream.

PROLOGUE

A late-night visitor rattled against our old oak door. Dad's muffled voice boomed through my walls, waking me from my nightly slumber. I tiptoed out of bed and went to Jake's door, opening it. Jake and I shared the second floor of a little cabin just on the edge of the mountains in Littleton, New Hampshire.

Jake's head popped up. "What's going on?"

I shook my head. "I don't know. Someone's at the door."

I squatted down and crawled over to the banister, pushing my face through the railing. Moments later, Jake joined me, and our gazes met. A man was standing in the doorway with Dad. His body glowed a slight gray hue, radiating dark intentions. With my body shivering, my witch instincts tingled down the back of my head, alerting me that our uninvited guest wasn't human.

"Bill! The war is here. They're out there looking for you. They know you live in a log cabin. They know you have a daughter. They know everything."

"No!" My father's voice boomed through the house. The walls vibrated, and the house flexed inward towards him. His body ignited a vibrant glow of pearl, shards of electricity flowing through his limbs. Dad lifted the man with one arm and trudged to the door, hurling him out. The door slammed, and the house crackled, shifting slightly before settling back down to the ground. Dad's head shot up, and he glared at us with glowing red eyes. "Go to bed!"

I scrambled to my room and jumped into bed. Restlessly, I

1

tossed and turned as the late-night visitor's words haunted me. *Who do we have to worry about? Why did Dad throw him out of the house?* I cocooned myself with covers and closed my eyes.

The next day, I woke up to the sun blazing through my curtains. I shot up in bed and ran over to the window. "Dad's gone." I dressed and knocked on Jake's door. "Jake, get up. We're late for school." As I walked down the stairs, the house seemed quieter than usual. Sunshine peeked through the drawn curtains in the family room. I let the light in and looked out into the yard. It appeared to be an average day, but I knew it wasn't. My instincts alerted me that something was off. The calm before the storm.

Our schoolwork began every day at the kitchen table. I opened my math book and grabbed a pencil and paper. Jake's footsteps creaked along the hall above my head, and then the bathroom door slammed. I looked up to see him enter the kitchen a few minutes later. We nodded at each other, and I went back to my book. We didn't speak to each other all morning, and then around three, we both jumped when the phone rattled on the wall. Our gazes met, and I stumbled over anxiously to pick it up.

"Hello."

"I'm going to be late. Don't go outside. I have something important I need to do. Don't go outside!"

"Dad, what's going on?"

"Adele! What did I just say? Stay inside! Don't answer the door. I'll be home soon."

The dial tone hummed on the other end. I hung up the receiver and looked over at Jake. He stared at me, waiting for me to say something.

"He said to stay inside."

"Did he say why? Or what's going on?"

"No." I shook my head and sat back down at the table. I stared down at my book but couldn't focus on the page. I propped my elbows up on the table to rub my face, and acid burned in my stomach as chunks rose into my throat. Swallowing, I exhaled a deep breath. Dad had never yelled at me like that before. I knew then that my instincts were right. Something terrible was going to happen, and it would change everything. I dropped my hands on the table. Glancing up, I saw Jake's glowing golden chestnut eyes. I stared back at him and felt my lip quiver. Tears welled up, and I gently shook my head. His eyes softened, and he nodded slightly. He studied me for a long moment before he looked away.

The sunlight was slowly dimming through the kitchen window as we sat down to eat dinner without Dad. He was late. Very late. We finished eating, and Jake restlessly started pacing back and forth in the kitchen. I kept looking from Jake to the phone, expecting Dad to call any minute. The clock's second hand clicked through the silent kitchen like a heavy drum. My parched lips ground together as I tried to swallow.

I stood up and walked over to the sink to fill a glass of water. My mind raced with questions as I held my cup under the faucet. *Where's Dad? What's happening? He should've come home by now.* Before I realized what had happened, glass shattered on the floor, and water splashed my legs. A sudden wave of despair struck me like a bullet in the chest. I sensed the presence of someone with magical abilities standing just outside of our house.

"Something's wrong. I feel . . . I feel them. They're here."

Jake sniffed the air, grabbed his bo staff, and handed me mine. A loud thump against the side of the house sounded in the family room. Jake looked over at me, and his facial features began transforming. A loud crackle echoed through the kitchen as his bones enlarged, doubling in size. A low growl ruptured from his throat, and his nose elongated into a snout.

His shoulders and chest broadened as his legs took the shape of an ebony beast. His furry paw grabbed my arm, and we ran into the family room.

The oak door burst open and slammed against the window, sending shattered shards of glass everywhere. Frozen, I watched as hooded men dressed in all black crowded into my house. A sharp pain blasted in the middle of my back, knocking me down on all fours. Jake pulled up the hidden door in the floor and shoved me in first. A cloud of dust swooshed up into my face as I landed hard against the cold floor. The heavy door slammed down above us, and I looked up through the floor cracks. Water splattered over my face and ran down the back of my neck. Jake stood under the door, holding his bo staff.

My lips quivered when I felt him drawing near. *Dad's coming home.* Moisture dampened my face as the tears rolled down my cheeks. Jake stood up and pushed on the door. I scrambled over to him, gazing into his eyes, and shook my head.

A blinding white light gleamed into the room above us, flashing through the cracks. The walls and floors vibrated, quaking the whole house, and shattering the windows. All the men in our house collapsed to the floor in one loud crash. Blood oozed between the floorboards and dripped down over our bodies. The house settled down, and everything went silent.

My father's pain radiated through me, paralyzing my body as I dropped to the floor. My lips trembled. I opened my mouth but couldn't speak. The vibrant light dimmed, and his body hit the floor. I was released and looked up to see a figure lying above me. I shook my head and raised my hands to cover my mouth, but the screams escaped my lips, burning my insides. My skin glowed a pearl-white light for a brief moment.

Jake crawled over and pulled me close. My face vibrated off of his furry chest as I let the tears flow. I couldn't feel him anymore. I couldn't feel anything. It was over. Dad was gone.

Chapter One: Adele

"**D**o you really want to live all the way out here by your-self? We're still driving and haven't even made it to your house yet. Like, what if there was an emergency or something? No one would know. Seriously, Del, I'm worried about you," Molly said.

"I'll be fine." I stared out the window, watching all the trees and remembered all the drives I took when I was a kid with Dad. Nostalgia struck my heart with a strong beat as I realized I'd been away for too long. The town had changed and grown into a new-age city with a hint of vintage flavor. Tension knot-ted in my stomach as I drew closer to where my life had started and changed so abruptly thirteen years ago.

"Mom would roll over in her grave three times if she knew I was letting you move out here by yourself."

I turned to Molly. "I'll be fine. This was my home. I want to try it out. It's all I have left of Dad." I looked away as the tears welled up in my eyes. I didn't want Molly to see how much it hurt me. She would never let it go. "It's been so long since I've been out here to check on the place. I appreciate eve-rything you and your mom did for me, but this is where I want to be now."

I watched out the window and gazed into the mountains as they drew closer. The peaks were layered with a white blanket hugged by a thick cloud. The sun was peeking over the top, smiling its light over a vast forest.

"The cable company said they'll install a satellite, so I can have wi-fi out here. They'll be out next Monday. The electricity and water should be on already. I called in last week to hook everything up."

"Wow. A satellite, Del? Next thing you'll say is that we'll have an antenna in the house to watch television. Come on, Del. Really?"

"Molly." I turned to glare at her.

We turned down an ominous looking road that parted through thick trees soaring overhead. Sunlight glistened off the frosted two-story roof as we arrived at our destination. The cabin didn't look as big as I remembered. I sat in the car and stared before opening the door.

"Adele!"

"What?" I jumped and looked over at her.

"It's awful. It's falling apart! You can't live here. Heck, you can't even stay here overnight."

"It's fine. Calm down, crazy."

Molly glared at me for a moment and then turned away.

"I'm sorry. Thank you for coming here with me. I know it was a lot for you to miss work and stay with me tonight."

I sensed her anger ease as she turned to look at me. I held my arms out, and she scooted over and hugged my neck. Molly was a little high-strung, and when she didn't want something, she would say it repeatedly.

I walked to the back seat of my SUV and opened the door. "Hi, Buddy! We made it." My dog's tail knocked against the leather seats. Buddy was a large Pit Bull mixed breed I'd rescued from the shelter a couple of years ago. "That's a good boy. We made it to our new home." I unhooked his seatbelt from his harness and snapped on his leash. He jumped down and pulled me back and forth with hard jolts. "Hey. Sit down. Sit." Buddy sat down with his rump bouncing up and down in the dirt.

Molly was already up at the house, waving her hands back and forth. She squealed and jumped back from the front door as if something startled her.

"Okay, let's go, Bud." Buddy galloped, pulling with everything he had up to the front door.

I dug through my purse and accidentally dropped the keys on the ground. I reached down to pick them up, and the old wooden swing clanked against the house as the wind picked up. A memory of Jake and me arguing over who would sit on the swing popped into my mind. He would sit on me and squish me until I got up. Smirking, I stared for a moment.

"What's wrong?" Molly asked.

"Oh, it's nothing. Just old ghosts." Shaking my head, I put the key into the lock and turned. The deadbolt clicked, and the lock jolted open. I turned the knob slowly, and a cloud of dust dropped into the doorway as I pushed the door. An icy breeze nipped at my face, welcoming me into the family room. My boots pushed through piles of damp leaves and old newspapers in front of the door.

Molly shivered and pushed past Buddy and me. "Well, at least there's a fireplace."

My gaze ran along the walls and stopped at Dad's bedroom door. I walked over to it and put my hand on the knob. My eyes closed, and I could see Dad smiling at me from his bed, smoking his pipe.

"Yuck." A kitchen cabinet door slamming echoed through the house. "The kitchen is so seventies! Ugh! I hope you remodel this!"

I took a deep breath and pushed open the door. The room looked untouched, with the bed made and pillows tucked under the covers at the top. I walked over to the bed and ran my fingers across the old quilt.

Molly stomped in and stopped in front of me with her hand on her hip. "The laundry is a tiny little hallway before you go out the back door. Which is attached to the kitchen. This is a weird little house." She looked around the room, huffed, and wafted the air in front of her. "Adele! Where do you expect to write? Are you sure you can work here? I don't know, Del. Is this what you really want?"

"Yes, it'll be fine, and it's called a mudroom, doofus. The room or little hall where the laundry is."

I headed back to the family room when the picture next to Dad's bed caught my eye. Mom and Dad were standing in front of their apartment in New York, smiling at each other. Mom's belly was enormous with me, and Dad's hands were around her. I walked over and picked it up. Dad said he'd always hated living in the city, so they'd moved out to the country right before Mom had me. Mom died a few years later of cancer. Dad never remarried and would always say he'd had his great love, and that was enough for him. I smiled at the picture and turned around to look at Molly.

She frowned and shook her head at me.

I walked out of Dad's room, walked past the stairs, and headed into the kitchen. Molly was right. The house needed some serious updating. My once-white kitchen had matured into a mustard mess with layers of dust and mildew. The mudroom was in front of the back door with rows of Dad's old heavy coats still hanging up. I grabbed the big brown jacket he favored and hugged it, inhaling the remnants of to-bacco and sawdust.

Buddy tugged and jumped onto the back door, pressing his nose against the glass.

"Okay, pup. Come on, then."

The deck was still standing six feet off the ground. The forest wall was a couple hundred feet from the back door. I scanned the tree line until I spotted the path we'd used to enter the forest on warm days.

Dad would say *It's just a little walk* when he really meant a full-blown hike to the river two miles from our house. If he wanted, we would go another mile to the mountains. Dad liked to take us fishing, or sometimes we would just explore the forest. He took the time to teach us the differences between berries and other plants.

I was staring at the path's entrance when a twig snapped and echoed to my right. Buddy and I looked over and scanned the forest. He huffed, and a little whine came from deep in his throat. "I know, I heard that, too." Drops of melted snow drizzled from the tops of the oaks and pines. I turned to head back into the house and heard another twig snap, but this time it was right next to us. Buddy pulled me towards the forest, whimpering. "No, Buddy, we can't go in there." I stared at the forest wall and sensed someone's gaze looking back.

I stopped, closed my eyes, and reached out, using my senses. It had been a long time since I'd used my power, but I knew it was still there. I focused and opened my mind, looking for anyone or anything watching us.

A cool breeze whistled through the air and tickled the back of my neck, and I opened my eyes when I felt sharp pains radiating down my head and into my spine. I hadn't flexed the muscle I used for my power in a very long time. I knew it was going to take some getting used to again. Dad always told me to never stop using my power no matter what, but after I lost him, I just stopped. I stopped everything and felt numb and empty inside. *But I'm here now, and I'll get back to who I really am. Who I was meant to be.*

"Del! Someone's at the front door."

"Okay, I'm coming."

As soon as I entered the house, I heard a man's voice talking. The ridge on Buddy's back fluffed out as a deep growl rattled from his chest. He pulled me into the family room to see a man chatting with Molly.

"Well, hello, Adele," he said.

He put his hand out for me to shake, but Buddy barked at him.

"No! Sit down, Buddy!" Buddy sat down, but he didn't

take his focus off him. "Hello, do I know you, sir?"

"Well, you and your brother were kids back then. My name's Mason. Everyone calls me Mace. I live out that way." He pointed his finger back towards town. "I worked with your dad at the Mylar Mill. It went out of business a few years after you . . . well, after you left. I'm retired now." His gaze darted around the family room, as if he was searching for something. He slowly turned his head and looked back at me. "So, what are you doing? Are you moving back here?"

"Yeah, she's—"

"No, I'm just cleaning up the place to sell it. Yep, we're just staying a couple of days." I glared at Molly for a long moment before she turned back to Mace and smiled. "Well, it was very nice to meet you, and I'm sure we'll see you around town." I pointed to the door and handed Molly Buddy's leash.

He looked at me for a minute and then back at the door.

"Well, if you need anything, I'm not far away. Don't hesitate to ask." He grabbed my hand and squeezed.

Shuddering, I pulled back my hand and nodded as he exited the house. The darkness inside him sent chills down the back of my head. I knew he wasn't there by accident and that I would have to be careful.

"Um, what was that? He seemed nice."

"Molly, how did he know we were here? Bad people always seem nice when you don't know their real intentions."

"What?"

"It's just, he shouldn't have been here."

"You don't know if he's bad and has bad intentions. You always do that with people. You need to be more friendly. He was just coming to greet his new neighbor, Del, and you just shoved him out the door."

I stared at Molly and knew I couldn't explain why I knew some people were dangerous. I'd looked inside his heart and saw the evil he was capable of. It was just easier to smile and nod.

"We have a lot of work to do. Can you help me get the rest of the boxes out of the car?"

"Yeah."

CHAPTER TWO: ADELE

I retrieved Buddy's kennel from the SUV and put him in it while unloading the car. After all those years of being away, I'd only ended up with four boxes, two suitcases, and one carry-on bag with my stuff for work.

After bringing in everything, I headed to the kitchen and turned on the water. The pipes grunted and sprayed brown sludge water, so I left it running. Walking over to the old refrigerator, I opened the door. Cold air greeted me as I put up the remaining *Sprites* from my bag. The water started running clear, so I grabbed a bowl from the cabinet and filled it up for Buddy. He gulped down eagerly and then head-butted my leg and snorted. He pawed my foot, looked up at me, and ruffed.

"What? Are you hungry? It couldn't already be dinner time?" I looked at my watch and realized it was already four o'clock.

"I'm hungry!" Molly yelled from the other room.

A loud thud hit the floor from upstairs. I jumped, spun around, and looked up and then down at Buddy. He was looking up and cocking his head to the side. "What was that?"

"Molly? Are you okay?" I walked out of the kitchen and headed to the stairs when Molly ran into me.

"Ow! What are you doing?"

She was carrying my bag with my work stuff in it. My eyes darted up to the ceiling and then back at her. "I thought you were upstairs?"

"No, I was unpacking in the family room. You're going to

13

take over the master bedroom, right?"

I looked up at the ceiling and then back at her again. She flipped on the light, pulled out my computer, and set it up on the dining room table.

"I figured you wanted to work here until you got a desk. Right?"

I shook my head and stared at her. My heart pounded in my chest as I inhaled deep breaths. She slowly nodded and looked up at me.

"What?"

"I heard something upstairs, and I thought it was you."

Molly looked up at the ceiling and then at me, shaking her head. "I haven't been up there yet."

Buddy barked and took off, running towards the stairs.

"Shit!" I followed him and stopped at the bottom of the stairs. He disappeared into my room. "Buddy?"

Buddy ran out of my room with his nose to the floor until he came up to Jake's room. He snorted loudly, blowing air through his nostrils, and then stood up on his hind legs and pawed at the door. He dropped on all fours and dug at the floor in front of the door. I ran up the stairs and noticed lights flickering from underneath Jake's door. I reached for the knob.

"Wait!" Molly whispered.

I jumped back, holding my chest. "Don't do that!"

I reached for the knob and turned it. The door opened, and a cold breeze greeted us from the window. The curtains fluffed out, showing glimpses of a hole broken at the top of the window. I exhaled loudly and pushed the door open all the way. Damp leaves covered the bed and floor. A thin layer of dust mixed in with a stench of mildew polluted the room. The armoire that Dad had built for Jake was ajar, and all of Jake's clothes were missing. I looked around the room and noticed a footprint near the window. I cocked my head to the side and stared. It looked like the print was from someone who'd crawled in through the window from the outside. I leaned down and touched the footprint. The mud had dried out and crumbled on the carpet long ago.

"Well, I need to call the window guy and have him come back out here to repair that window."

"Yeah."

"I can put some boards up, for now, to keep the critters out." Buddy jumped up and ran his nose along with the window. He followed the scent to the bathroom and stopped in front of the tub. It was an old clawfoot tub that Dad had found and installed. Dad was a man of all trades and could build or repair anything.

Buddy followed me out of the bathroom and into my old room. Everything looked the same, except for the layer of dust covering my furniture. The handmade quilt Dad bought for me was still covering my bed. My armoire was closed, and my dresser was untouched. I walked over to the window and looked down into the yard. The sun was going to bed for the night fast.

"Molly, let's go to the store before it gets too late."

Buddy had sniffed his way out of my old room and left me alone. I turned around to see another bare footprint. It was right in front of my armoire. I walked over and pulled the door open quickly. I jumped back and almost fell on my rump. My reflection greeted me as I swung open the door. Panting, I stared at my reflection, holding my chest. My long black hair had clumps hanging out of a rushed, messy bun. Dirt and cobwebs covered my t-shirt, and my tennis shoes had remnants of dried, moldy leaves. My height had altered a few inches, and my body had developed into that of a muscular Native American woman. Shaking my head, I closed the armoire and left my room. I walked over to Jake's door and closed it before going downstairs.

"Molly! Where are you?"

"What! I'm down here."

I ran down the stairs and looked for her. She was in the dining room finishing my computer setup. "Let's go to town and get some groceries and a pizza."

"Okay."

I put Buddy in his kennel, and we left for the store. Molly was quiet until we got back onto the road.

She finally turned to look at me. "Why didn't you tell me you had a brother? You cried for weeks about your dad, but you never mentioned a brother."

"Well, Jake wasn't actually my brother. My dad adopted him when his dad died, and he only lived with us for a few years before everything happened."

"Jake?"

"Yeah."

"I remember when you were in college, and Mom and I were visiting you. You had some paperwork on your desk about a guy named Jake. Is that the same Jake?"

I looked over at her and knew she'd been snooping in my things. I thought about snapping at her but knew we would have gotten into a huge fight if I had. Molly had always been nosey and rummaged through my things when I wasn't around or she thought she would get away with it.

"I just . . . I guess I don't understand how you can live in that house after your dad died there. It's kind of creepy."

I didn't answer and drove into town. I knew she wouldn't understand what I had to say. She'd never understand that Dad's old house was the only thing I had left of him. Even though he was gone, his memory was still very much alive.

We went to the grocery store, and I filled up the cart with everything I could think of so I didn't have to go back there for a while. When we walked out of the store, it was already dark outside. I opened the back, put the bags in, and hurried to jump in the car. Molly walked around the car and silently ignored me.

"What is it? If you have something to say, then just say it."

Molly exhaled a deep breath. "Why do you do that? You don't tell me the truth about things? For years, you never told me you basically had a brother. I don't understand that. I thought we were sisters?"

I shook my head, my mouth dropping open. I didn't know what to say to her. I knew I could never tell her the truth about everything. I could never tell her we were different and that my father's murder wasn't an accident. Something from his past killed him, and I had come back to find some answers. Deep down, I was there to find Jake, too.

"I'm sorry, Molly. It just hurts me to talk about it. Sometimes, I miss them both" — I swallowed hard. "I love you very much. I'm just not very good at showing it." I scooted over and hugged her. She didn't respond at first, and then she turned and opened her arms and hugged me back. She wiped her face and sniffed.

"Well, did you ever find him?"

I scooted back over to my side and turned on the car. "No. I don't know what happened to him after that night. I remember the police coming into the house and riding to the station with them, but I don't remember seeing him after that." I quickly changed the subject. "I'm hungry, and I saw a pizza shop around the corner. Let's go get something to eat, and I bought your favorite beer."

"Okay," she said.

The dark roads home winded around mountains, hugging the rock as the fog settled over the road. I crawled around the curve, blinded to oncoming traffic, and looked up to see the full moon ducking behind rows of snow clouds racing across the night sky. After a few more miles, I turned, and my lights illuminated the murky path leading to my cabin. The cabin was hauntingly dark, with a hue of caliginous light glistening through the fog.

I parked with my headlights shining and ran to unlock the door. I reached for the outside light switch and flipped it on. The light remained dark, so I walked over and saw the bulb had been removed.

Buddy pounded against his kennel, demanding to be let out. Howling, he dug at the plastic flooring. "I know, Buddy, it's okay. I'm coming."

Tingling crawled down my head as I rushed back out to the car. I felt someone or something lingering in the darkness. Molly looked up at me with frightened eyes in passing. Even though Molly was human, she felt it, too. I picked up my speed and jogged as I carried the last bags in. We unloaded the groceries, and I went to retrieve Buddy from his kennel.

"Oh, poor sweet puppy. Come on then."

He circled around me until I filled his food bowl and put it on the floor in the kitchen. He finished his food and followed me around until I took him outside to do his business.

"Come on, pup." I walked Buddy quickly around the back-yard. The wind picked up and blew the trees back and forth violently in the forest. Buddy nervously circled around several times and finally did his business. "Okay, come on." We jogged back inside, and I locked the door behind us. I kicked off my boots and dropped Buddy's leash and harness by the front door.

I took the pizza box, grabbed two beers, and walked into the family room. Molly was trying to light a fire in the fire-place when I walked in. She dropped match after match into the newspaper clippings with no luck. "Here, let me try." I motioned to sit down on the floor next to her. I turned the flue to open the chimney, grabbed the matches, and hovered over the newspaper with the lit match. The paper slowly caught fire and ignited.

Molly stood up, grabbed a beer, popped the lid open, and gulped a big swig. I lit another match, put the flame on the other side of the paper, and waited for it to ignite. I motioned for Molly to put the wood pieces into the fireplace. The wood slowly ignited, and I leaned in to blow.

Molly walked over and plopped down on the couch. I followed and opened my beer, drinking two big gulps before pulling out a piece of pizza. We both sat in silence, staring into the flames fluttering over the charred wood.

"What happened with Tommy? I thought you were in love and going to get married and all that jazz?" She turned up the beer bottle, and a loud hiccup popped out when she lowered it.

"Well, he wanted to live in the city, get married, have kids, and I said I wanted to be a writer and move back here to live in this house and write my novel." I turned up my beer and gulped the last bit.

"Well, that wouldn't have been so bad. He was really handsome and funny and good-looking."

"Oh, really now." We both looked at each other and laughed out loud.

Once we stopped laughing, she turned and looked at me seriously. "I thought you were going to marry him, really."

I took a deep breath and exhaled. "I realized I didn't love him, and we wanted different lives."

"Too bad, cause his bod is delicious."

"Yeah, but he was terrible in bed." We both looked at each other and busted out laughing again. Molly rolled back and forth, gasping for air. The laughter finally stopped, and I turned to Molly. "I'm exhausted. Let's go to bed."

"Where am I going to sleep?"

"With me, goofy. Come on."

"Okay."

I put the pizza in the fridge, box and all, and double-checked the lock on the backdoor. Then I headed back up front and checked the front door. Buddy followed me through the house and sniffed everything as we walked. I went into the master bedroom, undressed, and put my pajamas on. Molly was already under the covers and rolled over onto her side. I dug in my bag, pulled out my charger, and plugged in my phone. I pulled back the covers, pushed my feet in, and patted the bed for Buddy to get in.

"Good night." I rolled over onto my side, turned out the lamp, and closed my eyes.

"Del?"

"Yeah."

"Do you think about Jake? The guy you grew up with?"

I didn't know if I wanted to answer that. I inhaled a deep breath and exhaled loudly. My body slowly recovered from the booze high, and I could think straight again. I opened my mouth to answer and closed it.

Molly stirred in the bed and turned to face my back. "Do you think he thinks about you, too?"

"I don't know."

"What would you do if you saw him again?"

"I don't know."

"I bet he still thinks about you, too." Molly's voice grew softer as she yawned.

"Yeah."

"Love you, Del."

"Love you, too, Molly."

"Molly."

"Yes."

"I think about him."

"Yeah, I know."

"Night, Del."

"Night."

CHAPTER THREE: ADELE

The wind whistled outside, wailing in the darkness as its force shifted back and forth. My eyes flew open, and I shot up deliriously, looking around to see I was sleeping in my old room. A glimpse of moonlight peeked through the crack of my curtains. I crawled out of bed and reached for the doorknob. A blast of ice sent sharp pains down my forearm. Flinching, I quickly turned the knob and looked out into the hallway. Steam exhaled from my lips as I stepped into the darkness.

Jake's bedroom door looked miles away and was closed. My vision tunneled and steadily moved up and down like a funhouse at the carnival. I stumbled towards the banister and gripped the railing as I slowly walked down the stairs. The old steps creaked with my weight as I went down, step after step. Lights flickered outside and flashed shadows up and down my family room walls.

I passed the front door, through the dining room, and went into the kitchen. I walked over to the sink and filled a glass of water. Cool water ran down my mouth and covered the rim of my nightshirt. I wiped my mouth and looked up to see streaks of lightning flashing through the darkness. I peered out of the curtain and waited for the lightning to strike again. A rumble from deep in the earth rolled up and boomed off in the distance. Then the lights flashed a bolt of electricity off of the horizon. A loud ping struck the window and splintered a long crack across the window. The wind had picked up, carrying a limb, and hit the window.

"Shit!" Panting, I held my chest. My finger ran along the fine crack. "Great."

I turned around and headed back to bed when a loud rap knocked against the backdoor. Trembling, I turned and looked down the dark *mudroom. Shadows bounced back and forth in front of the little glass window. Three monotonous pings rang at the door again, only this time with more force. I lunged back. My heart thumped against my chest. The side of the house rang with rapping sounds as if limbs were bouncing off the house. I slowly walked to the door, opened it, and looked out. The wind furiously blew hard against the door, funneling gusts through the treetops and into the forest. I rammed the door with my shoulder and walked out onto the steps. My long black hair whipped into my face and stabbed my eyes. I hugged the railing as I slowly walked down the steps and out into the grass, gazing up into the sky.*

Thunder roared through the mountains vibrating the earth with its magnificent power. Hairs on my forearm stood up and reached for the electricity. Lightning flashed over the mountains and spidered out over my head. The energy ran over the peaks, calling me to succumb to its power. I looked back at the house, and it appeared miles away. A mirage floating further and further from my grasp. As I tried to keep my balance, my legs were heavy with every step, one step after another, reaching out with my hands to grab the railing.

The back door slammed shut. I dropped to my knees and crawled to the banister. My body lifted in the air as a strong gust of wind picked me up. The wind thrust against me, trying to pull me into the storm.

"No!" My voice echoed through the forest with a momentous howl. The wind abruptly stopped, and my body dropped into the dirt with a heavy hit.

"Adele." A soft voice whispered from behind me. I huffed, trying to catch my breath, and turned around. The backyard was still, with darkness crowding in around me. The backdoor light flicked off, and the back of my head tingled, alerting me that someone was nearby.

I jumped up to my feet and spun around, searching the backyard. It was calm and eerily quiet. My heart pounded in my chest as I exhaled steam from my lips. "Hello?"

A moment felt like an hour. I turned back to the house and started to climb the steps again.

"Adele!" *A gruff voice screamed my name in my ear. A hand grabbed my shoulder and pulled me back. I fell onto my rump and looked up to see a wolf. He wasn't an ordinary wolf. He was standing up like a man looking down at me. I slowly stood up and faced him.*

The majestic beast towered over my five-foot-ten body with glowing golden chestnut eyes. He didn't move his mouth when he spoke, but I heard him talk to me.

"It's not safe here for you, Adele. They've been searching for you for many years. You need to leave this place before it's too late."

"I don't want to leave. This is my home. If they want a fight, then a fight is what I'll give them. I'm not scared of dying!" I turned around, marched up the stairs, and looked back before grabbing the knob.

He disappeared, and the wind picked up right where it left off. My body slammed against the door, and I couldn't open it. I planted my feet firmly and pulled with all my might. The door finally opened, and I dropped inside onto the floor. The door slammed behind me. Panting, I sat up and put my back to the door. After I caught my breath, I stood up and looked outside. The wind whistled against the back door, begging to come in. I locked the door and went back to bed.

Chapter Four: Adele

I woke up early and walked into the kitchen to brew coffee. Buddy bumped his head against my legs, then pawed at my foot. "Ow! Okay. Okay. I'm coming." I slipped on his harness and grabbed one of Dad's old jackets. The cold winter wind greeted me at the door, and a blanket of white covered the ground from the night before. We walked around the back yard for a few minutes before Buddy circled several times and relieved himself.

Remnants of my dream haunted me as I swayed back and forth, waiting for Buddy to finish up. I looked back at the house and remembered today was Molly's last day with us. I would officially be alone and miss her chattering. She would return to school and her busy life as I to mine. Molly lived fifty miles away in the city, and honestly, that was the furthest I've ever lived from anyone I knew.

Buddy finished up, and we jogged back up the cabin steps. The back of my head tingled as I reached for the door. I slowly turned around and saw oaks thrashing in the wind. Footsteps sounded as if something was running just out of my sight. Buddy tugged on me and scratched the bottom of the back-door. "Okay. I'm coming."

I fed Buddy, poured a coffee, and watched out of the kitchen window.

"Hey."

"Morning."

Molly walked into the kitchen, rubbing her face. She poured a coffee and grabbed a slice of pizza from the box in the fridge. We followed her into the family room and sat on the couch. Buddy inched closer and closer to her pizza, trying to snag a bite.

"Hey, no, Buddy. Yuck, I don't know how you don't heat it up."

Molly shrugged her shoulders and took another bite.

"Wow, it's quiet without a TV. Hopefully, they'll be here tomorrow to put in your wi-fi." She drank a big swig and looked behind us out the window. "Are you going to be okay out here all by yourself? Maybe you should buy a gun or something."

I stared up at the mantel and thought of Dad. He would take us out every evening, and we would train with our bo staffs. I looked around the room and searched for mine. He'd made it for me out of a piece of a pine tree he found that had fallen in the forest one day. I stood up and walked into his room and looked around, and then I ran upstairs to my old room and looked around. I slowly walked back down the stairs and tried to remember where I last saw my bo staff years ago.

"What are you doing?"

"I'm looking for the old bo staff Dad made for me when I was little."

"Did you just say bo staff? Wow! That's funny!" Molly laughed hysterically, rocking back and forth.

"Actually, I was well trained. Dad always said that I needed to learn how to defend myself because I never knew when someone would hurt me."

"I just can't picture you with a bo staff. I'm sorry, it's just too funny."

"Whatever, Molly." I stomped into Dad's bathroom, turned on the shower, walked over to the long mirror, and undressed. I pushed down my pants, and when I stood back up, a deep purple bruise was imprinted on my shoulder. It was the shape of a long-fingered hand. Steam filled the bathroom and fogged the mirror. I grabbed a towel, and a spider dropped from it. I yelped a high-pitched scream.

"You okay?"

"Yeah, I'm fine." The spider was a giant wolf spider. He stopped and stood in front of me and acted like he was waiting for me to make my move. I shooed him with my foot, and he ran under the cabinets. I stepped into the shower and let the hot water run over my head. Flashes of my dream haunted me every time I closed my eyes. I scrubbed my body, turned off the water, and gently pulled another towel from the shelf.

Buddy scratched at the door and snorted the crack along the floor. I opened it, and he looked up at me with his big brown eyes. "Can I help you, sir?" I wiped the mirror with the towel and looked at my reflection. The handprint had disappeared. "What the?" I raised my hand up and gently touched my shoulder. "I must be losing my mind, Buddy." Buddy looked up at me and cocked his head to the side. I reached down and scratched behind his ear, then got dressed and went back into the family room.

Molly looked up from her phone and smiled. "You okay?"

"Yeah, just a spider. So I guess we need to get going soon. Huh?"

"Yeah, let me go get dressed."

I walked back into the kitchen and cleaned up, washing out the cups and coffeemaker, and then wiped down the counter. I glanced out the window over the sink, and something caught my attention. A deer was grazing in my backyard. Our gazes met briefly before it trotted off into the forest.

I was staring at the spot the deer had entered when I saw something move in my peripheral vision. My attention glided over to see someone standing just on the forest's edge, looking back at me. I stood completely still and gazed back, focusing on the outline of his body. A man with pale white skin wearing a long black cape and glowing blue eyes stared back. I focused and tried to use my magic and explore what he was. A sharp pain shot through my head, as if the person was purposely trying to block me. I squeezed my eyes shut for a single moment and covered my right eye to conceal the pain. When I opened my eyes back up, he was gone.

A heavy jolt against the window knocked me back. A sparrow slammed into it, breaking its neck and leaving a crack stretching from one side to the next. I looked into its face for a moment while it twitched. Death slowly took it as it slid down the glass and then dropped. My body was shivering, and my mouth dropped open as I stood there in shock. The crack looked precisely like the crack from my dream. Shaking my head, I swallowed hard and yelled, "Molly!" Molly walked over to me and stood there staring at the crack.

"Wowza. What happened?"

"A bird. A sparrow, I think, flew into the window."

"Weird. Well, another thing to fix on this old place."

My forehead creased as I looked over at her. She looked away quickly and walked back towards the family room. I shook my head and got ready to go. "Come on, Buddy." I grabbed Buddy's harness and slipped it over him, stepped outside, and let him do his business. Molly came out a few minutes later and put her sunglasses on. Buddy jumped into the back seat, and I went to lock the front door.

Once I was in my car, my fingers shook as I tried to put the key into the ignition. "I think I'll pay to put in a better deadbolt on the door next week."

"And buy a gun?" Molly asked, looking over at me.

Shaking my head, I exhaled loudly and entered the main road. My phone vibrated in the cup holder of the car. I looked down and saw that it was Tommy again. I shook my head and declined his call.

"You should just answer it and talk to him. Maybe he can

come to stay out here with you for a while."

I shot Molly a dirty look and looked back at the road.

"Come on, Del. He misses you."

"No, Molly. I don't love him, and I don't want to hurt him. I want to be a writer, and I want to live here. I don't want to be his little woman and live as a prisoner of his rules. No thanks! And besides, I shouldn't have to explain what I . . . wait, did you talk to him?"

She stared out the window and wouldn't look at me.

"Molly! Damit! You're supposed to be on my side. No matter what."

"He just sounded so . . . heartbroken. I think he just wants to talk to you."

"He treats me like I'm his property." I shook my head. "And I can't believe you."

We didn't speak for the rest of the trip home. I pulled up to Molly's apartment and parked. When I got out of the car, I walked to the back and grabbed Buddy. "Come on, Buddy." I walked him over to the grass under the trees in front of Molly's apartment complex. I closed my eyes and let the wind blow across my face. I inhaled the breeze and exhaled, opening my eyes.

"Hi."

I spun around, and there he was. Tommy was standing a few feet away from me. He was taller than me, with blond hair and bright blue eyes. "Tommy, what are you doing here?"

"I've really missed you. I wanted to see you. I tried calling, and you never picked up. I thought you just needed some space, but I think you never meant for us to get back together."

He walked forward, and Buddy jumped up onto his chest and greeted him.

"Hey, Buddy, good boy. I love you, Del. I can't think of my

life without you. I want you to marry me and have my babies. I want us to buy a big house here in the city and go to dinner parties. I thought that's what you wanted, too, but something changed in you. I don't know if it's something I did or what. Is it someone else? Are you seeing someone else?"

"No, I'm just . . . I want to . . . I want to figure out who I am. I want to be a writer, and you know that. When I talk about it, you act like it's just a hobby, but it's who I've always been."

I looked up into the trees and stared at the leaves fluttering on the branches. The wind blew again, and I knew what I had to do. I looked back at Tommy and exhaled. "I'm sorry, Tommy, I don't love you, and I don't want to marry you."

Tommy's forehead furrowed, and his nostrils flared as he started panting. He took a step forward and slapped me across the face.

I fell back, and Buddy leaped on Tommy and bit his arm. I almost lost Buddy's leash and pulled him back. "No! Buddy!" Tommy fell back onto the ground and held his arm.

Molly ran over and got on her knees, coddling him. "What's wrong with you, Del! He almost took his arm off."

"He slapped me, Molly!" My eyes welled up with tears. My nose and eyes burned as my lip quivered. "Molly!"

Molly stood up and helped Tommy up, and they walked towards her apartment. People gathered around us, watching. I ran towards the SUV and let the tears roll down my face. Buddy jumped into the front seat, and I buckled him in and then myself. I grabbed a tissue from my purse and dabbed it with water to get the blood from around his mouth. I swallowed hard, holding in the sobs, but tears rolled down my face. Buddy leaned over and licked my cheek. I wrapped my arms around him and held him. "You're a good puppy." I started the car, looked up at Molly's apartment window for a moment, and then pulled away.

Chapter Five: Jake

I clutched my ticket as I waited next to the empty track at the station. The smell of sweat and stale cigarette smoke polluted the air. My gaze darted back and forth, surveying the perimeter as I waited. *I'm so close to being out of this place forever. I have to keep moving because I know they're still looking for me.*

The train blew its horn as it sped around the bend. Smoke barreled out of the top, reeking of diesel fuel. I shifted my weight back and forth between my legs, waiting for the train to stop and open its doors.

Hissing, the cars pulled up and came to a stop. The automatic doors opened, and I trotted in, clutching my black backpack over my shoulder.

"One, two, three." I counted as I walked down the aisle. The rows of seats were blue with white stripes over the top. Lights dimmed over the seats as I crawled in and took the seat next to the window. I spun around and scanned the area to see the tops of two heads in the back. I set my bag across my lap with my arms folded over it. My eyes were heavy as I gazed up at the full moon peeking through the rows of snow clouds. Lights blinked in the aisles of the train, and then the doors closed. The engine pulled with a sharp tug, moving the cars along the track. The horn sounded its departure as we left the station.

I studied my reflection in the window. The wolf peered through my irises, begging to come out and take over, but I knew I had to keep it together. I rubbed my eyes, and my mother's smiling face flashed in my mind. She was a beautiful Latina woman who broke many hearts before my dad. My father was a great warrior reared in Canada who fought to defend my mother and himself till death. I learned the family secret and changed into a wolf on the first full moon of my twelfth birthday. I hid in my bathroom and stared at my reflection of the animal I'd transformed into. My mother came to me and explained that I was a Lycan and that it was a great honor passed on to me. She explained that I couldn't tell anyone and would always have to hide my true identity no matter what.

The next day, my mother and father died. Police told me that they'd had a terrible car accident, but I knew that was a cover-up. The police tried to take me in their car, but I broke free from their arms and ran. My legs throbbed in pain, but I kept running until I tripped and fell in front of an old, abandoned building. I crawled in through a broken window and collapsed. I remember the strong scent of urine and the cool, moist cement against my face. I curled up into a ball and vibrated as the sobs exploded into my palms.

Weeks went by as I wandered the streets searching for food. I didn't know if I would die soon, and honestly, I hadn't cared. Then everything changed. I met Bill. I'd been standing in front of a sandwich shop, staring at the food through the window. Bill, a giant Native American man, walked up and towered over me. "Hello," he said.

A girl carrying a bag walked out of the shop and handed me a sandwich first, then one to Bill. She walked over to the picnic table in front of the shop and sat down. Frozen, I stood there, shocked that they'd given me food. Bill waved for me to come over.

They saved me that day.

I looked around the train and saw emptiness. I unzipped

my backpack and pulled out a folded-up picture. It was the three of us. The last image we had together before . . . well, before everything happened. Bill took me in and made me feel like I had a family again, even if it was for only a little while. I stared at it for a few minutes, then folded it back up.

I knew I would always have to hide who I really was and what I could do. Sometimes I was proud to be the wolf, and other times I was just . . . tired. Tired of running. Fighting. I don't want that life anymore. *I want a home again. A family. I want to see Adele.* Even if it was for one last time. I had to tell her the truth about everything. I had to tell her how I felt, and then I could move on with my life.

Chapter Six: Adele

I stared at my phone while I ate my sandwich, expecting Molly to call, but it never rang. Buddy pawed at my leg and whimpered. He knew something was on my mind. "I know. It's okay." I locked up the house, and we went to bed for the night.

The next day, I cleaned to stay busy. Every time I stopped to rest, I saw something else that needed to be cleaned or repaired. People came and went for the next couple of days. My wi-fi got hooked up, and the windows were all replaced. I even found a couple of guys to put in a privacy fence for Buddy. Life seemed quieter and more peaceful. *Lonely.*

Molly's face flashed in my mind time and again, recapping what had taken place. I knew she would never forgive me for what happened. In her mind, I was at fault. I was the bad guy for letting my dog bite that jerk, Tommy, and no matter what I said, it wouldn't change. I shook my head and tried to erase what had happened. I tried to erase Molly.

I finished organizing the bottom half of the house and then worked my way upstairs. I vacuumed the second floor, washed the linens, and remade the beds. Looking around, I realized I had done everything I could. I dropped down on Jake's twin, looked over at the door, and saw him looking back at me, smiling. Shaking my head, I smiled back and inhaled a deep breath. Something inside me always told me he was still alive. I've always hoped maybe one day I would see him again.

I stood up, walked to the door, and looked back to check

the room one last time. A cold nose poked my fingers. I jumped back and held my chest. Buddy stood next to me, looking up. "Okay, okay. I'm coming down."

Evening came, and Buddy and I sat down to eat dinner in the family room. I opened my computer to turn on a movie when I bumped into my glass of water, spilling it onto the carpet. "Well, shit." The water was dripping down the table and saturating the rug. Of course, Buddy tried to lick it up. I ran, got a towel, and sat on the floor, dabbing up the wetness. A faint sound of water running echoed near me. I looked around, confused about where it could be coming from, and then it hit me. I realized what I'd forgotten.

I hopped up, pushed the coffee table out of the way, pulled back the rug, and there it was — the door to the hideaway in the floor. There was no handle, so I had to look around the house for something to pry it open with. I ran into the hallway and dug through Dad's tools until I found a pry bar. I ran back into the family room and pulled open the door just enough to get my hands under it and finish pulling it up. It was a hefty door. I didn't remember it being so heavy. A flash of Jake opening the door and looking at me popped into my mind.

Buddy dropped his front paws down on the first step to walk in, and I pulled him back and said, "No, Buddy! Stay!" I ran back into the hallway and grabbed a flashlight. Buddy was sitting with his rump bouncing on the ground. "That's a good boy." I rubbed his head and flashed the light down into the hole. The room was in disarray. A musky scent wafted in the air as I shined the light around the room's emptiness. Spider webs covered the turned-over table and chairs like in an old horror movie.

I cupped my nose, scooted to the edge, and put my feet on the stairs. Slowly, I walked down, following the beam of light to look around the room. Memories flooded in, and I saw glimpses of Jake sitting across from me. His body vibrated in our escape's darkness as the world as we knew it was ending. I blinked and heard Buddy woof at me. "Sorry, Buddy. Come on, pup." Buddy flew down the stairs, nearly falling, and spun around the room like a mouse on a wheel. "Buddy, calm down!" As the dust settled, I ran my beam along the walls and over the floor. I looked down and saw it lying under a layer of trash. At first, it didn't click what I'd seen, and then it dawned on me. "My bo staff." I walked over to it and held it in both hands. The flashlight dropped from my grip and hit the floor with a loud thud, rolling back and forth. "I can't believe it."

So many memories flooded my mind of Dad and my training in the backyard. Dad would take us out back to train after dinner. Jake and I would duel until dark.

Dad always said, "Someday, I won't be here, and you'll have to take care of yourselves. Some people will stop at nothing to take your power and kill you. Always hide who you are and never ever trust anyone."

I stared at the wall for a long time before bending down to get the flashlight. The floor slightly moved inward and shifted when I squatted down. I quickly stepped back and studied the floor. I stepped on the floor again, and it sank in slightly as if something was there. Something hidden. I wiped the dirt away until I found a crack in the foundation. I reached for the pry bar and tried to open it. "It won't open, Buddy. That's strange. It's like there's no door."

Buddy sniffed the ground and circled around it. He tried to dig but stopped and snorted. I settled down on my rump and shined the flashlight over it. I swiped more dirt away and leaned forward to examine the floor.

"I've got to be missing something." I swiped across the ground again and noticed the dirt sinking. "It's not a door. It's a box, Buddy. A large box. It's . . . it's iron. How the hell do I get it out or open it?" I examined the floor and ran my fingers along the sides. "I guess I'll just dig it out."

I scooped dirt out from around the box with my fingers until I had enough cleared to try to pull it out of the floor. With my legs braced on either side, I cupped the sides of the box with my hands and pulled with all my might. The box wasn't budging. I gritted my teeth and tried again. Nothing. The more I tried to move it, the more the dirt seeped back down into the holes around the box. I looked down at the box and then back up at the hole in the floor. "Why in the hell does Dad have a freaking heavy box in the floor anyway?"

Pacing back and forth, I stared down at the box. "I'll just open it."

I grabbed the pry bar, got down on my knees, and something stopped me. I looked up to see Dad. He was smiling at me from the family room. The lamp blinked three times systematically and then shut off. A vision of how to open the box flashed in my mind. I knew what I needed to do.

Closing my eyes, I inhaled a deep breath and then exhaled slowly. A tingling sensation ran from the back of my neck and traveled down my spine. Concentrating, I imagined myself opening the box with my power. My fingers tingled as my power grew. I looked down to see my hands begin to glow a white string of lightning bolts that flowed up my arms and down the rest of my body. Shivering, I laid my hands over the box and pulled up. The box trembled under my fingertips as it opened. Air released out of the top of the iron door and blew hot, musky air into my face.

A beam of light glowed from inside. Squinting, I looked down at a glowing white sheet with a fine piece of rope tied across it. I slowly reached inside and untied the rope. I peeled back the sheet, and a force of magic echoed through the room. A blanket of power released and rolled over me and through the house like a tidal wave. It knocked me back, and the power seeped into my body. I gasped, my body convulsing as my breath escaped my lungs. Seconds felt like minutes until I finally took in a breath. The lights flickered, and then the house went black.

After a few moments, I came to and opened my eyes. I looked up and realized the entire house was dark. Buddy was in the corner, shivering. Sitting up, I patted around the floor, searching for the flashlight. I touched my bo staff, and it glowed a vibrant white. Startled, I jumped, dropping it. The staff's light slowly dimmed and went dark. I reached down and touched it again. The light shimmered brightly as my hand wrapped around it and picked it up. I put both hands on my staff and watched my body glow as the electric charge surged through me and into the staff as I held it. I shook my head and gently laid my bo staff back on the floor. I walked up the stairs and into the mudroom to turn the breaker back on. The lights flashed on, and I walked back to the hidden room to see Buddy still shivering in the corner. "Come on, pup. Come out of there." Buddy ran up out of the room and bolted into his kennel. I slowly walked back down into the room and knelt.

I ran my fingers over the silky white sheet, and a memory surged through me of Dad walking behind me in the forest. I remember looking back, and he was bent over, picking up a piece of wood from the ground. I blinked, nodding, and looked over at the bo staff he'd made for me. I pulled back the sheet, and there were two letters with a special wax seal holding them closed. I cradled the letters in my hand, picked up my bo staff, and climbed the stairs enough to set everything onto the floor. I walked back down and closed the iron box. Then I covered it back up with dirt and put the stool on top.

I walked back upstairs and closed the trap door behind me. I pulled the rug over the door, picked up everything, and carried it to my room. I checked all locks on the doors and went back to my bedroom.

"Buddy! Buddy, where are you?" Buddy was sleeping in his kennel. "Really, come on, pup." Buddy just looked up at me. I crawled into bed and waited for him to join me. "It's okay, pup. Come sleep with me." Buddy slowly crawled out and joined me in bed.

I sat back and stared down at the letters. Both were blank on the outside, but I knew by feeling which one was for me. I broke through the special seal, and a wisp of steam rose from the letter. The smell of pine and Dad's tobacco tickled my nose. Smiling, I unfolded the paper to reveal the stationery that we used from our old writing desk. Inhaling, I held my breath as I looked up and swallowed. A lump formed in my throat, and my eyes filled with tears. Exhaling, I looked down and read the last letter my father had written me.

Adele,

If you're reading this, then that means I'm gone. I'm very proud of you, and I know you'll grow into a smart and brave young woman. I tried to teach you as much as I could to prepare you for the world's harshness, but unfortunately, I've run out of time.

Remember to never let your guard down and protect who you are, no matter what happens. You will grow into a powerful woman who will wield the same powers as mine. Keep training, and your abilities will flourish.

It was not by accident that you found Jake at the sandwich shop that day. Destiny sent us to rescue him. He's of royal blood and the last of his kind. A dark being has been lurking in the shadows, searching for us for quite some time. I wish I'd been honest with you and Jake about the dangers of this being. His name is Victor, and he's the man who killed your mother and Jake's parents. He will stop at nothing to find you and Jake, absorb your powers, and kill you both.

Someday he will find you as he found me. There's a hidden cave in the mountain that your mother and I went to. I pointed it out the last time we went fishing. I put a spell on the cave to keep you and

Jake safe.

Adele, don't be afraid to let go and use your powers to protect yourself. You are capable of much more than you know. Believe in yourself, and you will prevail in the end.

I have cherished all the time I've had with you and Jake. I love you both very much, and I know that you will stay together and be safe. Remember, you are survivors, and you'll know what to do when the time comes.

I love you,
Dad

I dropped my hands, still holding the letter. Moisture covered my face as my lips quivered. I looked over at Dad's picture and stared. Heat slowly started to burn my fingertips. Smoke rose from the letter, and then a white flame ignited at the top. I shuffled the paper back and forth between my hands, looking for somewhere to throw it. The burning grew hotter and hotter, burning my fingertips. I slipped off the bed and dropped the paper on the floor. The white flame grew into a ball of fire and engulfed the letter. Once it was extinguished, the white flame disappeared into thin air, leaving no fire remnants. I dropped to the floor and touched the spot where the fire took place. The floor was cold to the touch and unharmed. I wiped my face, slowly stood back up, and crawled into bed.

CHAPTER SEVEN: VICTOR

The earth vibrated, and a blinding wave of white light blasted into the darkness. A wave of immense power flowed over me and sputtered out over the horizon. I opened my eyes and saw him. An old ghost who had haunted me since the day I brought him down. He stood there smiling at me in the darkness. Taunting me. He couldn't have risen from the dead. I closed my eyes, followed the light to where it originated, and found her. *Adele.*

"Victor."

I turned my head and looked at my loyal servant, Rick.

"It's coming from his house, sir."

I nodded, walked over to the window, pushed the curtain to the side, and looked out. The night was dark as the moon wasn't full enough to light the lands. I shook my head and then looked back at Rick. "Have you located him yet?"

"No, but we think—"

"You think?" I closed my eyes and inhaled a deep breath. I dropped my head and let it hang towards my chest. My body pulsated with a vibrant green as I searched.

"Sir?"

My head shot up, and I sat down in the room's darkness. My eyes emanated power as they glowed in the shadow of the room. I looked for her and found her. "Go back to the cabin, and you will find her. Adele is living there now, and she's alone. He is . . . on the move. Traveling. Searching for her. Go now and bring her to me before he finds her." I looked up at Rick, and my eyes burned like fire. I blinked and jolted into Rick's face. "Now!"

CHAPTER EIGHT: JAKE

"*Jake.*" Adele's voice called for me in the darkness. I blinked my eyes open and looked around. I remembered that I was still on the train. I must've been dreaming. Her voice haunted me, whispering my name. "*Jake. Jake.*"

I looked into the window and saw her smiling face looking back at me. Yawning, I rubbed my eyes as the morning sun's rays warmed my face. I folded my arms over my bag and saw a sign that read *Welcome to New Hampshire*. Butterflies fluttered in my gut as the train came to an abrupt stop. The door creaked open, letting in the cool morning air.

A map of New Hampshire was located right next to the ticket booth as I stepped onto the sidewalk. Scanning the area, I slowly walked over and looked for Littleton. It was located in the northern part of the state. Nodding, I stepped down into the road and started walking. A bright yellow taxi pulled up, and a door opened. A woman stepped out and headed to the train station. I watched the taxi for a moment before walking over to it.

I rapped on the window, and a man with a white *New York Yankees* baseball cap turned to look up. "Hey, man, what can I do for you?"

"Can I get a ride to Littleton?"

He threw his head back and chuckled. I waited for him to stop laughing and gave him a half-smile.

"You're serious?"

"Yeah."

"Dude, that's a hundred and twenty miles away."

"Yeah."

"Well, it's going to cost you. Cash, too."

I nodded, unzipped my backpack, and pulled out a wad of cash. "How much?"

"Okay, we're going to Littleton."

I hopped into the taxi and sat my bag on the floor in front of my feet. Rain drizzled against the windows as we drove away from the train station.

"So, where are you from?"

I stared out of the window and watched the raindrops run along the side of the taxi's window. The town was busy, but traffic thinned out once we got on the main road. I closed my eyes, and the memories began to flood back in.

"Jake! Jake, are you listening?"

I looked up to see Dad standing there with my bo staff, and I looked over to see her. Adele stood there, side-eying me because Dad was teaching us something, and my mind was off somewhere else.

"Boy! This is important. Pay attention!" He walked over and pinched me on the back of the arm.

"Ow! Aren't I getting too old for you to pinch me?"

"Aren't you getting too old for me to have to pinch you to get your attention? Now. Pay attention! What do you do if someone comes up behind you and has their arms around you? Jake!"

"You hit them anywhere to pull free. Or you can twist your body out."

"Yes, nose, groin, feet, or if you can move enough, twist your body, throw them over you, and attack while they're down. Always go for a kill spot. Remember, they're trying to kill you."

Adele made faces at me, sticking her tongue out and crossing her eyes. I smirked and bugged my eyes out at her.

"Something funny, Jake?"

He bobbed his head back and forth between us, and Del looked down and put her hands behind her back. Dad stormed off, went into the house, and slammed the back door.

I walked over and pushed Adele. "Thanks, smelly. Now I'm in trouble." She smirked and laughed through her nose. I stomped inside, and Dad was sitting at the table with a cup of coffee. He had his tobacco pipe in his mouth, puffing away. He looked straight ahead as I walked in. Adele ran in, walking goofily until she saw Dad sitting at the table. He didn't say a word to us. He just sat there, staring.

I walked over, got a water glass, and drank it, looking out the kitchen window. The rain was coming down, drizzling drops of water down the windowpane.

"Dad," Del said.

Dad stayed silent and exhaled loudly. We both sat down at our little round table in the kitchen and looked at each other. Dad puffed his pipe and took a sip of his coffee.

"I want to go fishing. Del, will you get my pole and tackle box, please?"

"Yes, Daddy."

Del walked out of the room, and Dad looked over at me. "Jake."

"Yes, sir."

For a brief moment, he stared into my eyes. It was like he was trying to find the words, but he couldn't speak. He opened his mouth and then closed it again. Finally, he exhaled a long breath. "I won't yell at you anymore. If you don't want to learn, that's fine, but we have little time left together before – "

"Here, Daddy." Adele entered the room and looked over at me. I nodded, and she looked down at Dad.

"Okay, honey. Thank you." He grabbed Adele's hand and patted it, smiling. "Now, you two go get dressed. Del, will you make a couple of sandwiches for us if we get hungry, too?"

"Yes, but it's raining outside."

He looked up at the window and shook his head. "It's just a brief shower. It'll pass soon."

She nodded, and I waited for her to leave the room and stared at Dad.

"Dad, what . . . what were you saying?"

He stood up, smiled, and patted my back. "Let's go fishing. It's a *good day for it."*

He walked out of the room, and I remember looking up at the kitchen window. The raindrops rolled down the glass, distorting the forest behind our house.

I think about that day often. What if I'd just made him finish his sentence? Would things have turned out differently? Maybe he would still be here with us.

"Hey, buddy! Hey!"

The cab driver waved at me.

"Hey, man, I got to stop for gas and take a leak. Okay?"

"I'll take care of the gas."

"Okay, thanks."

He pumped outside while I walked inside, grabbed a couple of bottled waters, and paid for the gas. I headed back outside, and the rain was steadily pouring down.

"I'm going to go to the restroom. I'll be right back."

I nodded, stood outside the car, and pulled up my collar. I walked back and forth, stretching out my legs, and saw him running towards the car, so I got back inside. He crawled back into the car and grunted as he strapped his seat belt on. I leaned forward, handed him one of my waters, and nodded.

He looked back at me through his rearview mirror and nodded. "Thanks."

He started the car and got back onto the road.

"You okay, man?" Our gazes met through the rearview mirror.

"Yeah." The rain picked up, and the driver had to slow down and creep along the old road. It was a two-lane road, so the traffic was heavier than average. Wood lodging trucks passed us by, and the car moved from the wind, pushing against us. I settled down and stared out the window and thought of Adele.

She looked back at me, smiling, as we entered the forest for our last fishing trip together. Her smiling face was ingrained in my memory. Dad led the way down his usual path and looked back at us every so often. Adele was always behind him, and I followed. I remember something had felt different about that day. Dad acted strangely and waved for Del and me to walk up front with him. I looked at Del, and she shrugged her shoulders. Dad was panting, and his hair was all muffled around his face. He turned, looking up at the mountains and pointed.

"This mountain is important to me. It has a hidden cave in it that I used to go to with your mother when we first got married."

"Ew, Dad."

"Not ew, Del, listen to me. This is important. You can go up there if you need to. Okay."

I met his eyes, and he was sincere. His eyes moistened, and his scent smelled different.

He looked away, and I could see that he was wiping away a tear. His voice caught in his throat, and I saw his chest rise, taking in a deep breath. He clapped his hands together and motioned us towards the river.

"Okay, let's go fishing."

Del looked at me with her forehead furrowed. She knew something was up with Dad, too. Neither of us said anything. We just followed him to the river.

We stepped through the opening of the trees that led to the river. I stopped and dropped my bag on one of the big rocks. Dad laid his pole down and walked over to the rocks near the forest edge. He started picking them up one by one to look under. Dad pulled out a fat earthworm and tore it into pieces. He handed me my pole and a part of the worm. Del grabbed her pole and realized her line was tangled, so she plopped down to untangle it. Dad walked over and handed her the rest of the worm and talked to her.

I walked up the river some and cast my line out. The water sparkled as it raced over the rocks and flowed into the river's depth. I threw my jacket off, pushed up my sleeves, and reeled in my line slowly. Dad walked down a few feet, looked at me, and smiled. I remember his smile. It was the last genuine smile he had before he was *gone.*

I caught my biggest fish that day and rubbed it in to Adele. I walked around and shook my rump, saying how my fish ate her fish. Adele walked over and smacked me in the arm, and I chased her around with my fish. Dad pulled out his old camera, and we put our arms across each other's shoulders, laughing.

I looked down at the picture and smiled. It was the one thing I'd grabbed before I disappeared that day.

CHAPTER NINE: JAKE

I crossed my arms and watched the red and blue lights flashing in front of us. The taxi came to a standstill as the wreck completely blocked off the road ahead.

"Well, it looks like we will be here for a while."

The driver flicked on the radio, and I stared out my window, watching the raindrops roll down.

"Jake." Her voice echoed in my head. "Jake."

Rick waved at me. "Jake. Jake, did you hear me?"

We were sitting around a long rectangular table in a windowless room. I had a sad cardboard cup with a broken handle filled halfway with cold coffee and a half-eaten bagel.

"This is your objective."

Rick pulled out a long vanilla envelope and opened it. He laid out the pictures of the targets and looked up at me.

"Yes," I said.

Vahn looked over at me with his eyebrow arched. I knew it irritated him that I was zoning out. My gaze darted over to the door and then back down at the pictures. I wanted to shove the pictures away, walk out the door, and never look back.

"You'll go in at midnight. They'll wrap up —"

The car jolted, and my body jerked back into the seat. Traffic started to move again. A logging truck and an SUV with heavy damage were sitting on the side of the road. A woman was lying across a stretcher with a cold compress on her forehead. A sign reading *Littleton 50 miles* followed the accident.

"Almost there, sir. Just over an hour to go."

I nodded and went back to watching the rain drizzle down the window.

A blast of strong wind was blowing my hair as I stepped into the view of the cottages. Smoke billowed out the top of one of them, carrying the smell of pork roasting over a fire. Echoes of laughter alerted us to which house they'd all gathered in. The full moon smiled down, lighting the way to their doorstep. The wolf inside me ruffled anxiously as I knew the fight was drawing near. Vahn looked at me and pointed for me to go one way around the cottage while he went the other. We jogged down from the jungle's thick brush and ran around both sides of the cottage simultaneously. I slowly followed and peeked around the window to see how many assailants were inside. Six people, and two of them were our targets.

I jogged around the cottage and stopped, frozen in my tracks. Air caught in my chest, pounding against my heart. The ground was littered with slaughtered bodies. Hundreds of people were bloody and left for dead. Children's screaming faces looked back at me from stakes plunged into the ground where their decapitated heads were laid to rest. I shook my head and looked over to see Vahn shaking his head with his mouth open. He looked over at me wide-eyed and then back at the grounds of torture. It was a graveyard, and from the ripe smell, it was freshly laid.

"Please, help us. Please!"

I spun around, and there was a little teepee a few hundred feet away. The woven material moved outward as someone's body was slapping against it. I ran over, untied the rope, and looked inside to see people tied together.

"Please, let my daughters go. Please. I'll stay, but please just let them go." A woman pleaded with me as tears rolled down her cheeks. Her face was swollen with fresh bruises along her jawline.

I looked around the teepee, and Vahn walked up slowly behind me.

"This isn't part of the mission. We have to finish the job before

they leave," Vahn said.

I looked back at him and then over at the woman. My heart ached in my chest from the graveyard that I'd just seen. Dad's face flashed in my mind, and I shook my head. "No." I crawled over and untied the people in the tent. "Go. Quickly. Go."

"Jake, what are you doing?" Vahn grabbed my shoulder and pulled me back.

I slapped his hand off and gazed into his eyes.

"Help me."

"Jake. This isn't our problem. We need to do our job."

My face burned up with heat, and I felt the wolf teeter-totter inside me. I slowly turned to glare at my friend. He stepped back, shaking his head. I finished untying everyone.

"Go. You're free now."

A woman dropped to her knees, grabbed my legs, and cried. "Thank you, sir. Thank you."

I nodded and then looked up at Vahn. My anger flashed throughout my body as I let the wolf come out before I finished walking out of the prisoners' tent. "I didn't sign up for this, Vahn. I thought we were killing the bad guys, but we were the bad guys all this time." I stomped past him and headed for the cabin.

My body doubled in size, and I lunged toward the perpetrators. Vahn's body transformed, and he grew into a giant black bear. I sliced across the enemy's throats, squirting blood across my face, then ripped out the remainder with my jaws and spat out their rotten innards. I was moving in slow motion as my ears went silent to their bullets and screams.

I looked up to see Vahn as we met in the middle of the cottage. Panting, we both stopped and stared at each other. The floor was covered with bodies, and the job was complete. We nodded at each other as our inner animals slowly drifted back down into human form.

"Hey buddy, we're almost there. Look."

The driver pointed at the sign passing by. *Twenty miles.*

Adele and Dad flashed through my mind. I nodded and smiled, looking out the window.

Vahn and I started a fire and ate dried jerky in silence when we returned to our camp. I looked over at him a few times, and he looked away, shaking his head. I sensed his anger stewing as he chewed quietly. I opened my mouth to protest but knew he wasn't ready to listen. Vahn, after all, was like a brother to me. We'd been together since the beginning. He, of all people, knew what type of person I was. Honestly, I don't see how he could have just walked away from helping those people. I looked down at my hands, studied the marks and scars from past battles, and wondered if he honestly knew me at all. Not like she did.

Regardless of what he thought, I couldn't leave those people there to rot. I couldn't live with myself doing something so heartless. Maybe I didn't know Vahn as well as I thought if he could just walk away from them. I shook my head and stood up, stretching my limbs.

We set up our sleeping bags and lay down for the night. Looking up through the trees, I gazed at the stars. I was restless. The children's faces burned in my mind when I closed my eyes. I tossed and turned, waiting for Vahn's snores before I turned over and pulled out the picture. Dad, Adele, and I smiling at each other at the river. I held up the crumpled picture against the stars and fingered the outline of her face. I wondered what she looks like now. I wondered if she still thought about me.

A twig snapped next to where I was lying. I shoved the picture down into my bag and pulled out my hidden bowie knife in my boot. I looked back and forth, trying to locate where the noise was coming from. A human scent tickled my nose, and then I got a whiff of Rick. I grabbed a rock and threw it at Vahn. His snores stopped, and he lifted his head. My finger covered my lips, and I pointed in the direction where the men were walking in from. A tall, slender man with glowing emerald eyes stepped out from behind some trees. A cloud of smoke billowed from his mouth as he stared at me. The wind carried a peculiar smell of tobacco and someone I recognized but couldn't place where. I shot out of my sleeping bag and onto my feet.

Two men came from behind me and grabbed me by my shoulders. "We've got him."

I closed my eyes, and my chest and arms exploded as the beast emerged. A growl vibrated in my throat and rolled off my lips. My legs elongated and grew in strength as I lunged forward away from the men. I spun around, sliced one of their faces off, and ripped out the second man's throat with one swipe. Two more men came for me head-on. I pounced towards them, ripping one of their arms off, and broke the second man's back. I inhaled a deep breath and exhaled a monstrous growl, warning the rest of them to stay away.

"Jake!" A boisterous voice rang behind me.

A rifle was aimed at my chest. Before I could run, a sharp pain pinched into my abdomen. I dropped to the ground, and my body trickled back into human form. A tranquilizer protruded out of my human flesh. I ripped it out and threw it down. The man with the glowing green eyes nodded and smiled, watching me. I stumbled, trying to stand up, shifting my steps back and forth. My power fluctuated as I tried to heal myself, shaking my head fiercely to see straight. More men were marching toward me.

"No!" I screamed, holding up my hand. Tingling ran down my body as I fought the effects of the tranquilizer. The wolf took over, and I grew into the air as my body shifted back. My vision cleared, and I took back control.

The man with emerald-green eyes watched me with a devious smile. "We'll meet again, Jake. I'll find you."

My body flexed, and a monstrous growl bellowed from my chest. I dropped down onto all fours, ready to fight, and then looked down and saw my picture. It was lying on the ground next to my bag. I cocked my head to the side and stared at Adele's smiling face. I looked up at the man, grabbed my bag and picture, and leaped into the trees. I ran and didn't look back.

CHAPTER TEN ADELE

Blinking, I stared up at the ceiling and thought about Jake. My fingers slid down my moist panties, and I imagined his tall, dark physique lying on top of me, pushing his member inside my slit. Seconds passed, and I exhaled a long breath. My fingers satisfied my morning yearning. I sat up and wondered if he thought about me as much as I thought about him. *Jake*, his name echoed in my head. *Jake*.

I jumped out of bed and got dressed for the day. I wandered into the kitchen and opened the back door to let Buddy out. A week had passed since Molly cut me from her life, and now living here alone with Buddy felt like a new chapter in my story. The snow clouds raced across the sky as the sun peeked over the oaks and pines. Steam exhaled from my lips as I stretched my arms up.

Something felt different about today. My stomach fluttered anxiously as I turned around and closed the door. Buddy scratched at the back door after a few minutes, so I let him in.

I fed Buddy, brewed some coffee, and walked into the family room.

The flashlight sat on the coffee table, waiting for me to open the door in the floor. I pulled up the door, walked down the steps, and sat down on the little stool sitting in the middle of the room. A memory of Jake looking at me with his golden chestnut eyes flashed through my mind. Blinking, I shook my head and looked up to see Buddy. He poked his head down into the hole and barked at me.

"What?"

He lay on his belly and hung his head down, then pawed at me and whimpered.

"I'm okay." I walked around the room and straightened up the furniture, then headed back up, when a bright flash of light caught my attention from under the steps. I reached under the step and wiped the dirt away. "Jake's bo staff."

His staff was made out of an Albany wood Dad had crafted for him when he first arrived. I carried it upstairs, walked into my room, and propped it on the wall next to my bo staff. I returned to the family room, closed the door, and threw the rug back over it.

"Come on, pup." Buddy's tail wagged, and he followed me into the kitchen. I poured myself a cup of coffee and stared out the window when it dawned on me. "I can train. I can train and get stronger. That's what Dad always said. I'll get some work done first, and then I can train." I paced back and forth, nodding, and worked out the training details in my head. I remembered a lot of what Dad taught us, but I knew I would be really rusty at first. I picked up my coffee mug and headed into the dining room, where my computer was set up.

The clock read two when I heard a rapping at the front door. Buddy ducked his head down, and a low growl rumbled in his chest. The ridge on his back fluffed up as he slowly walked up to the door on alert. I leaned my ear against the door and listened.

"Who is it?"

Heavy knocking rattled the door again.

"Who is it?"

"Fed Ex, I have a package."

I grabbed Buddy's collar and held him as I opened the door. A man with a nametag that said *Fed Ex* and *Rob* was standing in front of the door. He looked up at me, holding a clipboard and a plastic pen.

"Sign here."

I signed, trying to hold Buddy back, and handed it back.

He said, "Okay, here you go."

"Thanks."

The Fed Ex guy stood there and stared at me. "Do you want me to leave it here or . . ."

"Oh, sorry. Hang on. I'll be right back. Come on, Buddy." I put Buddy up in his kennel. He howled and pushed his head against the door. I walked back, and the Fed Ex guy shifted his weight, holding a long rectangular box. The box was as tall as my height, five foot ten, and the width was almost as wide as my door. I leaned forward and grabbed the top half of the box, and the guy let go. I almost dropped it because it was so heavy.

He watched me and waited, shaking his head. "You okay?"

"Oh, yeah. Fine. I just need to . . . get my husband. He's in the shower."

"Okay, have a good day!" he yelled as he was getting in his truck.

"Okay, thanks. Come here, honey. I could really use your help." Dad always said to never let people know if you were alone. I wasn't exactly alone because of Buddy.

I pulled in the box and dragged it to the window. A picture of a desk with arrows pointed up on the long side was upside down. I smirked and shook my head. "Well, that's wrong." I laughed and shrugged my shoulders. "Oh well." I laid it down on its side and stared at it. When I was a kid, I always wanted a desk facing the window to enjoy the natural sunlight. Dad always made us do our work at either the dining room table or the kitchen table so we could both sit and spread out our books. My smile widened when I realized I was making it my own house now. I opened up the curtains above the box a little more and nodded.

I went to the closet where Dad's tools were stored and pulled out a flathead and Phillips-head screwdriver to start. I cut open the box, laid out all the pieces, and unfolded the directions. As soon as I sat down, there was a knock at the front door. Buddy slammed against the kennel door, barking. I walked over to the door and shouted, "Who is it?"

Silence.

I shouted again, shifting my weight from one hip to the next. "Who is it? Hello!"

I turned around, and more heavy knocking rattled the door.

"Who is it!"

"It's Mason from down the street."

I shook my head and stared at the door. "What do you want, Mace?"

"I need to borrow sugar. My daughter's making cookies."

"Okay, hang on." I stood at the door for a moment and hesitated. I looked over at Buddy. He was slamming his body against the door. I shook my head at him. "It's fine." I unlocked the door and opened it to see the guy from the other day.

"Hey, how are you?"

"Good, thanks."

"May I please borrow a cup of flour? My wife and daughter are baking cookies, and we didn't want to have to go all the way to town to pick up flour."

I cocked my head to the side. "I thought you said sugar?"

"Right, sugar. Right, right. So, where's your friend?"

"Oh, um, she's um." I looked around behind me, searching for the answer. "She went back home, but my boyfriend . . . my fiancé, is in the shower. Yeah, he's in the shower. Yep." I shook my head and looked behind me at Buddy. He was barking uncontrollably.

"Wow, he's upset. I wonder why?"

"He doesn't like you. And sorry, but I don't have any sugar. I actually need to go to the store myself." I attempted to close the door when he slammed his hand against it and stepped a foot inside. I looked down at his foot, gripping the door. "I said I don't have any."

He put his hand on my forearm. "Are you sure?"

Darkness radiated through his veins. My arm fluctuated with his dark intent toward me. He glared into my face, and his eyes flashed a cold, icy blue. "My boyfriend is about to be down, and he won't appreciate how you're acting." I stepped forward, meeting his gaze, and gritted my teeth. "You're not welcome inside!"

He stared back at me, letting go of my arm, and smiled. "Okay, then. I'll see you later."

He stepped back and turned to step off my porch.

I panted, my hands quivering as I closed the door and locked it. I let Buddy out, and he ran over to the door, dropping his nose to the floor and snorting. He looked up at me, whimpering.

"I know, he was a creep. I should've let you out. I know."

I crept over to the window and peeked out. Mace was standing in the driveway in front of my house on his phone. He turned to stare at the house while he was chatting. I hid behind the curtain and watched him as he talked. He nodded, put his phone in his pocket, and then stared at my house for a few more minutes. He finally turned around and left.

"You better leave, jerk." Buddy bumped against my legs and rubbed his head under my hand. I stroked his head and scratched behind his ears. "Let's go outside, Bud." I grabbed my bo staff, and we headed outside.

The middle of the yard was the usual spot where Jake and I trained. Dad would tell us what to do and then sit down in his old wicker chair to watch. I looked down at my staff and hesitated. I didn't know where to start. My hands hadn't gripped my bo staff or any other weapon in over a decade. After losing Dad and Jake, I didn't want anything to do with training. My heart was broken. I hid what I was, and I pushed away that part of me. After a while, I'd realized that part of me was lost, and I didn't know if I could ever get it back.

I closed my eyes and focused on my power. I tried to remember the warm-up that Dad taught us to start with. Flashes of Jake and me spinning our staffs from one hand to the other came into my mind. I opened my eyes and tried to let my hands guide the way. My staff flew through my fingers and soared into the air, hitting the side of the house. I cringed as it hit. Buddy lay down on the porch and cocked his head to the side. He yawned and stretched out his front paws.

"I'm sorry I'm boring you, pup." I walked over, picked up my staff, and tried again. Closing my eyes, I let the wood ease through my fingers, gliding side to side.

After a few dozen rounds, I crossed my staff in the air and let the moves flow naturally. I spun around and kicked in the air, holding the staff, punching, and jabbing.

The trees swayed back and forth, sending icy winds down my back. I was attempting one last kick and then a punch with the staff when I lost my grip. My staff flew across the yard, bounced off the fence, and landed on the other side. Buddy's head popped up, and he stood up and woofed.

"I know, I know. Come on, let's go inside and then I can go around and get it." I shut the door behind us and walked into the family room. "Stay, Buddy." I pointed and turned around to open the front door. I looked up, and it was him. My heart pulsated in my chest as the air left my lungs. I swallowed hard and licked my parched lips.

"Jake?"

CHAPTER ELEVEN: JAKE

"Hey man, we're in Littleton. Where do you want to go?"
"Just keep driving down this road."

The driver nodded, and we followed the road through town. Then we turned at the stop sign and headed outside of town towards the mountains. "Take this turn slow. People drive fast around it." The driver nodded, and I kept pointing straight ahead. I looked up and saw the rows of mountains ahead.

"It's lovely out here. Is this where you're from?"

"Yes. Up here, you're turning right in between those trees."

"There's a house down there?"

"Yes." We turned and followed the dirt road until we saw the old cabin. I leaned forward and gazed up at it. "That's it."

"Looks like they're expecting you."

There was smoke coming out of the chimney, and a black SUV was parked out front.

The driver pulled up to the front door and stopped. "Well, we made it."

I froze in my seat, staring up at the old place. It had been so long since I'd been back. Memories flooded in of what happened the last night I was here.

What if Adele is here? She's going to want to know why I left. I know she'll want answers, but I don't know if what I have to say will be enough.

My mind raced as I rubbed my face. Blinking, I shook my head. Exhaustion was wearing me down.

"Hey, man, you okay?"

"Yeah, sorry. Give me a minute." I pulled open my bag, pulled out a wad of cash, and counted out five large bills. "Now, who did you drive all the way out here?"

"A woman and her two kids. We went to the *Motel Six* in town."

I handed him another three bills and nodded. "Thank you. Be careful driving back."

The man nodded. "Thank you!"

I opened the taxi door, grabbed my bag strap, and threw it over my shoulder as I climbed out. The taxi driver waved, turned around in the driveway, and drove off. I looked up at the mountains and nodded as if I were greeting an old friend. A cool breeze blew through my long locks, sending chills down the back of my neck. I walked up the porch and remembered looking up at the old wooden door for the first time.

I was twelve years old, and Del drug me through the front door, holding my hand in hers. "This is the family room, and that's Daddy's room. Then over here is the dining room and the kitchen. We have two tables to eat at. Oh! I do all my schoolwork at home. I've never been inside an actual school with teachers. Dad teaches me at home. Before Dad, it was my mom, and she's — "

"Del, that's enough. You're going to rip his arm off with the way you're dragging him through the house. You can walk him up to his room and show him where he'll sleep, and then when you come back down, we'll talk. Okay, Jake?"

I looked down at the knob and began reaching out when the door opened in front of me. It was her. *Adele.* She looked up at me with her magnetic brown eyes and smiled. My gaze took in every inch of her matured figure. Her body had transformed into a beautiful, tall, slender Native American woman. She kept her black hair long, shimmering in the sunlight as it flowed down to her curvy hips. Her waist was petite, and her bosom had grown into a full set of succulent breasts. I looked into her eyes and smiled.

The girl I fell in love with so long ago grew up into a stunning woman. My body yearned to wrap my arms around her and hold her tight. I opened my mouth to tell her I'd wanted to come back so many times, but I couldn't bring myself to say the words. I knew she might never forgive me for leaving her so long ago. She might never understand why I had to leave her and run. Even though I'd left, I wanted to tell her that a day hadn't gone by that I hadn't thought about her and wished I'd done things differently. I wished I'd stayed.

Moisture grazed my brow and dampened my palms as I fidgeted in the doorway, hiding behind my stoic gaze.

CHAPTER TWELVE ADELE

I looked up at Jake, gazing into his eyes. My mouth dropped open as I tried to inhale a breath. Jake looked down at me with his glowing golden chestnut eyes. A slight smile tilted his full lips as he towered over me. He pushed back his jet-black mane, scratched his scruffy beard, and shifted his weight to adjust a large black bag hanging over his shoulder. Jake had changed for the better. My dreams of him were nothing near the handsome man that stood in front of me now. His black shirt clung to his broad ripped chest, and muscular thighs snuggly filled his tight blue jeans. His golden chestnut eyes glowed a wild intense gaze that hid the wolf he kept at bay.

Wincing, he shrugged his shoulders slightly. "Hi, Adele."

"I-I can't believe you're here." My chest fluttered as I gazed up at him, searching for the boy I once fell in love with as a girl. My body yearned to hold him and inhale his musk. I'd dreamed of this moment time and time again, and now, he was here, standing in front of me.

Jake fidgeted and stumbled slightly towards the door. His hand reached out, and he grabbed the frame to brace himself. My hands reached to help him, but I stopped myself. I knew I couldn't let myself get hurt again. I had to put up a wall and protect my heart. Parched, I swallowed hard, trying to mouth the words. "Sorry, I'm just . . . come in."

I opened the door all the way and pointed to the family room. He sauntered in and looked around the house cautiously. His masculine body walked past me slowly, and I felt aroused by the pure physicality of his matured muscular body. Every movement and step of his stride bulged muscles through his snug jeans that clung to the tight roundness of his rump. He was a prowling wolf walking into his domain. A sense of his raw nature made my insides boil with excitement.

I turned away, shaking my head, and pointing. "I have to, um, I'll be right back." I ran outside to the back of the house and searched for my bo staff. It was lying in some tall grass next to the forest edge. I picked up the staff and looked back at the house. The place looked a hundred miles away.

My head swam with questions. *Where has he been? Why hasn't he contacted me? Where did he go the night Dad died? Does he still think about me because I honestly never stopped thinking about him?*

I stopped at my door, straightening out my hair and shirt. "Here we go." I opened the door, and Buddy was lying on his back at Jake's feet, getting belly rubs. "Really, Buddy. You're supposed to be a guard dog." Buddy slowly crawled over to me on his belly, dragging his legs behind him. He rolled over onto his back, showing his belly.

Jake was sitting on the couch with his bag on the floor in front of him. I slowly walked past him, studying his existence as I sat on the other end of the couch. I watched him, still not believing my eyes. Buddy walked back over and sat next to Jake. Jake leaned forward and scratched behind his ears as he looked around the room. Buddy looked over at me with his tongue hanging out the side of his mouth.

"You're such a spoiled puppy."

Jake's gaze stopped and lingered over my body. I waited for him to say something, but his focus darted back to the room.

I finally broke the silence. "Are you okay?"

His eyes were heavy as his head kept nodding forward. He looked like he was about to pass out on the couch.

"You can go rest in your old room if you like. I washed

your linens and vacuumed your room when I moved back in."

His head shot up, and he looked at me. "You moved back in here?"

"Yeah, I wanted to fix it up and live here again. I haven't decided if I'll stay or sell it."

"Why?"

"Why . . . why, what?"

"But this is where your dad died."

"He was your dad, too. He loved you like a son." The letter popped into my mind, and I opened my mouth to tell him about it, but something stopped me. I closed my mouth and waited for him to say something. He shook his head, and a yawn rattled his whole body. He stood up and wobbled back and forth.

"I think I'll take you up on that offer and get some sleep."

"Oh, okay."

Jake took a step and stumbled forward.

I jumped over next to him, putting my body under his arm. He leaned against me and wrapped his arm over my shoulders, pulling me into him. His tight grip around me sent shivers down my spine. I breathed in his musk, and he smelled sweet with a faint hint of something wild and untamed. My body shivered from arousal, and I tensed up as we walked up the stairs.

CHAPTER THIRTEEN: ADELE

I *opened my eyes to the darkness surrounding me. A cool breeze nipped at my shivering body as I squirmed. A tent door flapping haunted me as I opened my eyes. I tried to stand up, but my wrists and ankles were bound by a connecting rope. My toes and hands sank into a mound of dirt as I moved back and forth. The wind picked up, and the tent door flapped opened and closed, sending chills down my spine. I stretched my body out as far as I could to look behind me and see the light beaming in and out of the door. Flashes of the full moon sitting ominously behind streaming clouds, leering down at me.*

"Adele! Adele! Wake up. Del, wake up. It's me, Jake." My eyes opened to see Jake looking down at me. Frowning, I shot up in bed and slapped his hand away.

"Hi. I think you had a bad dream. Sorry, I could hear you crying and came to wake you."

"I wasn't crying." I slipped out of bed and went into the bathroom, slamming the door.

Sweat moistened my brow as I felt a sharp pain twinge in my wrist. I looked down to see it was nothing and swiped away the sweat from my temple. I stared at my reflection, panting as my heart pounded against my chest. I knew my nightmare was a premonition. A warning of what was to come.

Shaking my head, I looked back at the door. Jake was back. *Why? Why, after all this time? I dreamed about this moment so many times, but now that it's here, it feels too good to be true. Where has he been all these years? I needed him when Dad died, and he selfishly left me and didn't look back. What does he want? My heart wants to embrace him open-armed, but my head says not to trust him.*

I leaned over and splashed cold water on my face. Exhaling, I dressed, walked through the family room to the kitchen, and made a cup of coffee. I cradled my steaming mug and turned to the window, gazing out into the forest. Jake let Buddy in and walked over to the coffee maker.

"May I?"

"Of course." Nodding, I knocked the spoon onto the floor. Fidgeting, I reached down to pick it up and hit Jake with my head as I came back up, dropping the spoon again. I stood up and gazed into his eyes. They were glowing as he smiled down at me.

"Here, let me." He bent over, and his round rump popped into the air.

I turned around and gazed out the window again. My body heated up, and I felt my cheeks burning. Sweat pooled under my arms and dampened my palms. Everything was moving so fast. I felt like my grip on reality and control of my life was slipping away. The nightmares were coming more frequently now, taunting my mind with the faint sound of flapping.

"So," Jake said. "How have you been?"

"Um, I'm good. Actually, I've—um, I've been busy. I've been working on the house, and I work from home. I—"

A loud knock at the front door stopped me in mid-sentence. Buddy sounded off and ran towards the family room.

"Are you expecting anyone?"

"No. Are you?"

"No." I followed Buddy into the family room and stood in front of the door. Another round of knocking bounced against the wood.

"Who is it?"

"It's, it's me, Molly."

I unlocked the door, and Jake walked up behind me. I pulled Buddy back, holding his collar. "Will you take him to my room? Please."

"Yes, I guess so. Who is it?"

"It's — um. It's a long story. Please just take Buddy to my room, and I'll explain later."

"Okay." Jake nodded and did as I asked.

I opened the door, and Molly was standing there shivering. "Hi."

She walked in, grabbed me, and pulled me into a tight hug. I hugged her back slightly and wondered what she wanted. Then Tommy stepped into the doorway, smiling the same self-righteous smile he wore when he'd slapped me across the face. I stepped back away from both of them, crossing my arms.

"What's going on?"

Molly smiled up at Tommy and then back at me. "We're getting married."

"Oh. Okay."

Molly held up her hand and showed me a sparkling diamond on her left ring finger. "Oh, great." I forced a smile. Molly half-smiled at me and looked up at Tommy, who was staring at me with a malicious grin. She frowned, put her arm under his, pulled him close, and shook him slightly. He looked down at her and his eyebrows creased together.

"That's great, Moll. Really, I'm happy for you two. What's it been? A week since I last saw you two? Or were you two dating while we were dating? Oh, I guess that's it. Well, good. Good. I'm just so happy." I rambled hysterically, not knowing what was wrong with me. I finally closed my mouth and waved for them to come inside. Buddy was howling in my room and jumped onto the door, vibrating his body against it. Tommy flinched, looking back and forth. "He's put up. He just remembers what you did to me and doesn't like you."

Molly's forehead arched as she blurted, "I can't believe you kept that beast. He's aggressive and already hurt someone!"

I shifted my weight and exhaled loudly. "So, when's the big day?"

"This summer. I like it when it's warm. Tommy's parents will pay for us to have a trip to Hawaii for our honeymoon."

"Well, you have it all planned out. That's great. So are you going to finish school, or just give up, I guess?"

"I was going to finish in the fall."

"Oh, okay. Well, I'll believe it when I see it. I'm pretty sure once Tommy gets you knocked up on your honeymoon, you'll have to quit and be the little wife. I guess that's what you've always wanted, though, huh?"

"Del."

I turned around, and Jake walked out with Buddy. Buddy ran towards Tommy like he was fresh meat.

Jake said, "No, Buddy." Buddy stopped in his tracks and sat down.

Tommy turned around, started for the front door, then stopped, holding the knob. He shivered as he turned around and watched Buddy. I felt a small glimmer of happiness as I watched him on high alert.

Molly stared with her mouth dropped open. I smirked, looking back at Jake as he strolled up to me like a wolf. He looked down and winked. A smile twinged, and then I looked back at Molly with a straight face.

"I'm sorry, honey. I didn't know we had company. My name's Jake."

Jake held out his hand for Molly to shake. Molly held out her hand and gently touched his. Tommy walked over and went to shake Jake's hand when Buddy started growling.

"No, Buddy," Jake said.

Tommy flinched and jerked back his hand, staring at Buddy.

"So why didn't you just call me, Molly? I tried calling and texting you, but you never responded. I guess your phone isn't working. Hmmm."

Molly glared at me with fire in her eyes. "You never apologized, Adele."

"Apologize for what, Molly?!"

"Apologize to Tommy about your beast! He could've killed him!"

"Tommy slapped me across the face, and Buddy defended me. Which is more than I can say for you! You dropped to the ground and didn't even ask me what happened! You didn't return any of my calls or texts!" I turned around and rubbed my face. I could feel Jake staring at me, but I couldn't look at him. My eyes were burning, and my bottom lip quivered as the tears welled up in my eyes. I inhaled a deep breath, shook my head, turned back around, and smiled.

"Congratulations. Thanks for stopping by, but I don't think I'll be attending the wedding." I pushed past them, walked over to the door, and opened it. I waved my hand for them to leave and looked outside. My eyes blinked tears down my cheeks. I brushed them away quickly, staring out into the road.

First Molly brushed past me, then Tommy. He turned around, stopped, and smirked at me. Jake walked up and stood next to me, staring him down. Tommy made eye contact with Jake for a split second, then spun around to leave. They both hopped into their truck and pulled away.

I slammed the door and went into the kitchen. I refused to shed any more tears for Molly and Tommy. They deserved each other after what they'd put me through. I wiped my face and stared out the kitchen window again.

Jake followed and walked up behind me. "Del, who was—"

I darted away from his questions and walked over to the

coffeemaker to pour another cup. I paused with my hand resting on the handle of the coffee pot. "I'm going to go sit outside for a bit. Come on, Buddy." I just wanted to be alone. I didn't want to try and explain what had happened between Tommy and me. Honestly, it was none of his business.

I let Buddy out first, then walked over to one of Dad's old wooden chairs. He'd built them before I was born, and they still sat strong. I eased down into it and sat quietly with my thoughts.

A few minutes later, I heard the back door close. Jake walked outside quietly and sat in the chair next to mine. I looked up into the sky and saw the treetops swaying in the wind. A gentle breeze fluffed my hair into my face, cooling my neck with its whispers. I felt Jake's attention on me. I looked over and met his gaze. Buddy walked over and touched my hand with his cold nose. I smiled at him and scratched behind his ear. "You're a good boy."

Jake broke the silence. "It's nice out here. I remember when you and I would train out here when we were kids."

I nodded and looked towards the mountains again.

"Why did he hit you?"

I inhaled a deep breath and then exhaled. My mouth opened, but nothing came out. I couldn't talk about Molly and Tommy anymore.

We gazed into each other's eyes for a long time, and then I had an idea. "Do you want to train with me?"

"What?" Jake asked.

"Hang on." I ran into the house, changed into a long-sleeved shirt, and put on my sneakers. I pulled my long hair up and checked myself in the mirror. Nodding, I grabbed our bo staffs and ran back outside.

Jake looked up and laughed. "Wow! Where did you find those?"

"I—I just found them while I was cleaning. So, do you want

to?"

"Yeah, let's do it. But you know I'm going to kick your butt. Just like the old days."

It felt good smiling with Jake again, and I enjoyed the playful banter between us. It had been a long time since I could be myself again.

"We'll see." Laughing, I walked out to the middle of the yard and started warming up the way Dad taught us. Jake stepped up and didn't miss a beat. He was right next to me, and we were in unison. I spun my bo staff, switching back and forth between hands. I eased into punching my staff and spun around, using it to jab. Jake looked over at me and nodded. I panted with sweat dripping down my brow. I nodded back and stopped, spinning my staff. "Are you ready?"

"Are you sure you want to do this?"

"Yes," I said. "I haven't trained since . . . since before the last night I saw you."

Jake stopped spinning his staff. "What? You know Dad said to always keep up our skills. That was one of his many rules. Remember?"

"Yes, Jake. Really. Let's just do this."

"Okay, I guess I'll have to go easy on you then." He smiled at me, but it was beguiling. I felt aroused by his confidence and wanted to win against him more than ever. I used my sexual frustration, channeling it into power against him. We faced each other, and I swung up and spun around and went in strong against Jake. He stomped backward and smiled at me. I smiled back, and he hit my staff with his. I pushed him back and swung to hit him. Jake dropped back, and I missed. He lunged at me, and I dodged. He jabbed, and I jabbed.

We went back and forth for a couple hours until Buddy started whining. I stepped back, panting, and lowered my staff. "Okay, pup, let's go in for a bit." I lunged at Jake one last time, flipping him over my back and dropping him hard on the ground. I smiled down at him. He grabbed my hand and pulled me down, and I landed on top of him. Our gazes met, and we burst out in laughter.

"You're squishing my bladder!"

I laughed, bouncing against Jake's diaphragm. "Sorry. I'll get up." My body temperature rose, and a surge of electricity bolted through my limbs and down into my groin. I hesitated for a moment, gazing into Jake's eyes. He slowly blinked, and his eyes started to glow. His smile faded, and he looked into my eyes with a hunger I'd never seen before. My groin throbbed, and I felt a rush of heat flush through my body. I stared down at his lips and wanted to push my mouth against his. His body was magnetizing, pulling me into him and opening my heart. His head started inching towards mine, and I could feel his warm breath blow against my bottom lip.

Buddy barked and jumped up onto the back door. Smiling awkwardly, I shook my head to dismiss my desires. I pushed myself up onto my feet, put my hand out, and pulled him up.

Jake smiled, hunched over, and used his staff as a walking stick.

"Really, come on."

He nodded, and we both walked into the house. I looked up at the clock, and it was almost one in the afternoon. "Wow, we were out there for a while."

Jake nodded, walked over, and got himself some water. I did the same, and we both gulped it down.

"Hungry?"

"Yeah. What can I do to help?"

"Nothing, I've got it."

"Okay."

I made us sandwiches and chips for lunch. Jake followed me into the family room, and we sat down by the coffee table to eat.

"It's weird being back here. It's been . . . it's been a long time," Jake said.

"Yes."

"How long have you been back?"

"A week. Molly drove down with me and stayed the first night."

"Was she your best friend or something?"

"Yes, something like that," I said.

I finished my food, gathered the plates, and walked them back into the kitchen to clean up. I prepped dinner and walked back into the family room. "I have to get some work done. I'll be in the dining room if you need anything."

"Work? What kind of work?"

"I'm a writer. I write stories about love and romance," I said. My cheeks heated up as I said it.

"I remember you always writing stories in your journal," he said. "Have you ever been in love?"

"Just make yourself at home, Jake."

Jake's smiling face popped into my mind from when we were kids. I knew that in the back of my mind, the only person I'd ever been close to being in love with was him.

"Del?"

"Yes."

"Was Tommy your lover?"

I looked away and then back at Jake and exhaled. "He wanted to get married, but we wanted different lives. I wanted to move here and be a writer, and he wanted to live in the city and have a family. When I told him that, he laughed and said being a writer was just a hobby. I told him we needed to take a break, and then I moved here." I looked away and then back at Jake. "He wanted me to be his little wife and settle down and have kids. I want kids, just . . . not with him. I didn't love him, and when I told him that, he hit me, and my dog attacked him."

Jake nodded, reached down, and petted Buddy. "You're a

good pup."

Buddy flopped over and exposed his belly.

"Really, Buddy? I need to work for at least a couple hours." I smiled at him, walked into the dining room, and started working.

CHAPTER FOURTEEN ADELE

A few hours went by, and I heard noises coming from the family room. I got up and went in to see Jake on the floor. He had my desk box opened and was putting it together. "Hey, what are you doing?"

"Well, I saw the box and thought I could put it together for you. I figured you wanted it in front of the window."

"Yes, thank you."

"It gives me something to do. How's work?"

"It's good. Well, I guess I'll get back to it then."

Jake organized all the pieces and had Dad's tools laid out and ready for use. An image of Dad and Jake standing together and working on a coffee table popped into my mind. I wanted to walk over to Jake, wrap my arms around his back, and hug him, but I knew I couldn't.

I went back into the dining room and worked for a while, and then Buddy came in and pawed at my leg. I looked up and saw the clock read five-fifteen. I closed my laptop and went into the kitchen to check on my food in the *Crock-pot*. Steam rose from the pot as I picked up the lid and smelled the meat cooking.

I glanced out the window to see the sun was resting over the mountains. When I turned to walk back into the family room, something caught my eye. A man was standing on the edge of the forest, watching me. He was very tall and dressed in all black. I wouldn't have seen him, except his pale white skin and bright blue eyes glistened from under his black hood. I cocked my head to the side and stared at him. Then it dawned on me. That looked like the same man from before. When Molly was still here, I'd seen a man standing on the forest edge watching me.

That couldn't be the same man from before. Could it? I shook my head. *No, it can't be.* It seemed like whoever he was, he was staring at me or my house again. He stepped backward and was absorbed back into the darkness of the forest. A feeling of dread ached in my stomach.

I looked back towards the family room and started to get Jake, but something stopped me. Shivers ran down my spine and tickled the back of my neck. My psyche alerted me that someone with magical abilities was near. *Is that who Dad was warning me about? Should I go get Jake and tell him that someone's watching my house? What if Jake goes out there and gets himself killed?* I looked out the window, and the man had completely disappeared. I pulled the curtains shut and spun around to see Jake.

"Hi."

I jumped. My heart boomed in my chest. "Are you . . . are you hungry? I made beef in the slow-cooker for dinner. I just need to make the sides."

"Yeah, that sounds great."

I spun back around and walked over to the pantry. I kept busy and didn't look over at Jake. He stood behind me and watched me for a few minutes before he walked over and washed his hands.

"Let me help you do something."

"I, um, I think I've got it. You can feed Buddy. His food bucket is in the pantry. I usually pour some beef juice over his food when I make it. You can grab a spoon out of the drawer," I said. "He has a food bowl in the pantry. I wrote his name on it."

"Really?" Jake chuckled as he walked over to the pantry.

"Yes, he's a good boy. Yes, he is." I smiled down at Buddy. His rump bounced on the floor as he watched Jake and me.

The window haunted me and drew my gaze over. The curtain closed out the night, but the image of the man burned in my memory.

Jake fed Buddy, and we sat down and ate dinner at the round table in the kitchen. I looked back at the window and then glanced at Jake. He looked up at me, cocked his head to the side, and looked back at the window and then at me. I didn't know how to tell him what I'd seen outside. I finished my food, cleaned my plate, and put it in the drainer. I walked over and let Buddy out the backdoor.

The trees swayed in the wind as I walked out onto the porch. Tree limbs crackling and breaking rattled through the forest. Shivering, I walked back to the door and whistled for Buddy to come. I could hear the ground ruffling as he ran around in the yard.

Jake ran into me with the door as he opened it. "You okay?"

"Yeah, why? Aren't you cold?"

Jake cocked his head to the side and smiled. "I don't really get cold."

I wrapped my arms around myself and bounced.

"So, why did you put the fence in?"

"Um, well, it's a long story. Mostly because of Buddy. I was afraid of him running into the forest and getting eaten by something. Come on, pup. It's cold." Buddy ran up the steps and shook off. We walked back in, and Jake started cleaning the kitchen.

"Thank you. So where did you learn to do that?" I smiled, playfully pointing at Jake washing up in the sink.

"I know how to do the dishes. You were always . . . just better at it."

"Wow, thanks, Jake."

I walked over and opened up the dishwasher. "I had a dishwasher installed. I never actually need it because it's just Bud and I. Technically, we can use it tonight if you want."

"I'm almost done, and there really aren't a lot of dishes to do."

Nodding, I close the door and walk over to the coffee maker. "Do you want some tea?"

"Tea?"

"Yeah, sometimes I have green tea and watch something on my computer after eating."

"Okay. I don't think I've ever had tea."

"It's good and helps you sleep."

I made us each a mug of green tea, grabbed my computer, and walked into the family room.

I checked the locks on the front door and peeked out the window. The road was dark, and the wind blew leaves and dead limbs across my porch. The window was fogged up from the cold outside, so I wiped it and looked again.

Jake walked up behind me and looked over my shoulder. "What are you looking for?"

"Oh, nothing. Just checking outside."

He looked outside and looked down at me with his eyebrow raised. "You okay?"

"Yeah, of course." I walked over to the couch and realized he'd finished putting my desk together. It was a beautiful pale oak with three drawers going down each side. It fit perfectly in front of the window. Smiling, I ran my fingers over the soft finish of the wood. "Thank you, Jake. It's beautiful! It would've taken me a while to get it together."

He nodded and took a big swig of his tea. "I know."

"What!" I smiled. "Well, not that long. Just . . . you, know." I shrugged my shoulders and blew on my tea.

"It's okay, Del. I wanted to."

His eyes started glowing again as he looked at me. My heart thumped in my chest, and my face heated up again. I quickly walked over, sat on the couch, and turned on a show on my computer.

The wind picked up and pushed against the cabin, squealing as it went inward. My gaze darted to the front door again, watching the shadows bounce in front of the window.

Jake's focus darted back and forth between the door and me. "What is it, Del?"

"Nothing. It's nothing." I looked at him and then back at the door.

"Is there someone outside?"

I shook my head and didn't want to answer. I didn't know exactly who or what I'd seen earlier.

"Del! Did you see someone outside? Do you feel someone out there?"

"I don't know."

Jake stood up and walked over to the door. I jumped off the couch and followed him over. I grabbed his arm, turning him to face me. "Don't."

"Del, is there someone out there?"

"No. Well. I don't know, Jake. Okay, I don't know. I don't feel anyone anymore."

"But you saw someone, didn't you? Didn't you?"

I hesitated. I didn't want to answer. "I'm not sure. I think I saw someone out the kitchen window next to the forest. It was only for a second. I honestly thought I was seeing things."

"I'm going to go check."

"No. Really, don't, Jake. I . . . just wait." I exhaled and looked at the door. "I think I saw someone a week ago when Molly was here before. I remember it was strange, because he was very pale with bright blue eyes. I didn't think much about it, but tonight I saw a similar-looking person in the same location again, except I felt him watching me this time. I felt that he was different. He had abilities like us."

"It'll be fine. Just let me check. Okay? I promise. I'll be careful."

He gazed into my eyes, and my heart fluttered. I didn't

want Jake to get hurt just in case the person was still out there.

"Why won't you let me go outside to check?"

"I don't know . . . I'm afraid, Jake."

"It's okay. I'm not scared."

Jake reached over, grabbed his bo staff, and walked up to the front door. He unlocked the bolt, looked at me, and smiled provocatively as he opened the door. He walked out onto the porch, stood on the steps, and sniffed the air. A gust of wind blew a drizzle of moisture, dampening my hair. Steam exhaled through my dry lips as I stood completely still, listening to the night. The wind died down, and an owl sang in the trees.

"I don't see anyone. Did you say you saw someone at the backdoor?"

"No, the kitchen window, but it's too dark to see anything now."

Jake walked back inside and nodded. He looked toward the back of the house. I walked over to the couch and sat down. Jake locked the door and sat down next to me.

"So, it was the kitchen window, and you said you saw him before today?"

"I was looking out the kitchen window and saw a hooded man with bright blue eyes and pale skin stare at the house. He stepped back into the forest and disappeared before I could get a good look at him. Honestly, he was probably just a hunter."

"Yeah, but this is the second time you saw this guy. Right?"

"Yeah." I nodded, yawning, and sat cross-legged on the couch. I turned the show back on my computer and felt myself zoning out.

I kept thinking about Dad's letter and what he wrote.

Should I tell Jake about his letter? Maybe that's why he's here now? He was meant to come back into my life, and we're supposed to find each other again. But Dad also said to be careful because people aren't always what they seem.

I looked over at Jake, staring at him. Wondering.

Is he truly here because he missed me, or is there something else?

He looked at me, smiling. "What is it?"

I smiled, shaking my head.

"What? What is it?"

"I'm glad you came back. I've missed you."

"I've missed you, too."

"I'm pretty tired, and I need to get some rest for tomorrow. I actually have a lot of work to do before my deadline."

"Okay."

I stood up, yawned, and stretched.

"Del?"

"Yeah?"

"Thank you for letting me stay here for a couple of days. I've wanted to come back here for a while and see the old place. You know."

"Yeah, I'm glad you did."

"Anyhow, I just need to get my assets in line, and then I can get going."

"Jake, you're welcome to stay as long as you like. It's honestly nice having you here. I have Buddy, but sometimes it gets a little lonely."

"Del?"

"Yes."

"Can we go fishing tomorrow?"

"Sure. Sounds fun."

"Okay, night."

"Night."

CHAPTER FIFTEEN: JAKE

My eyes opened, and I turned to see I was in my old bedroom. I rolled over and put my feet on the floor. A cool breeze nipped at my bare toes, pushing air up my pants. A giant yawn shivered through my body as I twitched from the cold. A small crack of light escaped the curtained window, lighting up the doorknob to my room.

A voice whispered behind my ear, calling my name. "Jake . . . Jake." I jumped up, swirling around with my fists up. I slowly crept towards the door and realized I'd recognized the voice calling for me. It was the man with eyes that glowed emerald-green in the darkness. He came for me the last night I was a Merc. He spoke my name and smiled perniciously as I ran into the woods.

I walked to the top of the stairs and was greeted by another cool breeze blowing back my mane. I jogged down the stairs and glanced toward Del's room. Her door was closed, and the light was off. The clock over the mantel read three AM. Nodding, I continued into the kitchen for a drink. I grabbed a glass, turned on the faucet, and gulped several sips of water.

"Jake." Another whisper tickled my lobe right behind my ear. I whipped around, but the room was empty.

"Who's there?" I demanded as I searched the darkness for my stalker.

A loud crash against the back door rattled the walls of the mud-room. I tip-toed over to the door and watched shadows racing back and forth through the window's curtain. Unlocking the door, I stepped outside. The wind whistled through the trees, whining, as another gust of air pushed against me. The door slammed behind me, and I whipped around to see the door turn into dust. The house slowly faded away, and a solitary tent appeared. The flap of the tent door crackled violently against the wind.

Three men appeared from the darkness and entered the tent. I ran up to the tent, and the minute I touched the flapping door, everything went still. The wind's groans ceased and came to a complete halt.

I walked inside, and blood-curdling screams bellowed from the center of the room. Chills shivered down my spine as I approached the three individuals. They were surrounding a man hovering over a person sitting on the floor. His sharp talons were extended as a bright blinding light flowed into the palm of his hand. As I inched closer to get a better look, I realized the person screaming was Adele. He was drawing power from her forehead into him. His body began to glow a vibrant emerald green to match his florescent eyes. Blood oozed out of Adele's orifices as her body trembled under his control.

My parched lips graded together as I mouthed the hushed words. I inhaled a deep breath and screamed. "No!"

I shot up in bed, panting, and looked around the room. My heart pounded in my chest as sweat dripped from my brow. I jumped out of bed, slammed the door open, and walked to the stairs.

The house was still asleep but fully lit with natural sunlight shining through the windows. I inhaled deeply and walked into the bathroom to do my business. *It was just a dream. It was just a dream.* I chanted the words in my head.

I faced the sink and turned on the hot water. Steam filled the bathroom, fogging up the mirror. I swiped the glass and gazed at my own reflection. Shaking my head, I attempted to stand up straight, and a flash of the tent door flapping burned in my mind. A sharp pain pierced through my chest, and an image of Adele's helpless body ached in my heart. I squeezed my eyes shut and swiped handfuls of water over my face. I knew that my dream was a warning. A premonition of what was to come if I couldn't protect her. *Something brought me back to her, but I don't know if that's enough. I don't know if she'll let me back into her heart after leaving her so long ago.*

CHAPTER SIXTEEN: ADELE

I opened my eyes and saw darkness surrounding me. Cool air blew, nipping at my ears as I lay in the dirt. Déjà vu. I've been here before. I looked over and saw the tent door flapping in the wind. A tiny bit of light peeked through the door, casting shadows across the walls. Another cold breeze wafted through the door and blew the perfume of meats sizzling over a fire. I tried to sit up, but sharp pains shot through my wrists and ankles. I squirmed over to the tent door and looked out to see men standing around a long table. They were all wearing black pants, boots, and long black jackets with hoods covering their faces. The wind picked up, and the door slapped my face.

"Del!"

I opened my eyes and blinked up at Jake.

"Are you okay?"

"Yeah, I'm fine." I sat up, and my head pounded. I lay back and held my forehead with both hands. Buddy crawled up to the top of the bed, licking my chin. "I'm okay, pup." I sat up, climbed out of bed, walked into my bathroom, and started the shower.

A knock rattled the bathroom door.

"Del, are you sure you're, okay?"

"Yeah, I just need a shower. I'll be out soon." I rinsed off and smelled coffee when I turned off the water.

I got dressed, walked into the kitchen, and saw Jake feeding Buddy. "Thank you." I grabbed two *Advil*, poured myself a coffee, headed back into the dining room, and sat down.

"So, I guess no fishing today?"

"Oh, yeah. Of course, we can fish. Just let me drink my coffee."

My headache cleared up, and I hopped up, grabbing my hiking boots, winter hat, and gloves. I grabbed Buddy's harness and walked back into the family room. It had been a long time since I'd been on a walk in the woods, especially with Jake. After Buddy was ready, I paced back and forth and looked up to see Jake walking into the room. A flash of when I first met him as a boy went through my mind.

I saw my younger self standing next to him at the front door, making faces. Shaking my head, I grinned.

Jake was freshly shaven, and his hair was combed back. His six-foot-four body seemed dark and mysterious under his long mane of hair as he leaned over to pet Buddy. Strands of thick black locks masked his animalistic features, concealing his true identity as the wolf. His black long-sleeved shirt clung to his body enough to outline his six-pack abs and reveal that his manhood grew, bulging out his pants. I tried to narrow my eyes and not look so obvious, staring. "You, um, you look nice."

"Where are Dad's poles and tackle box?"

"I moved them to the closet."

He turned and walked over to the closet to reveal his tight rump, firm and barely contained in his jeans. He opened the closet door and leaned down. I shuddered and forced myself to turn and walk toward the kitchen. My body heated up, and I yearned for Jake physically. Images of him naked and ready, laying across my bed, flashed through my mind. Blinking, I squeezed my eyes shut and pushed the thought out of my mind.

I put together some sandwiches and reached up into the cabinet's top shelf when Dad's old lunch bag fell onto the counter. Pausing, I looked down at it for a long moment. My fingers ran across his faded name, *Bill*. I patted the bag and brushed off all the dust and cobwebs.

Jake's feet echoed down the hall, and I stopped and threw the food inside and grabbed a bag of chips, four water bottles, and a plastic bowl for Buddy. I grabbed my keys, shoving them into my pocket.

"Are you ready then?"

Jake nodded, and we headed out of the house.

I followed him into the forest, and we took the same old path we always took with Dad years ago. Once we entered the forest, it was like we were kids again. Smiling, I looked over at Jake. "I'm glad we're doing this. It's been too long."

The morning was early, with dew still covering the ground. The forest was quiet as the birds and squirrels were still waking up from their nightly slumber. Dad led the way, then me, and then Jake when we were kids. This time, Buddy was the leader, dragging me and sniffing everything as we walked.

"Why don't you just let him go, Del? He'll be fine. I'll help you watch him."

Jake grabbed Buddy's leash, leaned down, and unhooked him before I could argue. "Damn it, Jake! I don't think that's a good idea. What if there's a bear or badger? Or something worse?"

"He'll be fine. I'll help you watch him. I promise."

At first, Buddy didn't realize he was free and slowly trudged along. Then he shot away from us like a bullet. Leaves sailed into the air, and he jumped head-first into a pile and lay there with his legs sticking out the back. Laughing, I threw my head back and chuckled. Jake walked over and stood next to me. We looked at each other, smiling.

"Come on, silly pup," he said.

Buddy ran up to Jake, walking side by side, and I followed them until we made it to the river.

Jake walked out to the river and stood on the water's edge. "This was his favorite spot. Or at least I think it was."

I walked out of the trees and looked up to see Dad's face smiling back at me. "It's right."

Jake nodded, sat down, and opened Dad's old tackle box. I walked over, pointed to a lure I liked, and handed Jake my pole.

He smiled at me shaking his head. "Just like old times, huh?"

"Yep." I walked over to the river and stared out over the water. The water glistened in the morning sun as its peeks of ice sparkled like crystals. Buddy galloped out of the forest and aimed for the river at full speed. "Buddy, no." He came to a halt and walked in halfway, drinking and walking simultaneously. He coughed and snorted as he choked gulps of water. "See, that's what you get, doofus."

Jake walked over and handed me my pole. I nodded, turned to the river, cast out, and then reeled in slowly. Jake headed down the river to cast.

There were patches of ice on the bank's edge clumped up with mud. I held up my pole and tried to stay away from the ice. Jake's line spun and seized as he pulled back his rod. A fish was fighting him on the other end, trying to get away. After a few times of pulling and reeling, he finally won and held up a giant catfish.

"Wow, just like old times. You and Dad catching all the fish and me watching." I honestly didn't mind. It was nice being out in the sunshine, back at Dad's old spot with Jake.

Buddy walked over, bumped his head against my leg, and looked up at me. "Really, spoiled pup. Do you just need some scratching? Hmm." I scratched behind his ears, and he did three circles before he finally lay down in a dry spot on the ground to sunbathe. I reeled in my line, walked upriver a few more feet, and cast out again. Slowly reeling in, I looked over at Jake and watched him. He reminded me of the same old goofball I knew as a kid, except now he was grown into a strong, handsome man.

He used to smile and play pranks on me when we were young. He called me Deli smelly and pulled my hair or made silly faces. Now he was cautious and reserved around me. His demeanor suggested a kept man with little to no worries, but I knew that something was going on with him.

Why would he show up out of the blue? Is he running from something or someone?

After an hour of no luck, I reeled in my lure and sat down on a flat rock, sitting over the river. I laid my pole in the dirt behind me, wrapped my arms around my knees, and sunbathed. Closing my eyes, I listened to the water rushing over the rocks and the warmth on my face.

Jake startled me when he sat down behind me on the rock, holding his pole.

"What's wrong?"

I opened my eyes, smiling. "Nothing. It's nice being out here with you. I'm glad we came."

He looked at me with a big smile.

"I was thinking about eating a sandwich. You hungry?"

"Sure," he said.

Jake got up and fetched my bag. I pulled it open and retrieved the sandwiches. We ate quietly, and then I grabbed the water to wash them down. Buddy walked over and sat as close as possible to my sandwich. "Really? You know human food hurts your tummy." He cocked his head back and forth, listening to me. I pulled a few bites of my sandwich off and gave it to him. "You're a spoiled puppy." I stared out over the water for a long moment, then looked at Jake.

"Jake." He looked at me. "Why did you leave all those years ago when Dad died? You and I could have both been in the same foster home with Molly. Molly isn't the best person, but her mother was really kind to me. She would've taken you and I both in."

"I'm not like you, Del. Dad was different, and he under-stood what I am and how we're different. I was fourteen and thought I could take care of myself . . ." He stared out over the water. "When Dad died, I got scared, so I ran."

I looked out at the river and then back at Jake and shook my head. "For years, I thought you were in foster, so when I turned eighteen, I started looking for you, using websites to locate you. It was like . . . you just disappeared. I honestly thought you died." I patted my chest and swallowed hard. "But I felt you were still alive. So, I just stopped. I stopped looking and moved on. I thought you would come back, and . . . you never did. Not until now. Why?"

Jake looked out over the river, took a deep breath, and then looked back at me. He put his hand on mine and looked into my eyes. His intense eyes glowed as he opened his mouth, creeping toward me. I felt his power peak. I shivered with ex-citement and waited for him to say something.

"Del. I—"

"Excuse me!"

We both turned around, and a man with a gun exited the forest and walked over to us. Jake stood up first, and then I stood up behind him. It was Mace.

Buddy woke up, recognized him, and started barking hys-terically. I walked over to Buddy, grabbing his collar. "No, Buddy. Sit." I clipped his leash on his harness and turned around to Mace, who was walking up behind me. Jake was right next to me in seconds.

"Well, hello there, young lady. What are you doing way out here?"

"I, um, we're fishing." I stepped away from Mace, pointing my hand over to Jake. "Mace. Meet my . . . fiancé, Jake." Jake didn't take his eyes off Mace and walked over and put himself between Mace and me. Buddy pulled me, growling at him.

"No! Buddy! Sit!" Jake put his hand out, and Mace slowly reached his hand up and gripped it, squinting.

"Jake, huh? Wait, are you? Jake, her brother? Yeah, yeah. I remember you."

"Um, no. I'm her fiancé. We're going to get married in a few months."

"I'm Mace from down the street. I worked with your dad. Don't you remember?"

Jake shook his head and looked back at me.

"Sorry. You have the wrong Jake. My brother moved away a long time ago, and I don't know where he is."

"Uh, huh." Mace nodded and eyed both of us. "I'm pretty good with faces, and you sure look familiar, Jake."

I watched Mace look back and forth between us, and then I realized I remembered him. His face flashed in my mind from the night before Dad died. He was the man Dad had forced to leave. My heart pounded in my chest as I swallowed hard, trying to collect myself. My mouth dropped open, and I turned to Jake.

"Sorry, man, you have me confused with someone else."

"Uh, huh? Well, you two be careful. The forest is full of dangers."

"We were just leaving. Are you ready?" I threw my bag over my shoulder, grabbed the poles, and handed them to Jake. Mace stared at both of us for a long moment and then focused on me and smiled.

"Bye now."

Jake put his hand on the small of my back and guided me into the forest. I shivered and walked as fast as I could to get away from there. We didn't speak, just walked until we made it back. The walk to the cabin took just over two hours, so it was dark when we reached the house.

We both went straight to our rooms when we got home. I used the bathroom, kicked my shoes off, and pulled the covers over my head. I didn't know what to say to Jake. Everything felt like it was out of control. Jake came home after disappearing for over a decade. He expected me to greet him with open arms, but I really didn't know who he was or where he'd been. Then Mace, the man who was there the night before Dad died, showed up—twice now—and warned us about the dangers. *Is he a part of the reason why Dad was killed?* My bedroom door creaked and opened slowly.

"Del? Are you asleep?"

Part of me wanted to turn over and invite Jake into my bed. All those years of thinking about him and wondering if he was alive. *Did he think about me as much as I thought about him? He touched my hand and acted like he wanted to tell me, but I didn't know if I was ready to hear what he had to say.* Exhaustion weighed heavy on my shoulders as I closed my eyes and tried to lie still until he walked out of the room. My heart pounded in my chest as I felt my eyes fill with moisture. I wanted Jake in my bed more than anything but feared he would be gone in the morning if I did.

CHAPTER SEVENTEEN: VICTOR

The wind picked up and whistled against the thin glass. The sign outside rocked, flashing the neon red words *Littleton Motel*. I inhaled deep and exhaled dark grey smoke at the window's frame. My weight shifted in the unforgiving motel chair as I inhaled another puff of my cigarette. My phone vibrated on the table, flashing in the darkroom.

"Yes."

"Victor."

"Yes."

"He's with the girl now. I followed them into the forest, and they're together now."

I inhaled another long drag and exhaled loudly, blowing the hot air against the window. The steam fogged a portion of the window and slowly faded away.

"Sir?"

"We move in tomorrow. Get the men together. We leave in the morning."

"Yes, sir."

"Don't kill them. Capture them both. We can use tranks. I want them both alive. Understand?"

"Sir? What if they —"

"Do you understand?"

"Yes."

Click.

Chapter Eighteen: Jake

I walked into the kitchen and turned on the faucet to fill up Buddy's water bowl. As I stared out the window over the kitchen sink, memories struck my heart.

For a year after Dad died, I wandered the streets, lost and heart-broken. Begging and stealing became the only way for me to survive.

One day, a man came up to me and put his hand on my arm. "Hey, man, do you want to go get something to eat?

A sensation shot down my arm when he touched me. I instantly knew he was different, magical. I slapped his hand away. "Fuck off. Not interested, asshole."

"Jake, I know who you are. I've been looking for you for a long time. Come with me, and let's go get something to eat."

His eyes flashed a crystal blue. I glanced around and saw two other men standing near us. My chest rose and fell as I inhaled their scents. Fear tainted the air as they looked at each other nervously and then back at me. I was young then, and the wolf was building more vital every day. My control over him emerging was chaotic.

I closed my eyes and breathed deep, keeping him at bay. My eyes opened. I cocked my head to the side, glaring at him. "What do you want?"

"I just want to talk and have lunch. I'm hungry, and I bet you are, too, from the looks of it. Come on. We can walk right over there to that diner."

I looked around and then over at the diner. The scent of burgers cooking on the grill wafted towards us. The man talking slowly turned his head toward me, grinning and shrugging his shoulders.

"Smells good," he said.

We walked to the restaurant, and he got us a long, round booth.

He pointed for me to sit, but I shook my head and held my hand out for them to sit first. We ordered our food and handed the waitress back her menus.

"We've been looking for you for a long time, Jake." He looked around at the other men and then back to me. "I have a business proposition for you. I want you to come work for me. We're in a special line of work called mercenaries. Do you know what that is?"

I shook my head and eyed all the men around the table.

"A merc is a person who's a hired hitman. It's a soldier who goes in and kills people for money." He looked at me and then over at his friends and smiled. "They sent me here for you. Your father was a merc. Your grandfather was a merc, and we want you to follow in their footsteps."

"They?"

"I'm not at liberty to say. I just know that you were born to follow in their footsteps."

Our food arrived, and I stared at him. The waitress sat my plate in front of me. Steak, a large baked potato with butter and cheese, and a large helping of steaming green beans with bacon. My mouth watered as I cut into the rare piece of meat. Three bites and I devoured it. Everyone stared at me as I gobbled down my food. I gulped my water down and wiped my mouth and hands on the napkin. The man watched me eat and waited for me to finish before speaking again.

"Jake, I know you don't trust me, but is this life really what you want? You want to freeze to death every night, not knowing where you're going to sleep or if you're going to have something to eat the next day?"

I looked past him and gazed out the diner window. Del and Dad's faces danced in front of me. I nodded slowly, turning to him. "How does this work?"

He reached his hand out, smiling. "My name's Rick. This is Vahn and Scott." He looked at the two men and nodded.

"I need to go use the restroom." I walked into the bathroom, turned on the water, and splashed hot water over my face and hands several times. The heat burned, but I wanted to wash off any

remnants of the emptiness that filled my heart. A tear rolled down my cheek, and my chest tightened. Squeezing my eyes shut, I aggressively swiped more hot water over my face until my skin burned. I looked up and saw myself distorted in the reflection.

CHAPTER NINETEEN: ADELE

I could hear Jake in the kitchen with Buddy, feeding him. I listened for Jake's footsteps going upstairs before I slipped out of bed and put on my pajamas. I walked into the kitchen, got a drink of water, and turned around to see Jake standing behind me. I jumped back, holding my chest. "Ugh! You scared the crap out of me."

"Are you okay?"

I nodded my head and looked away.

He walked over and stood in front of me. "Why won't you look at me?"

I shook my head. I couldn't look at him. My heart was confused about how to feel.

"Del. I—"

I looked up, and his eyes were glowing.

"Del . . ."

He stepped closer to me.

"Del, I left because I knew I could never go into the foster system. I wanted to come back sooner. I—"

I shook my head and looked away. Tears welled up in my eyes as anger burned inside my chest. I bit my quivering lip and looked back at him. "Don't give me that shit. If you wanted to come back, then you would have. You ran and didn't look back. You were a coward. I needed you, Jake, and you left me." I pushed him away and put my back to him. "I lost everyone I loved."

He grabbed my shoulder and spun me around. "I couldn't come back because I . . . I didn't know what to do, so I ran. I

ended up starving and living on the streets. Then I met someone who gave me a job. He wanted to help me, or at least
that's what I thought . . . I trained to be a soldier, and then . . .
I worked. They knew what I was, and they —" He exhaled a
deep breath. "I thought I was doing some good, but I realized
I was being used for my gifts."

My mouth dropped open. I couldn't believe what I was
hearing. Jake paced back and forth, looked over at me, then
paced some more.

"I didn't leave on good terms. I couldn't . . . I didn't follow
orders, and I'm scared they'll follow me here. They know exactly who I am and where I'm from. I'll have to leave here,
and I can never come back. I just . . . I just wanted to see you
one last time. I wanted to tell you I'm sorry for leaving you all
those years ago. I wanted to come back before, but I couldn't."

Jake walked out of the room and headed for the family
room. I shook my head in shock. I couldn't believe what I was
hearing. After all this time, he wanted to come back, but he
couldn't. Shaking my head, I rubbed the tears from my eyes.
I inhaled a deep breath, followed him into the family room,
and sat next to him.

"All this time, I thought you were dead. I'm glad you came
back." I leaned over, put my arms around his waist, and laid
my head on his shoulder. He wrapped his arms around my
waist and squeezed.

My eyes burned as I pulled away from him. Jake leaned
forward and stopped right before putting his lips to mine. I
closed my eyes and felt a tear roll down my cheek. Jake's hand
swept under my chin, and he gently pressed his lips against
mine. He wrapped his arms around me and pulled me into
him. A warm sensation flowed from my lips down to my toes.
I pulled my lips away quickly.

"I have something for you, Jake. Let me go get it. I'll be
right back." I stood up, walked into my room, grabbed the

letter from under my bed, and laid it on top. "Jake," I called from my room.

Jake walked into my room and sat down on my bed. I crawled into bed, pulling the covers over my legs. I pointed to the letter. "Dad wrote us letters." I handed Jake the sealed letter.

"Where did . . . where did you find this?"

"It's a long story. Just read it."

Jake slowly sat down next to me on my bed, crossing his legs. He looked over at me and then back down at his letter. I watched his face as he opened it.

Chapter Twenty Jake

Adele had sounded so urgent as she told me there was something for me. As soon as I saw it in her hands, I knew. I trembled as I reached for it. The minute it touched my hand I felt his presence. *Dad.* I looked up, and he was standing at the end of the bed, smiling at me. A special seal covered the lip to close the envelope. I broke through, opening the letter.

Jake,

If you're reading this, then I'm gone. You've grown up into a strong, brave young man, and it's been an honor to be your father. I have cherished every moment of teaching and preparing you for the harshness of the world.

I'm sorry I never told you the truth about the day at the market. Adele finding you wasn't by accident. You see, the thing is, your parents and I were best friends. I swore to protect you if anything happened to them. You're of royal blood and one of the last of your kind. A man named Victor murdered your parents. He's a very dark and powerful being who drained your parents of their powers and left them for dead. I wish I could be there to help you fight against Victor when the day comes, but I know that you and Adele will stay together and protect each other. Adele loves you very much and will die for you. All I ask is that you love and protect her in return.

Eventually, they'll find you as they found me. Take Adele and go to the place I told you about in the mountains. I put a spell on it to protect you when the time comes.

I have always been proud of you and loved you very much. Take care of each other.

Love,

Dad

I couldn't hold back as tears flooded my cheeks. I nodded at Adele and looked down at the letter again. A white flame ignited, and then smoke billowed into the air. I dropped the note on the ground, and before I realized what was happening, the letter disintegrated into nothing.

I looked up and met Adele's gaze.

She patted the bed. "Lie down with me, Jake."

When I crawled into bed, she yawned and cuddled up against me. I pulled her closer, holding her for the first time in a long time. In that moment, I realized how much I had always loved her. I always wanted this life with her. I closed my eyes and listened to her breathing until sleep took me.

CHAPTER TWENTY-ONE: ADELE

My eyes opened to the darkness surrounding me. The wind swooshed through the tent and slapped the flap back and forth, taunting me. Sharp pains shot through my wrists as I squirmed over to the door. A dozen men dressed in all black stood next to a row of long industrial tables with bulletin boards attached. The boards rocked back and forth, threatening to collapse with one strong gust of wind. I scanned the grounds and saw someone lying next to a bonfire in the dirt. I squinted and tried to sit up to make out who it was. The person shifted their weight and looked up at me. "Jake."

"Adele! Wake up. Del, wake up!" I opened my eyes to see Jake lying in my bed next to me.

"Were you having another bad dream?"

Panting, I sat up, rubbing my face. The image of Jake lying in the dirt beside the fire burned in my mind. Shaking my head, I squeezed my eyes shut and held my face, leaning over into my lap.

He rubbed my back with long broad strokes. "Are you okay?"

Nodding, I turned back to look at him, and he was smiling at me. My body warmed up with excitement. He gently pushed my hair out of my face and guided me back onto my pillow. My heartbeat pounded, deafening my ears. I played this moment over and over again in my fantasies, and it was finally happening. Shivering, my body trembled with anticipation as I knew this would change everything. Jake leaned over my body halfway and gazed into my eyes. His hand grazed my forehead and swept across my cheek. A smile creased his brow as his eyes glistened down at me. My mouth dropped open, gasping for deep breaths of air. My lungs quickly filled and exhaled as I wet my lips. I craved Jake's touch, the tenderness of his flesh against mine. He inched over me and pressed his manhood between my legs. Electricity flashed inside my tummy and fluttered down into my groin.

"Del?"

He put his hand up to my face, ran his fingers down my chin, and touched my neck. Chills shuddered through my body as I trembled. "Yes."

Jake leaned in and put his lips to mine. I closed my eyes and tasted his sweet nectar as he ran his tongue gently inside my mouth, tangling them together as one. I broke free and inhaled a deep breath, taking in his musk. His scent deepened with the release of his endorphins. He ran his lips down my neck, shoved my shirt up, and found my nipples erect and ready. He suckled them and nibbled gently, making me squirm. I leaned forward and connected my lips to his again.

Jake rubbed his bulge against my groin and—

Knocking rattled my front door. We both jumped and stopped abruptly. Our hearts pounded in unison as we both stared in the direction of the front door. Buddy sounded off, barking as he ran towards the door. The front door rattled again, but it was a much heavier knock this time. Jake got out of bed first, and then I did. Shaking, I stripped off my pajamas and put on my jeans and t-shirt. I followed Jake into the family room and peeked out of the window. "It's my creepy neighbor, Mace."

Jake pulled me away from the window. "No, it's not." He pointed to the windows on the side of the house. Shadows of several men were walking along the house, holding guns.

"Jake, what's happening?"

"They're not here for you. They're here for me."

Jake's body moved so fast that I didn't realize he'd picked me up until my feet were off the ground. His hands gripped my rump as he carried me over his shoulder to the bedroom and sat me down. "Stay here. This isn't your fight, and I don't want you getting hurt."

"Jake, please, I can fight."

"No."

"You can't tell me what to do, damn it." I pushed against his chest, and he put his hand on my forearms and held up my arms.

"I can't lose you again, Del. I—" He stopped, and I could see the emotion in his eyes. He loved me. He almost said it. My heart skipped a beat when I realized what he was about to say.

"Stay here. I'll take care of it."

I stepped back, dazed. I didn't know what to say. Jake opened the bedroom door and brought Buddy in. He marched over, grabbed me by the waist, and pulled me to him, pushing his lips against mine.

"Stay here. I mean it."

CHAPTER TWENTY-TWO JAKE

I opened the front door, and men flooded into the cabin. Rick strolled out in front of them and glared at me, holding his rifle erect. He nodded to some of his men to crowd around me, then met my gaze.

"Jake! We've been looking for you everywhere. Where have you been?"

"What do you want?"

"You know what we want."

"Well, too bad, 'cause I'm not coming back. So get the hell out of here. Now!"

"Sir, he wants them brought back alive."

"Go see where the girl is." He pointed towards Adele's bedroom.

"Yes, sir."

I looked at Rick and cocked my head to the side.

"Oh, don't you worry. We won't hurt her." He mischievously chuckled. "Too much. Right, boys?"

I let out a monstrous growl and stood in a fighting stance, waiting for them to attack. I would die before letting them pass me and get to Adele. Gunshots fired, filling the wall to Adele's room with holes. I turned to stop the man shooting when another man came at me from the side and hit me with a silver bar in the abdomen, throwing me back against Del's bedroom door. A sharp pain pinched my side. I looked down to see a tranquilizer sticking out of my rib cage. I ripped it out and threw it on the ground.

"You shouldn't have done that." My body rose into the air,

and then my limbs grew to complement my height. The beast emerged, and I looked down at Rick first.

"Calm down, Jake! Calm—" His eyes bulged, and he tripped, trying to run towards the door.

I slapped his body, knocking him through the window next to the front door. I peered out the hole to see him lying on the ground, motionless. A heavy blow hit the back of my head, vibrating my body with a burning sensation. I turned to see a man holding a silver bar. I swiped my claws and threw him against two other men, knocking them over like dominos. One by one, they rose and came back for more. The men ganged up on me, hanging onto all my limbs, trying to hold me down. My bo staff sat against the wall next to the front door. I swung my arms back and forth, throwing two men off and lunging for my staff. I uppercut the first one in the jaw and splattered blood across the wall. I slammed my staff down, knocking the second one to the ground. Third, I dropped my staff and twisted the man's neck until it popped.

The first man stood back up and punched my back with the silver bar. My body vibrated again, with tremors rolling throughout my limbs. I slapped the silver bar from his grip, ripping a hole in his chest. He dropped to the ground, cupping his hands over his chest as the blood seeped through his fingers. The second man stumbled forward, and I sliced across his throat, cutting open his jugular. He wobbled back and forth, finally hitting the floor.

I stumbled through the front door, looking for Rick. He'd disappeared. There was blood splattered on the ground where he'd landed. I walked out into the road and looked around for him. Del's creepy neighbor, Mace, looked back as he ran down the road. I weaved back and forth, walking back into the house.

My heart filled with rage. I'd always thought Rick was on my side as a friend and confidant. He'd betrayed me and hunted me down like a dog.

I sauntered to Del's room and waited for her to come out. Inhaling deep breaths, I calmed the beast and eased back into my human form. I knew that more was coming, and we didn't have much time left before they would return.

Chapter Twenty-Three Adele

I was so shocked my mouth dropped open. My ears were numb to Jake's muted words as I gazed around the family room. Dead bodies and blood littered the floors and walls. I was lost for words. My mouth was parched as I swallowed back tears. I didn't know what I was supposed to do next. Everything was changing so fast. Shaking my head, I looked around the room and was reminded of when Dad died. Flashes of him lying on the floor gazing at me with a hollow stare burned in my heart. I squeezed my eyes shut and slowly started to hear Jake's voice speaking to me.

"Del, are you listening? Adele! Snap out of it!"

He grabbed my shoulder, shaking me hard. Pain shot through my arm, and I looked up and yanked myself away from him. "No, we need to clean this up." I leaned down and grabbed broken pieces of furniture from the floor.

Jake squatted, meeting my eyes with a calm voice. "Del, we have to leave. Now. They're coming back, and next time there will be a lot more men and weapons. Are you hearing me?"

I stood up and ran into my room, grabbed my phone, and dialed the police.

Jake grabbed my phone. "What the hell are you doing?"

"I'm calling the police, Jake! They destroyed my home. Everything. Everything Dad built is gone. I don't know what else to do—" My bottom lip quivered as the words came out of my mouth. I blinked, and a stream of tears rolled down my cheeks. I dropped the wood pieces on the ground and cupped my face. Jake put his arms around me and held me. I let go and bounced against his chest. After calming down, I pulled back from Jake's hug. "This is your fault. This wouldn't have happened if you hadn't come back!"

Before I knew what I was doing, I was driven by rage and slapped my hand across his face as hard as I could. I stepped back and looked up into his eyes.

He looked heartbroken and hurt more by my words than my slap. His forehead furrowed as he apologized with his eyes. Then he looked away.

I knew I'd gone too far. I instantly regretted saying it, but I wanted to hurt him. I wanted him to hurt as much as I did.

Jake walked away from me and looked towards the front door. "We have to leave, Adele. I promised Dad a long time ago that I would take care of you, and that's what I plan to do. Now get your things. We're leaving. Now."

"Don't give me that shit. You left me a long time ago and didn't look back." I stormed over to him, standing behind him with my finger pointed.

He swirled around, and his eyes were full of moisture. "I will never leave you again, Del. I . . . I'll be with you until the end."

I stopped, and my anger slowly deflated. I sensed Jake's power fluctuate as he spoke the words. I knew he meant it. Nodding, I walked into my room, grabbed a bag, and filled it with clothes. Adrenaline kicked in, and I picked up the pace. I ran into the dining room, grabbed my laptop bag, and packed my work equipment. Jake darted past me, carrying the bag he'd brought in the first night he knocked on my door. I dropped my bag for work and a bag full of clothes by the front door. Jake stopped in front of my things and peeked out the window. He nodded and continued towards the kitchen.

I ran over, grabbed Buddy's harness, and called him over. "Buddy, come on, honey. Come out." I slipped the harness over his head and clipped his leash on. Jake came from the kitchen and set another bag down with food.

I walked back towards the family room and the sensation ran down the back of my head—I sensed them surrounding the house. My breath caught in my throat as I swallowed, trying to mouth the words. "Jake."

Jake was walking down from upstairs. "Are you almost ready, Del?"

"Jake, they're here."

Electricity vibrated through my body. My limbs ached as the volts blasted from my head, traveled through my body, and rested in my fingers. A static charge glowed a pearl hue as it rolled over my digits, quivering with anticipation. My emotions flooded my heart as I panted uncontrollably. The pain cascaded, burning my insides, begging me to come out and destroy. I couldn't control my limbs. I couldn't control my power. Moisture flooded my eyes, blurring my vision.

"Jake, no. Don't go." I whispered the words so silently as he walked towards the door. Everything slowed down, and I was stuck standing there. Frozen in time, watching in fear of what would happen if I moved. My power was like a volcano, ready to erupt at any minute.

Jake opened the front door, walked outside, and stood on the porch. The wind picked up, and he lifted his head and inhaled. He looked back at me and stared for a long minute before turning to go down the steps. I forced my feet to move and exited the front door, following Jake. I wasn't going to let him do this alone. I knew the dangers that awaited us before I turned the corner. A mob of men dressed in all black, armed with heavy artillery and two Jeeps, were parked next to the forest wall.

Jake slowly stopped, looking back at me. His eyes were glowing, and I heard him say in his head, "I'm sorry."

Again I sensed his power fluctuating inside him, begging him to let the wolf out.

"Well, well, well. If it isn't the little woman. She's beautiful, Jake. Is this why you left?"

A man wearing all black walked toward me with a mischievous grin. He nodded his head, and he looked me up and down.

Jake walked over, stepping in front of me. "What do you want, Rick?"

"You know what I want. We own you. Mercs for life. Remember?"

The man reached into his pocket, pulled out a pack of cigarettes and a lighter, and lit a smoke. He drew in a long drag and blew it out in front of him, aiming for Jake.

Jake took a step forward. "I'm done. I'm not coming back."

The man took another long drag and exhaled. "You're done when I say you're done. Got it!"

He threw his cigarette in Jake's face and lunged for him. I stepped backward and ran into Buddy. I grabbed his collar and saw men hovering around Jake and Rick sparring.

"Go!" Jake turned around and pushed me down. I stood up, turned around, and ran into the house.

"Hey! Stop!" A man yelled.

Buddy followed me in as I turned around to shut and lock the door behind us. The front door rattled the wall as someone beat on it. I spun around, grabbed my bo staff, and stood in front of the door. Buddy lowered his head and bared his teeth as his ridge raised on his back. I slowly walked back, one step at a time, gripping my bo staff, and waited for who would come bursting through the door. My heart pounded in my ears as screams from outside grew closer and closer. Then, all of a sudden, the door stopped vibrating. Exhaling a sigh of relief, I lowered my staff slowly and waited. I knew Jake must have fought everyone off. I clutched my staff and waited for Jake's command.

The glass next to the door shot through the window as

someone's boot kicked through the hole. The curtain pushed over, and a man looked in. He turned his head, said something to another person, and stepped inside the house.

Oh no. Jake. Where are you?

Trembling, I watched as two men crawled into my home uninvited. I was trapped and alone. Jake was outside, and I was in here.

One of the men walked over to the front door and unlocked it. Four more men entered my house holding rifles. Panting, I whipped my head back and forth between them. My hands gripped my staff, squeezing it. White light flickered from inside my fingers and then went dull. I couldn't breathe. My chest rose and fell, trying to inhale a full breath. My power was chaotic, and I knew I would explode at any moment. Six heavily armed men slowly surrounded me. Tears rolled down my cheeks as my lips quivered.

"Get out of my house!"

Buddy snapped at the men crowding around me. One man raised his gun to shoot Buddy. "No! No!" I ran over and thrust my bo staff into the guy's head, knocking him back. His legs flew up over his head, slamming him against the wall. I spun around and hit the guy next to him across the face. Blood spewed from his nose and dripped down his chin and shirt. I jump-kicked the last guy on the left in the chest, knocking him off his feet. The last three men glared at me with bulging eyes. Panting, I backed up, clutching my staff.

"Get her!"

I shifted my feet back and forth, waiting for the next round.

The last three men standing raised their guns. "Get down!"

I nodded and looked down at the ground. One of the men slowly stepped toward me. I waited for him to get close enough and smacked my staff upward into his nose. A loud crack, and then blood was pooling from his face. He screamed as bright red covered his hands and shirt.

"Get out of the way, Chris! Move!"

I hovered behind him, waiting for the next guy to attack me. One of the guys grabbed my shirt and held me. I swung up, popping him in the nose. A shrill scream rattled as he shuddered, holding his nose, and ducked down. Bullets flew past my head, pulverizing my family room wall. The gunfire stopped, and I looked up to see a fist coming down on my face. A heavy blow against my cheek blurred my vision. I blinked and tried to focus, but another blow hit me in the stomach. I dropped to the ground and rolled over onto my side, spewing acid in front of me. Panting, I flopped over onto my back. Another man walked over and leaned down, smiling. Pain seethed, burning from my insides out.

Buddy lunged over me and clamped down on the man's forearm. The guy raised his arm, swinging him back and forth. The guy next to him raised his gun to shoot Buddy.

"No!" I jumped up, punched him in the stomach, and then uppercut his chin, knocking his teeth together. "Buddy! Down!" Buddy dropped off the guy, and I spun-kicked him in the chest.

Another man stepped in and side-swiped me. He punched me across the face, and I dropped hard, hitting the floor with a loud thud. I clutched my stomach, rolling onto my side. He walked over to me and slammed his boot into my stomach. I coughed, blood oozing onto the ground in front of me. Slowly, I scooted up onto my knees and brought my face up. A blow sent me backward, throwing me onto my back.

Gasping for air, I rolled onto my side and vomited blood and acid again. It flowed out of me like lava. Buddy nosed my face, pushing against me, and I put my arm around his neck and held him. A loud squeal pierced through my ears, and Buddy was gone. I reached for him, but he'd disappeared. I blinked to see my dog lying on the ground across the room.

I reached my hand out and felt my eye explode in pain. I looked up, and another guy's fist was pounding my face.

Closing my eyes, I rolled up into a ball. My bo staff rocked back and forth in front of me. I extended my arm out and grabbed it. Sparks tingled through my body like lightning striking across the clouds. I squeezed my bo staff and turned off the pain pulsing through my limbs. I inhaled a deep breath, breathing easy, and focused.

Two of the men walked over and pulled me up by my arms. I held my bo staff with one hand and refused to let go. One man tried to pull it out of my fingers, but I gripped it tighter.

I felt my power peak, and then electricity vibrated through my veins. I squeezed the bo staff, inhaled a deep breath, and exhaled again. Buddy was crying out in pain right behind me. My body boiled with rage. "Get Out! Now!"

A man threw his head back and cackled. "We will kill your wolf, and then we're going to have some fun with you before we kill you."

The man pressed his lips to my face. His hot, pungent breath against my skin was souring my stomach. Laughter echoed through the house.

I blinked my eyes, looking around, panting short spouts of breath as the room closed in around me. Swallowing, I pushed down the lump forming in my throat and forced my eyes to open wide. I shifted my head back and forth, looking up at the monsters holding me. A tear rolled down my cheek, and I felt the electricity rushing through my shoulders. "No."

The men continued to rattle on to each other, ignoring me. I opened my mouth and felt the word leave my lips. "No!" My power boiled and shot through the rest of my body. My instincts activated, and I pushed everything inside me through my fingertips.

The men holding my arms started vibrating next to me. I looked over to see bolts of electricity traveling up and down their bodies. The men's mouths dropped open, and a fire was igniting inside their mouths, racing up over their faces and down their bodies. A white flame caught, and they were burning alive. Their arms dropped, and their bodies molded into a lump of flesh and melted into the floor.

Screams rang through the house as I stood up straight. A man standing next to the front door opened it and was halfway out before I shot bolts of electricity from my staff, piercing him with shards of white fire. The guy beside him tried to run, and I opened fire on him. He dropped to the floor, convulsing. His body glowed a pearly white hue as electricity rolled over his skin. He scratched at his eyes and screeched squeals of anguish as I was unleashing my fury. I redirected my electric stream and was shooting at every man until I was the only one left standing. Panting, I watched them all melt into the ground as their bodies burned from the inside out.

The door pushed open, and I aimed my bo staff up. Jake stared at me in wolf form, gaping at everything I had done. I felt the electricity inside me die down and finally stop. I collapsed to the floor, quivering all over.

"I'm so tired, Jake." My fingers trembled, clutching my staff. The air reeked of sulfur and burned human flesh. Jake's body trickled down to normal size before he walked over to me. I lay on the floor holding my staff. My head rolled over, and I spotted my dog. I crawled over to him and lay over his body.

"Del, are you okay?"

I didn't answer.

"Del, come on, we have to go."

"I can't leave him, Jake."

"We won't. I can help him."

"What do you mean?"

"Let me help him."

Jake lay down and put his head up to Buddy's face, holding him. He rested his arms around his midsection and whispered into his ear. It was too quiet for me to make out, but I felt something peculiar when he began whispering. I inhaled deep breaths, watching Jake as he lay over Buddy. After a few minutes, Buddy lifted his head and shook his ears back and forth. He looked into Jake's eyes and licked his nose.

Jake looked back at me. "Del, we have to go now. There will be more coming soon."

CHAPTER TWENTY-FOUR ADELE

I grabbed some of our bags, walked out onto the front porch, and saw more bodies littering the grounds around my house. My head swam as I struggled to put one foot in front of the other. Jake carried Buddy outside and sat him on the porch. Buddy slowly stood up and wobbled down the steps and into the driveway as he shook from head to toe, then started trotting down the road.

"I didn't know you could do that." I inhaled loudly and leaned against the house.

"Yes. We need to get going, Del."

I walked over to my SUV, popped the hatch open, and threw the bags into the back. My legs were dragging underneath me like heavy boulders as I turned around to go back inside. A peculiar noise caught my attention, causing me to look back at the road. A low humming whirled nearby, like a lawnmower engine just out of sight. I stepped out from under the porch, standing next to the car. A small private plane appeared through the trees and soared overhead. The aircraft flew so close that I could feel the wind off the propellors. The plane flew over the mountains, turned around, and came back towards us.

Jake grabbed my hand and pulled me towards the house. "Come on, we need to go." I tripped and fell over the porch steps.

Buddy ran back and forth, barking at the plane. Gunshots from an automatic weapon blew a circle around Buddy and up the porch. I covered my head, waiting for the gunshots to stop. Once the plane was out of sight, I jumped up and ran into the road to see it turning around to come back again.

"Get out of the road!" Jake said.

Jake was running towards me. I waved my hands for him to run into the house.

"Not without you!"

The plane came back and unloaded another round of bullets into my SUV. I ran up the steps and dropped into the door of the house. The car sounded like it was being hit by little meteors as it was rocking back and forth from the firing. When the shots stopped, I picked my head up and smelled gas.

"Oh, no." I sat up and crawled into the house. "Buddy!" Buddy ran inside with his tail between his legs. I slammed the door, sitting against it. The car exploded, and millions of pieces of it shot all over the house. The curtains caught fire and quickly spread up the wall to the house's ceiling.

"No!" I cried. "My dad's house! No!" I spun around, confused. I ran back and forth, searching for something to put out the fire.

Jake grabbed me by the shoulder and shook me. "We need to run now. We'll have to run into the forest, Del."

"I can't run into the forest! I have a life here! I have a job! I can't just run away!"

"Del, we have to go now. You can contact your job in a couple of days. If we don't go now, we will die."

Tears rolled down my cheeks as I looked around my old house. I walked over to the fireplace, grabbed the picture of the three of us, folded it , and put it in my bag. I wiped my face, picked up the only bag I had left, and looked at Jake. He put his oversized backpack on as I grabbed Buddy's leash.

"Let's go out the back door and through the fence. We can sneak into the forest quicker that way."

"I need to check out the front and see if my bags are still

there. Maybe, we can stop the fire." I walked towards the front door.

Jake grabbed my arm and shook his head. "Del, we can't. We have to go now."

"My laptop was in there. My work and just . . . just everything, Jake." Tears rolled down my cheeks as my lips quivered. "I don't know what to do. I don't know . . ."

Jake grabbed both my arms and gazed into my eyes. "It's going to be okay. I won't let anything happen to you. But for now, we need to go. We need to run into the forest. Okay?"

He pulled me close to him, hugging me tightly.

My body vibrated as I laid my head on his chest. Finally, the sobs ended, and I pulled away, wiped my face, and nodded. Jake led the way to the backdoor, stopped, and looked at me. I nodded, and he slowly turned the knob. We cautiously walked outside and scanned the sky.

Flames engulfed the roof, and black smoke was rolling up into the clouds. My heart pounded in my chest as I stared up at my house with moist eyes. Jake put his arm around my waist and led me out of the gate with him. We walked up to the trees and entered the line of tall oaks guarding the forest. Soon, my childhood home with my mother's, father's, and Jake's memories would burn to ash.

CHAPTER TWENTY-FIVE VICTOR

I cracked the window, flicking the ashes from my *Marlboro red*. I gazed up at the full moon, smiling down over the mountains. The truck slowed down and turned onto a dark dirt road. Trees kissed the sky, hiding the path until it opened, revealing what looked like the remnants of a cabin. Several men, trucks, and jeeps were standing around chatting as we pulled up. We stopped, and I opened my door, exhaling another drag of my cigarette. Smoldering ashes were dying down from a previous fire. I flicked my butt as I walked over to the stacks of burned lumber and steel.

"Sir."

Anger built up in my chest and rushed through my limbs, flushing electrical pulses through my body.

"Sir?"

I swiftly turned and wrapped my fingers around Rick's neck, picking him up and holding him in the air. The darkness inside me begged to squeeze his neck until it popped off, but I eased my grip. "Where's the girl?"

Coughing, Rick gasped for air. "They got—"

"Where's Jake?"

"They got away . . . sir . . . please . . ."

My body towered into the sky, and I watched my arm start to glow a green hue that erupted with my rage. "I distinctly remember saying that I wanted them alive and held captive until I arrived, yet I see no one here. You know what I see is the debris of what used to be Bill's cabin!" My voice vibrated off the trees, shaking excess clumps of snow onto the ground.

I shuddered as my fingers tightened around his neck. The feeling of squeezing the life out of him satisfied the demon inside me, begging to come out.

"Victor, please," Rick gasped.

Releasing my grip, I dropped Rick onto the ground. He rolled around coughing and expelled bright red acid from his mouth.

"Now, you and your men will hunt the girl and Jake. I don't want to see any of you until you have found them. Do you understand?"

"Yes-yes, sir."

"Good. Now get this place cleaned up and set up camp." Pulling out another cigarette, I puffed on the butt until it started smoking. I walked back to the truck and sat inside with the door open.

CHAPTER TWENTY-SIX ADELE

Moisture drizzled down, showering us as we walked deep into the forest. The sky peeked through the branches swaying in the wind as a cool breeze chilled my spine and swirled my long black hair through the air. We followed the familiar path Dad had made for us so many years ago. Buddy pulled and tugged on his leash, trying to gain freedom.

"Well, I'm glad you feel better, Bud."

"Del, just let him off his leash. He'll be okay."

"No, Jake, with everything going on, I don't think it's a good idea."

"I think he's just going to slow you down. Just take him off, and I'll make sure that he stays with us. Okay?"

I shook my head, and Jake walked over and leaned down to unhook him. "Damn it. No, Jake!"

Jake looked up at me as he unhooked him. "I promise I'll help you watch him." I opened my mouth to argue, but I knew he was right.

An hour passed, and I stopped and sat on a fallen tree. Panting, I wiped my brow with the back of my arm. Jake handed me bottled water, and I gulped long drinks, drizzling water down my neck and dampening my shirt collar. I cut the top off my water and held it for Buddy to drink. Buddy lapped the water and then plopped down on his hip, grunting from the pain. I leaned over, kissed his head, and scratched behind his ear.

I looked up, meeting Jake's gaze briefly before tearing my

eyes away. I didn't want to look at him. I didn't know what to say. Anger rolled through me as I peered into the forest. I couldn't help but think that if he hadn't come back, none of this would have ever happened. My house was gone. My work was gone. My life had been turned upside down, and now I was running into the forest because I had nowhere else to go. Images of my home burning flashed in my mind. I squeezed my eyes shut, swallowing a lump forming in my throat. Moisture filled my eyes, burning my nose as a tear rolled down my cheek. I swiped it away aggressively and inhaled deeply, trying to calm myself.

"We need to keep moving."

I turned to glare at him and said, "I know. I just needed to rest for a minute."

Jake looked back, scanning the forest. He inhaled a deep breath as the wind picked up and blew through the trees.

"They're not far behind us."

"I know. I know," I practically growled.

I got up, pulling my bag over my shoulder. I didn't know what was going to happen next. I didn't know if following him would lead me to a life of continuously running and hiding from people who were trying to kill us.

The mountains were a three-hour hike from my house one way. The sun was settling quickly, darkening the forest and leaving us to only use our memories of where to go. The cold winter wind blew, drizzling rainy snowflakes in our eyes as we trudged along.

Gunshots blasted behind us, echoing through the forest. Critters scattered throughout the trees knocking clumps of snow over our heads. Jumping, I looked back to see the gloomy forest haunting our escape. Jake held a finger up to his mouth and held the other hand out to stop me. He tilted his head back, sniffing the air.

His eyes widened, and his mouth dropped open. "Run,

Del. Run."

My feet fumbled over some twigs, and I almost fell, but Jake caught me. I looked up at him, meeting his ghostly stare. He pulled me to my feet, leading the way. I was barely keeping up as he weaved in and out of trees. I looked back to see Buddy had turned around and was staring toward the gunshots.

"Buddy! Come!"

We stopped at the foot of the mountains. Huffing, I let my hands drop to my knees as I gazed up at the colossal rock.

"Come on. They're right behind us."

Jake started up the mountain first. I tried to follow closely behind, sinking down into the snow with each step. Before I realized what was happening, Jake had disappeared into the darkness.

Snow flurries picked up, pummeling down into my eyes. Warm tears ran down my face and burned my nose. The mountain's steep slope was growing more treacherous, causing my feet to slip and fall forward. I continued on my hands and knees, peering through the darkness as stars filled the sky. I clawed against the floor of ice and gritted the sharp pain shooting through my digits. I tried to stand up, but gravity teased and pulled me back down, sinking into the sea of snow. My legs were heavy boulders as I gasped for air, swallowing salty liquid through chattering teeth.

"Jake."

Blinking, I peered up, staring into the darkness as the wind whistled down the side of the giant rock.

"Jake. Please." I wiped my face aggressively and shouted, "Jake!" My voice was hoarse, echoing through my head. *Jake. Jake. Jake. Please, Jake.* I didn't know if Jake could hear me anymore. The cold rattled my body as I gripped the rock under the ice. I knew if I tried to stand, I would fall down the frozen rock to my death. Peering up, I begged for a shimmer of hope.

"Del. Del, I'm here."

Quivering, I blinked as warm tears stung my cheeks.

"Del, come this way. Follow my voice."

I continued to crawl upward until I felt Jake put his hand on my forearm. I wrapped my arms around his arm, holding onto him. My body trembled as I hugged his warm limb. He pulled me up onto my feet, and I wrapped my arms around his waist as he led me around the side of the mountain into an opening. My heart raced, pounding against Jake as I pressed my body firmly against him.

"It's okay, Del. We're here."

I looked up and met his glowing eyes. His face had changed slightly, mimicking the beast he had hidden within. I slowly eased my grip from around him and held his fiery muscular biceps briefly before stepping back into the darkness. My body yearned to keep him in my grasp, even though the hurt was still very raw. Chills shivered through my body, drumming against my chest as my heart fluttered to the thought of his flesh against mine. I crossed my arms over my chest and watched him walk away.

Jake turned to look back and said,

"Wait here. I'll be right back."

Nodding, I looked up at the moon, peeking ominously around a row of winter clouds. A few minutes later, Jake walked back through the door with Buddy in his arms. Buddy's nails clicked on the floor as he approached me. I squatted down onto the ground, and Buddy sat back with his rump on my foot. I put my arms around his shivering body and sat there quietly.

The sounds of heavy winds whistled against the mountain, whirling snow over its peak. The cave seemed very secluded from the outside, its room quiet and undisturbed by the winter storm. Jake's footsteps echoed off the cave's walls as he walked around in the darkness. He unzipped his bag, pulling out something. A clicking noise bounced off the walls, and then a beam of light shined down in front of him. The light flashed towards Buddy and me, then up along the walls. The room appeared to be filled with wall-to-wall supplies.

"I think this is where Dad would sometimes come when he said he was going for a little walk," Jake said.

I nodded, watching as his beam ran along the walls. He stopped on an enormous cooking pot hanging from metal poles in the shape of a teepee. It looked like an old cast-iron pot that had been very well maintained. It had a big hook that held the pot handle, and feet on the bottom to sit over the fire. Large stones stacked on top of each other surrounded the fire pit.

Jake walked over and crouched down, picking up the pot and hanging it from the hook. He fingered the dirt on the ground under it and smelled it. "Ash."

Jake grabbed his backpack, sat down next to the fire pit, and dug around in his bag until he pulled out some paper. He leaned over the paper and ashes and struck something together. Sparks spat from Jake's hands, and then a tiny flame started on the ground in front of him. He sat up, giving the flame a minute, then he leaned over and gently blew on the fire. Light filled the room as the fire grew. Jake and I gazed at each other in silence. I glanced at the door and then at the fire.

"Do you think they can see us from the forest? Do you think they can see the fire?"

Jake shook his head and looked at the door. "I don't know."

He walked outside, disappearing into the darkness.

A few minutes later, he returned. "You can't see anything. Dad was right. It's hidden from the forest."

Jake walked over to the wall and grabbed a handful of wood. He set the wood in the fire and watched the flames ignite it from the kindling.

I stared at him, watching him work until his gaze met mine.

Quickly, I stood, walked over to the cave wall, and looked around. I could feel Jake's eyes on me, watching me as I walked along the wall. I didn't know what to say to him after everything. I didn't know how to feel. My heart still craved Jake, and it wanted me to open up and forgive him, but my head couldn't get over the fact that no matter what happened, my father's house was gone, and I could never go back.

As I walked along the wall, I ran my fingers over what appeared to be shelves carved into the rock, stocked with so many different items. I stopped in front of a wooden box with a lid and admired the fine craftsmanship of the wood. I pulled the top off and looked inside to see blankets and clothing stuffed down into it tight. I reached in, pulled out a blanket, and inhaled its scent. It was a soft, thick black fur from a bear.

A memory of Dad surged through me. *He was scraping the inside of a hide. He stopped to look at me, smiling. "This makes it soft, so you can use it. Feel."* I smiled and pressed the hide against the side of my face for a moment.

I looked over at Jake and held it up for him to see. He nodded and watched me walk a few feet away from the fire to spread it out on the ground.

I went back to the box and pulled out another blanket. It was wool. *Dad's voice spoke to me again. "This is one of the warmest and best blankets you will have, because it's water-resistant."* I *looked up to see Dad with his old smoking pipe in his mouth, smiling and nodding.*

I looked back to see Jake watching me again. His brows were furrowed, and when my gaze met his face, it softened, and he nodded. "You okay?"

"Yeah, I'm fine."

I lay down on the bearskin and pulled the wool up over my head. My head fell back onto the ground, and I sat up, walked over, and grabbed my bag to use as a pillow. I put my back to Jake and melted into the blanket from pure exhaustion. The minute I closed my eyes, I felt myself drifting to sleep. Buddy crawled up, slithering on his belly, and lay beside me on the blankets. I could feel Jake lie down behind me on the bear skin, squirming around to get comfortable.

"Del?"

"Yes."

"Are you warm enough?"

"I'm fine."

"Okay, good night."

"Night."

Chapter Twenty-Seven Jake

I stared at Del's back and wanted to reach out and hold her. My fingers stretched across and stopped just before touching her. She twitched in the blanket and shifted her legs. Buddy crawled over on his belly and rolled over onto his back for belly rubs. I laid my head down over my shoulder and snuggled the dog. He licked me in the face as I stared at the back of her head.

So many nights, I would lie awake and think about this moment, sleeping beside her. I would think about finally telling her how I feel, but now that I'm with her, I know I can never tell her the truth. I saw the way she looked at me. Pure hatred radiated from her beautiful eyes, and nothing I have to say will never change that. In her mind, I took everything from her, and the minute I returned, I was a burden on her.

I sat up, rubbing my face. The sound of snow falling hummed against the cave walls. I walked over to the entrance, peering out at the rows of mountain peaks, and watched the snow gliding over the rock like blankets of white as it drifted down to the floor. I walked out onto the ledge and walked around to check the forest. Lights twinkled through the trees, showing that there were men still hunting for us. I stood watch for a while and waited. *Dad said he put a spell on the cave, but I will stand out here all night if I have to make sure that she's safe.*

I may have run like a coward ten years ago, but this time I'm not going anywhere until I know she's safe.

CHAPTER TWENTY-EIGHT ADELE

Darkness surrounded me as I blinked my eyes open. My wrist was throbbing from pain, and my legs were battered and bruised. I looked around the room and tried to see where I was. The tent door was flapping freely in the wind. Muffled shouting echoed outside, and then I heard his voice. A bright light blasted through the tent door, blinding me. I blinked and tried to focus on who was entering the room. Three men walked in first, and then a tall figure ducked down and glided over to me. My gaze roamed his tall, slender body and stopped on his glowing emerald green eyes. My senses were on high alert blasting electricity through my body as his evil intentions seeped from him. I swallowed hard and waited for him to make his move. I tried sitting up to scoot away from him. He leaned down, and I sensed him looking inside my head.

"Where do you think you're going, girl!" he gritted through his jagged teeth.

He motioned to the two men he'd brought in with him. They stomped over and pulled me up by my arms. A squeal slipped my lips as their sharp talons dug into my flesh.

"Adele, wake up."

I flew up into a sitting position. The blankets were wrapped snugly around my neck, choking me. I thrashed around and pushed my arms out. Pain shot through my legs and back as I moved around on the ground. I stood up, swaying back and forth from my lightheadedness. I looked over at Jake, swallowing back the acid in my throat.

"Are you okay?"

Nodding, I started to fall over. Jake leaped over and caught me by the arm. I pulled away and wobbled to the door, looking out. A cool breeze wafted in my face through the row of neighboring mountains. I blinked at the bright sun's rays reflecting off the peaks like little diamonds over a blanket of white.

My stomach eased, and I turned back to Jake. "I'm sorry. I didn't mean to wake you. I keep having the same bad dream, over and over again." I stared back out at the mountain. "A lot has happened, and I don't know what I'm going to do now. I've always had a plan and a backup plan to that plan. Now I just don't know."

Jake walked up and stood behind me. "It'll be okay. I'll take care of you."

I snapped around and glared at him. "I don't need you to take care of me. I've been alone for a long time."

I walked over to my backpack, pulled out some fresh clothes, turned around, and stared at him.

Nodding, he walked out of the cave and let me have some privacy. A lump formed in my throat as I took in a deep breath. Blinking, I let the tears roll down my cheeks. I inhaled deeply and calmed myself before walking out of the cave.

The cave looked completely different in the daylight. The sun's radiant rays shined down, warming the mountainside. What had seemed like a treacherous climb was actually a steep slope covered in ice and snow. I followed the ledge out, and the wind caught me as I turned the corner. It blew hard against my body, knocking my footing off balance. Wobbling, I looked over the ledge to see a drop-off going down the side of the mountain. I leaned back against the rock and walked to the path we were on the night before.

Jake was busy working on something as I walked down. I approached him to see that he was pulling the feathers off a bird.

"Hey, what are you doing?"

"Breakfast."

"Where did you get that bird?"

"I didn't. Buddy did."

I looked down at Buddy, and his rump was bouncing on the ground as he watched Jake pull the feathers off the bird.

"Wow, good job, Buddy." I scratched behind his ears.

I looked back at Jake, but he didn't look up at me. He continued to pull feathers out of the bird until it was clean, and then he headed back into the cave. He left me alone, looking down the mountain and into the forest. A sea of white covered the slope all the way down to the forest floor. I followed it, spotting blackberry bushes a few feet away, and wandered over to it. Handfuls of berries were visible on the bottom half of the bush, wafting a sweet perfume in the wind. Excitedly, I popped them into my mouth, and the juices flowed over my tongue, exploding in my taste buds.

Dad had made us read books about survival and taught us to distinguish between good berries and poisonous ones. I leaned over and ate another handful when I sensed something peculiar. Slowly, I stood back up and inched around to see a bear cub. Holding my breath, I looked both ways and searched for the mother. She was nowhere in sight, so I stepped forward and tried to walk away when I heard a twig snapping right behind the berry bushes.

At first, I heard grunting, and then I felt the bush move towards my body. The bear cub stood on its hind paws and sniffed the air in my direction. I held my breath and stood perfectly still. The bush moved again, and the grunts turned into a monstrous growl. I threw berries at the bear cub and dropped to my knees, hiding in the bush. The bear cub dropped, sniffing the ground, and started eating the few berries I threw. The mother bear stopped pushing the bush and stood on her hind paws, sniffing the air. I knew she could smell me. She grunted again, and I felt the earth shake when she dropped onto the ground. The bear cub finished the berries and walked away slowly. I turned my head to look through the bushes and saw the mother bear following the bear cub, leaving the bushes. I exhaled loudly and stood up quietly.

"What are you doing?"

I jumped, holding my chest. "Nothing. I was eating berries and . . ." I looked around and answered, "Just—nothing." I walked away from the bushes and looked back behind me to see the bears were long gone, leaving me looking like a fool. I wanted to tell Jake about the bear, but he probably didn't want to listen to me right now.

"Did you try to get ahold of your work?"

I shook my head. "No, not yet."

"We need to prepare. I need to make some traps, and Dad has ready-made spears in the cave. We can use them for traps."

Jake looked around and headed back toward the cave. I nodded and followed.

"I also put the turkey in the pot for food later."

"Okay. Jake, listen . . . I'm—"

"We also need to make a plan. Where do you want to go? I can get you there, and then I can go on my own."

"Jake . . ."

Jake ignored me and walked ahead to the cave. I slowed down, looked up, and watched him enter the cave. I shook my head and looked back down into the forest, rubbing my face and forehead.

I don't know what I want. I know that I care about Jake, but I don't know if that's enough.

I turned around and started walking again. A loud creak rattled right behind me. I whipped around, and the wind picked up, blowing my long black hair in my face. Scrambling, I pushed my hair down and scanned the forest. Clumps of snow fluttered from the treetops, littering the ground. Shaking my head, I headed back up to the cave. Buddy was standing guard in front of the cooking pot. The pot had a long black cast- iron spoon handle peeking out from one side. The smell of delicious turkey and onion soup filled the room. I raised my hands to warm my body over the firepit. I looked back up to see Jake watching me. I gazed into his eyes, and he quickly looked away and acted like he was doing something.

"Jake. Can I help you?"

Jake kept his back to me. "No. Go call your job."

"Okay, I will." I stomped off, pulling my phone out of my pocket. *He can't just tell me what to do. I had planned on calling my job before he said anything.*

As I walked outside, I looked down at my phone and saw two bars blinking at the top right-hand corner of the screen. "Shit." I dialed my agent, and all I heard was silence. The phone beeped after a few minutes and then disconnected. I walked further out onto the mountain and tried again. No signal. Shaking my head, I walked back into the cave and pushed my phone down into my pocket. "No signal. I'll try when I go down to the forest in a bit."

"Whatever." Then Jake grumbled something under his breath.

Anger boiled inside me. I stomped over to him and got in his face. "Hey! Hey! Look at me when I'm talking to you!"

Jake spun around and glared at me. "What!"

"You don't have to be rude!"

Jake threw his head back and cackled. "I'm rude. Wow. You're a piece of work. You're the one who's casting blame on me and then crying *oh, poor me*. Well, guess what, honey. Life isn't as easy as you've had it. In the real world, there are people out there who kill, hurt, and take what they want, when they want." As he spoke, he walked towards me, putting his face into mine. I could feel the heat from his breath

132

blowing against my lips as he glared down at me. The anger that burned in my belly slowly started to dissipate, developing into a burning desire to push my lips against his. I wanted to be mad at him, and only minutes prior I'd been furious, but when his body threatened to touch mine, my will was taken over by lust. Squeezing my hands into fists, I exhaled deeply and calmed myself.

He turned around, walked towards the cave entrance, then walked back to me and gazed into my eyes. "I know you don't want to be here with me. It's fine. Figure out where you want to be, and I'll try to get you there. Okay?"

His eyes were glowing, and his musk was seeping through his long-sleeved shirt. A glimpse of him lying with me in bed flashed through my mind. I opened my mouth and licked my lips. "I never said that, Jake! I said that I didn't know what—"

"Yeah, I know what you said. Save it."

He stomped away and went out of the cave. Buddy followed him, and I stood there.

I walked outside and saw him walking back down into the forest. "I'm not done talking with you, Jake."

"Well, I'm done arguing. We have a lot of work to do."

I kicked the snow and paced back and forth. In my heart, I knew I'd been the jerk and that he didn't deserve my emotional outbursts, but after everything that had happened, I couldn't help but be angry with him. I waited a few minutes and walked down the mountain to find Jake. He had a little shovel and spears lying in a pile on the ground next to him.

"What are you doing?"

"I'm going to dig a hole and push spears down into the bottom so that someone would get impaled if they fell in."

"Please let me help?"

I grabbed the shovel and dug. The fresh snow on the ground was easy to dig up, but the ice underneath was tough.

I had to plunge the little travel shovel Dad had left us into the ground and try to break through the frozen earth. Grunting, I slammed the shovel down into the ground, making little indentions.

"Del! Just . . . just give it to me, woman!"

"No, I want to do it!"

"Adele!"

"Just let me try to do this, Jake."

"Let me break the ground for the hole. Okay?"

"Okay." I nodded, handing him the shovel. Jake smiled at me, and I backed up. He punched the shovel into the frozen ground and scooped out a clump of dirt. He repeated and started a hole and then handed me the shovel.

"Jake."

He looked down at me.

"I'm sorry."

His eyes glazed over as he looked into my eyes.

My senses fired as his emotions fluctuated.

He stepped back and shifted from one foot to the other. His eyes darted up to the trees as he shook his head. "It's fine."

I straightened upright. "No, it's not. I shouldn't have . . . I didn't mean it. I didn't mean it. You know I'm hot-headed. I'm just sorry I—A lot has happened, and I don't—I don't know how to feel about everything. I'm sorry."

He met my gaze with a half-grin. "Get back to work, Del."

I smiled and nodded. The shovel plunged into the ground more easily after Jake started the hole for me. I pulled out soft earth and laid it on the ground next to me. My body was halfway deep into the ground when I stopped for a break, crawling out. Jake and Buddy were nowhere in sight, so I jumped back in and continued to dig. The depth of my hole was at my shoulder when I decided to stop and go look for the boys. I pulled myself out and wiped my brow with my forearm. I looked up into the trees and saw the sun glaring down at me.

I walked around, looking for Jake and Buddy. About a hundred yards away, I spotted them. Jake was standing on a rocky hill, rolling a boulder back. I jogged over and climbed up.

"What are you doing?"

Jake grunted as his hands gripped the boulder. "I'm trying to set up something. By my calculations, this can work."

"Huh?"

"Just come here, woman."

I walked over, standing next to him, and pushed at the boulder. Its weight was tremendous. I knew it would run over me if I was left to hold it on my own. I pushed with everything I had, and it wouldn't budge. A low growl came from deep within Jake's chest. I looked over, and his eyes had changed shape, turning black and his facial features slightly altered, resembling the wolf. The boulder rolled backward and up onto an incline. He huffed, pushing until the boulder wouldn't move anymore.

"Del, go get that beam. I left it down on the ground. Go!"

I hopped down, climbed back up with a thick piece of oak, and held it out for Jake to grab. He released one hand from the boulder and held the vast rock, mounting the beam against it. He slowly stepped back, letting go of the rock and the wood.

He turned around, smiling. "There."

I nodded and smiled back, looking at him. My mouth gaped open as I gazed over his muscles protruding through his t-shirt, outlining rows of sweat that traced through the material. He looked away, wiped his hands on his sweaty shirt, and hopped down. He grabbed his jacket and carried it while walking away.

"Come on, pup."

I hopped down and jogged to catch up with him. We walked over to my hole, standing there, and looked down into it.

"You didn't finish it."

"Well, I—I didn't know what you wanted me to do next."

He hopped down into the hole and held his hand out. I handed him the shovel, and he dug more dirt out. It only took him a few minutes to get the hole a few feet deeper. His shirt was damp, clinging to his six-pack abs. His body didn't look like he had an ounce of fat on it except for his round, succulent buttocks. He looked up and caught me staring. A smirk arched the side of his mouth before he went back to digging.

I turned away and cleared my throat. "So, what are we going to do with the hole?"

"I plan to put spears at the bottom, so if someone falls in, it will kill them. We need more holes, though."

"Oh, so how many do we need?"

"At least three."

"Oh."

He stopped, nodded, and pulled himself out.

"Let's go check on the food. I'm hungry. We can finish the other two holes after we eat."

"Okay."

We walked back up to the cave, and the smell of the pot cooking made my mouth water. Buddy ran past us, nearly knocking us over. "Watch it, Buddy!"

Jake walked over to the jug of water and gulped some down. Then he washed his hands and face. He pulled his shirt off and used a small towel to dry off. He walked over to his bag, pulled out a fresh shirt, and put it on. I watched him get dressed and walk away after he pushed his head through.

I walked over to the pot and stirred it with the long cast iron spoon. The turkey meat was falling off the bone and looked cooked through.

"We can eat. Wait, where did you get the vegetables?"

"There's canned food in that crate."

I turned and walked over to the crate, pulling the lid open. It was full of canned food and dry rice put in *Zip-lock* bags. "Wow, I didn't see this. Dad really set us up well, didn't he? Do you think any of the canned food expired? It's been sitting here for years."

"Well, I guess we're about to find out, huh?"

I turned back to Jake and walked over to the pot. Jake handed me a wooden bowl and spoon.

"Where did you find these?"

"Over there in that corner. Dad made bowls and cups and brought some spoons and forks up here for us, too. It's all over there. You should look around. I woke up before the sun came up and looked around. I think Dad knew that we would have to run and hide here one day, either with or without him."

With or without him. The word caught in my throat. I swallowed hard and slowly walked over to the pot to scoop food for us. *Maybe the people trying to kill us are the same people that killed Dad?*

I stared down at the bowl and slowly handed it to Jake.

"What's wrong?"

I looked up at him and shook my head. "It's nothing. Here, eat." I didn't want to talk about the past. I wasn't ready to talk about Dad with Jake. Just saying his name out loud brought tears to my eyes after what happened.

I put a bowl on the ground for Buddy and handed Jake his. Then I made my bowl, walked over, and sat down on the bearskin we'd slept on. Jake followed me over and sat across from me. We ate in silence.

I finished my lunch and set it on the ground for Buddy. Jake did the same, and we looked all around the room except at each other. Buddy walked over, plopped between us, cleaned our bowls, and then lay down and got back scratches from both of us.

Jake looked up at me, smiling. "Did you have a nice foster

family after Dad died?"

I inhaled a deep breath and exhaled. "Yes. My foster mom, Beth, was nice to me. She made me chocolate cake a lot and let me read to her. I liked that. Her daughter, Molly, was always competing for her attention. I would tell Beth something happened at school, and Molly would try to top the story to make herself sound better."

"Did you ever use your power around them?"

"I wanted to sometimes, but I stopped using it altogether after a while."

Jake stopped eating and shook his head at me. "Why?"

"Because I didn't really need it."

"But Dad always said if you don't use it, you lose it."

"Well, I didn't, did I?"

"No, but you could have."

"Seriously, you saw what I did to those men back at my house. I cooked them from the inside out. I haven't used my powers in years, and now, I need to protect us from whatever's trying to kill you!"

"Trying to kill *us*, Del. You're in this now whether you want to believe it or not."

I got up, grabbed my bowl, and walked to the entrance.

Jake stood up and grabbed my forearm. "You did what you had to do. They were going to kill us."

I shook my head and pulled my arm away from him. "You don't understand. I don't know what I'm doing. I'm dangerous. I could've killed you or Buddy. I don't know how to control it."

"So, don't. Get stronger and learn to control it. Stop the *poor me* crap! Damn it, Adele. You're the strongest woman I have ever known, and you don't even—"

Jake threw his bowl in the corner and walked out of the cave. I stood there staring at the entrance with my mouth open. I didn't know what to say. I cleaned up our bowls and walked down the mountain to find Jake digging another hole.

He was aggressively stabbing the shovel into the dirt. He looked up, pointing. "Go get the spears and jab them down into the ground of the first hole and find some limbs to cover up the hole with."

"Jake?"

"What?" His eyes glared at me.

I spun around and went back for the spears. I grabbed a handful and went to my first hole, dropped into it, and positioned them in the ground. Then I searched for some limbs and covered the hole.

I walked back over to Jake, and he was just about finished digging his hole. The wind picked up, and the oaks swayed back and forth violently, creaking as the branches slapped together. The sun was making its way quickly behind the mountains. Jake pulled himself out of the hole and stood upright in front of me. He was so close that if he wanted to, he could kiss me. I opened my mouth, licked my lips, and stepped back.

I raised the spears up towards him.

"You can do that. I'm going to dig the last hole."

I nodded, dropped into the hole, and plunged the spears into the ground. Then I walked around and found some limbs to cover up the hole. Brushing off, I looked around the forest for Jake. He was gone.

"Jake. Jake." I called for him and listened. Footsteps crunched down into the snow behind me. I spun around, but it was too dark to see anything now.

A gunshot was fired just a few yards away from me. Shivering, I slowly walked back the other way. I turned around and tried to remember which way the cave was. Panting, my heart pounded in my ears. My eyes darted back and forth as my feet moved forward. I was lost, and I didn't know which way to go. Rustling sounded right behind me again.

A hand gripped around my mouth and the other hand around my waist, just below my breasts. I struggled at first, and then I smelled Jake's musk.

"Shh. There's someone right over there."

I nodded and felt my body tremble under his strong fingers. His lips brushed against my ear, shooting tingling vibrations down my back and into my groin. He removed his hand from my mouth and moved his other hand down to mine.

He grabbed it, pulling me. "Come on. This way."

We jogged back to the cave and stood inside the entrance, listening. Two more gunshots sounded just at the foot of the mountain.

"What is that?"

"I'm not sure. It could just be hunters."

Jake stood by the door for a while. I sat down on the bearskin, folded my legs, and cupped my arms around them. The cave was dark without the fire, and the cool wind blew in, making it chilly.

Jake shifted his weight, sniffing the air.

A couple of hours passed, and we were still waiting. I was fighting to stay awake. My head dropped forward every few minutes as I drifted to sleep. I finally stood up, walked over to Jake, and looked out. I couldn't really see anything in the darkness.

He looked down at me, nodding. "Let's go to sleep. I think it's just hunters. I just needed to wait a while to be sure."

We walked over to the blanket, and I unfolded it over the bearskin. I lay down first, then Jake lay on his back, leaving a few feet between us. My body shivered as I tried to warm up under the covers. Jake scooted over, wrapping his arms around my waist and arms. He felt safe, and his body heat warmed me like an oven. I closed my eyes and let the sleep come.

CHAPTER TWENTY-NINE: ADELE

I opened my eyes, and darkness filled the cave. My arms and legs were weighed down by the heavy wool blanket. Lightning flashed outside, and then a monstrous growl followed. I jumped, pulling the covers up to my chin. I turned to see Jake lying on his back with his head turned toward me. My gaze ran down his perfectly arched brow that accentuated the curvature of his full lips, stubbled mustache, and chin. His mouth was slightly parted, drawing in small breaths, raising his muscular bare chest up and down. I let my gaze follow his chest down to the top of his rippled abdomen, where the blanket slightly hung over his manhood. My heart fluttered in my chest as I inhaled a deep breath. My face warmed up, and my groin sizzled with excitement as I followed the bulge over Jake's groin, down to his toes. I looked back up, meeting his eyes. He cocked his head to the side, grinning. He slowly turned over and lay on his side, not parting from my eyes.

"Hi," I said.

"Hi. Are you okay?"

I nodded. Jake propped up on his elbow, looking down at me. Blood pumped into my heart, throbbing beats in my ears. His eyes started beaming an intense golden chestnut brown in the darkness. One of his eyebrows peaked as he gazed into my eyes.

My head tingled, sensing his erotic intentions. Shivering, my hands fidgeted, trying to pull up the covers. "It's freezing in here. Maybe I can start the fire now?"

"Girl, you were cooking me all night."

Jake stood up and was in a tight-fitting pair of black boxer briefs. I cupped the covers under my chin and watched him walk around the cave. The lights flashed, and gusts of wind started whistling through the mountains. Hard rain beat against the side of the cave. Jake was quick on his feet, hopping back when the wind blew in a sheet of rain. I threw my head back, cackling.

Jake shot a smile. "You like that, huh?"

I stood up, walked over to the fire, and tried to help him. He pointed, and I saw chopped wood lying against the cave wall. Nodding, I grabbed three chunks of wood and walked them back over to him. He squatted over the fire with the flints and knocked them together. A spark finally lit some of the ash, igniting the flame. Jake leaned over, blowing on it to help it grow. Shivering, I ran back over to the blanket and nuzzled under the covers. Jake walked over to the door, pulled down his shorts, and peed.

"Wow. I wish I could do that. Now I have to pee, too."

I got up, ran outside of the cave and walked only a few feet before dropping my pants. The wind blew the rain sideways, and I was getting drenched. I bounced twice and then hopped up and walked back to the door. Jake was waiting at the cave entrance, watching my drenched body walk up. I gazed into his eyes and felt the rain drip down my face and neck. Jake's eyes looked down at my see-through shirt, staring at my erect nipples. I glanced down at his manhood, which protruded from his shorts. I closed my eyes, swallowing hard as my heart hammered in my chest.

"Excuse me." I bumped past him, went to my bag, and un-zipped it. I turned around, looking at him.

"Of course, sorry."

I changed into a shirt and pajama pants, walked over to the bed, and lay back down. Jake stared out into the storm and waited for me to finish.

"Okay, I'm done."

He lay a foot away from me and stared at the ceiling, panting with heavy breaths. I turned over, propping my head on my hand, and leaned on my elbow to face him. The storm outside was merciless, dumping gallons of water in front of the cave as the mountain vibrated from its fierce growl. A cluster of blinding lights flashed, and an explosive howl grumbled outside the door. My eyes were drawn to the door. I gazed out into the violent storm, feeling drawn to its chaos.

Shaking my head, I look back over at Jake. Staring, I wanted him to look at me.

He turned his head over. "What?"

"Nothing."

"I just . . . what did Dad say to you in your letter?"

"Why?"

"I'm just curious."

"None of your business." Jake grinned mischievously, looking up at the ceiling.

"Wow. Okay, then." I lay back flat, putting my arm under my head, and stared at the ceiling.

"What about you?" Jake asked.

I shook my head, smiling. "Nope."

My smile faded quickly when Dad's face came to mind. I remembered my letter and turned over, staring at Jake again. As I looked at him, a lump caught in my throat. Blinking my eyes, my tears flooded down my cheeks. I quickly turned my face away from him as I lay on my back. I didn't want Jake to see me tear up. I couldn't control the pain seething in my chest for him. For Dad. For everything. It felt like it was all coming down on me at once. I inhaled, and my breath caught. Swallowing, I swiped the tears away and sniffed loudly.

Jake sat up on his side and looked at me. "Hey, what is it? Are you crying?"

"I'm not."

"Really? I can see the tears, Del."

"I'm fine. I'm just tired."

Jake scooted closer to me, pressing his body against mine. I tried to turn away from him, and he pulled me back down. He caressed my foot with his foot as he leaned in, pushing my hair behind my ear. An electric current tingled through my body as his touch fired into my groin. I craved the sweet juices of Jake's mouth and the raw heat of his warm body lying against mine. I wanted to feel his bulge burrowing deep inside me. My senses were on fire. The electricity was flowing through me on overdrive.

Jake's eyes were fluorescent, fuming with ravenous desire. My heart raced in my chest as he inched closer and closer to my lips. I opened my mouth, licking, and tasted the salt from my runaway tear as it rolled down my cheeks. He gently wiped my cheek with his finger.

His mouth opened slightly as he exhaled. "What's wrong?"

"It's just . . ." I swallowed hard, trying to push down the lump in my throat. "I've missed you and Dad so much, Jake, and now you're here after all this time." I exhaled, blinking my moist eyes. My body trembled as I gazed up into his eyes. I wanted to tell him the truth, but my lips were paralyzed. I wanted to open my heart to him, but I couldn't take him disappearing again. My mouth opened, and I licked my lips and inhaled deeply . I couldn't find the words.

Swallowing, I panted deep breaths. I wanted to give myself to him. I wanted to touch him, but I knew it would change everything if I did. It would change us. I'd imagined this moment hundreds of times, but now that it was here—I was afraid. I was afraid of what it meant or what would happen next.

I stared up into his lustrous eyes, and my heart was overflowing. I couldn't take it anymore. I wanted him more than ever, and I would rather have this than nothing at all. I closed my eyes, leaned in, and put my lips to his, pulling him against my body. He embraced me, wrapping his arms around my waist. I knew I was taking a risk but I wanted everything Jake could give me. I wanted him to open up to me. I wanted him to see me for who I really was. I wanted him to love me as much as I loved him. Fear consumed my heart, but I didn't care anymore. It was just him and me now. Our bodies intertwined, and we were one.

Everything moved so fast. The heat of our mouths, panting against each other as our hands explored each other's bodies. Jake climbed on top of me and forcefully pushed my shirt up, revealing my erect nipples. I gasped as he gently squeezed my nubs between his fingers. His boiling lips pulled back my bottom lip with his teeth. He nibbled down over my chin and ran his lips to my neck, kissing down my shirt line.

Jake sat up and pushed his boxers down, exposing his throbbing organ. He pulled me up, ran his fingers under my shirt, and pushed it over my head. He dove toward my abdomen and suckled my navel area. His fingers slid into my pants, pulling them down, revealing my pulsing groin. Jake stopped and gazed at my naked body. His eyes glistened with hunger as he followed my curves up to my eyes. His large, ruff hands stroked my thighs as he pushed apart my legs and gazed down at my crevice. He lay down on top of me and pressed his mouth against mine. His monstrous shaft rubbed against my clitoris, teasing the crease of my groin. I wrapped my arms around his waist, vibrating for his entry.

I pulled my lips away from him. "I want you inside me."

My hips rose towards his groin, begging for him. Jake pressed his body against mine, gazed into my eyes, wrapped his muscular arms around my waist, and slowly entered me. Gasping, the pain and pleasure from the enormous size of his manhood exploded inside me. My juices were gushing and drowned his rigid member.

My fingers clawed into his back, pulling him harder against me as my breath caught, exhaling a deep groan. He finally pulled himself all the way out and thrust slowly back in. Jake cupped his lips over mine as he picked up speed, pounding me against the ground. He suckled my neck, ran his tongue up my chin, and pressed his lips against mine.

I wrapped my legs around his buttock, squeezing his tight rump. I felt my climax rise and arched my back, pulling away from his mouth and groaning.

Jake sat up and thrust himself inside me, pounding my groin. I squeezed my legs around his back and felt his manhood harden as he climaxed. Panting, his body melted into me. He pulled himself out of me and lay down next to me. I rolled over onto one side, resting. Then I stood up, grabbed a dirty shirt from my bag, and walked to the door. I was headed outside when Jake grabbed my hand and pulled me back.

"No, stay in here."

I turned around, and Jake pressed his lips against mine again. He raised his hand and cupped my cheek, pulling me close . I felt his length grow and push into my abdomen. I pulled away, looking down to see his member ready to go again.

I smiled up at him. "Aren't you tired?"

Shaking his head, he pulled me back to the bed.

"I'm a mess. I need to wash off."

"No, you're perfect," he said.

He lay down, this time with his shaft erect and waiting. A low growl rumbled inside his chest as he looked up at me. The animal inside him was peeking through his eyes, hungry and waiting. I climbed on top of his muscular body and slipped his erection inside me. At first, I went slowly, and then Jake grabbed my hips, rocking my rump back and forth on top of him. He grunted and moaned, exposing his fangs.

Tingling rushed through my body, and I took control and

lay down over him. I cupped my lips over his and rode him hard, slapping my hips up and down over his length. He squeezed my rump tight, forcing himself deep inside me. I felt my climax rise, and I stopped, letting my juices flow down his member as I vibrated over him. Jake sat up, wrapping my legs around his waist, and bounced my body up and down. Our bodies slapping together echoed off the walls of the cave.

Jake suckled my neck and gently nibbled down my collarbone. He ran his fingers down my back, cupped my rump, and picked up speed, thrusting me on top of him. I felt his sex harden, and he erupted, exploding his juices inside me. I went limp and laid my head on his chest, panting. I pulled my legs from around him and lay next to him. Jake reached over and kissed me. He wrapped his arms around my waist, and we both fell asleep.

CHAPTER THIRTY: ADELE

The next morning, I woke up with Jake's arms still squeezing around my waist. My bladder was about to explode, so I snuck out and relieved myself. The morning was damp, with a thick layer of dew on the ground. My foot squished down into the mud as I trudged back to the cave. The boys were sawing logs, and the sun was just peeking over the mountains. I pulled out some fresh clothes and found my phone.

"Hmmm, still no bars." I walked out, holding up my phone and waving it back and forth. "Nothing." Nodding, I looked back at the cave and turned to go down the mountain. *I can be back before they even wake up.* I trudged through puddles of water that littered the ground from the night before.

A forty-minute walk later, I heard the water crashing into the rocks on the bank. A wall of trees stood guard, concealing the ice crystals floating in the brisk morning pool. The sun met my eyes as I pushed through the brush, blinking and blinded by the vibrant rays.

I shielded my brow with my forearm as I walked out to see the river was wide opened on both sides of the water for miles. I cautiously checked both ways, following the river upstream towards the city. I pulled out my cell, and it showed bars, so I dialed the number to my agent. Nothing. I walked along the river a few more feet and kept dialing. The circular asterisk would spin and spin and then read call failed. Exhaling loudly, I stomped further upstream and stopped when I saw a boulder sitting on the water's edge. I climbed up onto it and could see the rolling rapids for miles.

I held my phone up, reaching to the sky. "Finally. Three bars." My fingers scrolled down the list of names and clicked on my agent's number. The asterisk spun for a brief moment. Dialing . . . dialing . . . dialing . . . a ringing sound rumbled on the line. "Yes!"

"Sorry, this voicemail box is full. Please try back again later."

"What! Seriously. Come on!" I huffed loudly. "Okay, fine, I'll call the office and leave her a message. I can't believe this is happening right now!"

I rang the office, and a machine picked up. "Hello, I'm sorry we're not in the office today. A tragedy has occurred, and we'll be out for the rest of the weekend. One of our beloved writers, Adele Wolf, has passed. I'm so sorry for the inconvenience. If you need to talk to your agent, please dial them directly, and they'll get back to you as soon as they can. Thank you, and take care."

I dropped down hard on my rump. My arms dangled to my sides as I stared out over the water.

"Oh, my . . . I can't believe this is happening. I can't believe this is happening. This can't be happening. I'm not . . . I'm not . . ." I was speechless. Shaking my head, my mouth dropped open. "I don't know how to fix this. I don't know what to do. Wait! I'll call Molly. That's it. I'll call her." I dialed her number, and it rang four times before she finally picked up. "Molly! Molly, it's me, Del! I'm not dead. Listen, I've little time. These men blew up my car and burned down my house. I, um . . . I don't—"

"Adele?" A man's voice on the other end of the phone spoke. "Adele?"

"Yes," I said.

"Hello there. I was wondering when you were going to call. I've been waiting for you. This is your uncle Victor, and

I'm here with your foster sister, Molly, her family, and your agents. Well, a lot of humans . . ." His voice trailed off into a dark, rapacious tone. Trembling, I gripped my phone with both hands. Victor's dark intentions seeped through the receiver, and the image of his malicious face flashed in my mind.

"I-I-I know who you are. And you'll pay for this. Do you hear me! You'll pay!" My teeth chattered as I stuttered the words.

"Don't worry, girl. I'll find you and your wolf, and then you'll know what real power is. Your father was a minion compared to what I can do to you."

I shook my head, swallowing hard. My throat was as dry as the desert as I tried to inhale a breath. The trees towered over me, closing in around my spinning head.

"Oh, and one last thing. Ask old Jake what the truth is about why we know each other. I think you'll be interested to know the truth about your dumb wolf."

"What? What?"

"Oh, I don't want to spoil it. I'll let Jake try to explain his way out of that." He chuckled and sighed. "Well, it's been a pleasure talking to you, and I need to go now. Bye bye, then. I hope to see you soon."

The dial tone rang, echoing in my ear. My phone slipped out of my hands, dropping into the sand. My arms hung lifeless as warm tears rolled down my cheeks. A burst of salty liquid burned my tongue and sent a shiver down my spine.

I shook my head with my mouth gaping open. I stood up, stumbling off the rock, and tripped into the sand. I pocketed my phone, crawled over to the river, and splashed cold water on my face. The water drizzled down my face for a moment before I went for another scoop. I scrubbed my eyes, mouth, and cheeks aggressively, trying to wash away what had just happened. I fell back onto my rump and used my sleeve to dry off. His evil green eyes flashed into my mind. Shaking my head, I squeezed my eyes shut and pushed myself onto my feet.

I stared blankly ahead, walking back to the wall of trees. My feet tripped over something, and I stumbled forward onto all fours. I looked back to see I'd bulldozed over a bear cub eating a fish. He looked up at me, and a piercing scream bellowed from his mouth.

"Shh. No. No. No. Shh. It's okay." I held my hands up, stepping backward, but it was too late. The mother bear barreled from the forest's trees, bee-lining for me. I spun around, tripping over my feet, and fell forward. Forcing my body up, I ran back towards the river. My feet skidded through the sand, not getting any traction, so I zig-zagged over to the tree line to enter the forest. My feet pounded down into the mud as I swayed in and out of oaks and pines.

I abruptly stopped in front of a large oak tree that had fallen over. I tried to climb over it, but the bear caught up, slapping me with her giant paw. My head smashed against the log, knocking me down. Ringing echoed through my head as the bear pummeled against my body like a punching bag. Wetness flowed down my head, dripping over my shoulders and soaking my shirt. My arms were heavy and collapsed over my chest. I tried to focus, but my eyes grew drowsy, fluttering closed. I knew I was losing the battle. I was dying.

The bear opened her mouth and scalded my skin with her angry growl. Her fangs were exposed as she pressed her snout against my forearm, preparing to sink her teeth into my flesh. A faint noise triggered me to blink my eyes open. A dog barking off in the distance grew closer and closer.

The bear spun around and howled another monstrous roar. She lunged forward, and I caught a glimpse of my dog standing in front of her.

"No! No!" I sputtered the silent words. I grabbed a stick

lying on the ground next to me and hurled it at the mother bear's rump. Spinning back around, she came for me again. I lifted my trembling hand up and waited for her to finish me. Closing my eyes, I felt my hand drop into the mud.

A tingle tickled my fingertips. I wiggled my digits, and the electricity sparked, fluttering up my forearm and into my chest. My power fluctuated inside me, building, begging me to not give up. I opened my eyes, staring into the mother bear's face as she opened her mouth and exhaled a monstrous roar. Her razor-sharp paws sliced into my chest. She opened her mouth and dove into my side. An earsplitting scream echoed through the trees as my body trembled in pain. I wrapped my hands around her head and let go. A pearl hue glistened through my skin as the electricity in my body actuated. The bear's body seized, trying to pull away. I electrocuted her, cooking her from the inside out. She dropped over me and melted into the ground, covering my body. My hands collapsed, and I closed my eyes.

CHAPTER THIRTY-ONE: JAKE

My face pressed against the cold dirt as I opened my eyes. The cool wind picked up, blowing flurries against my bare buttock. I squirmed to move, but my hands and ankles stung from their tight bounds. I lifted my head, drawing my legs in to prop up onto my knees. I looked around and saw white tents parked everywhere. Hundreds of them put up like circus tents awaiting a show.

"Jake." A deep raspy voice called out my name.

"Who's there?"

"Jake, I've been waiting a long time for you."

Anger radiated through my body as the beast emerged. I soared several feet into the air, and my mane flooded with ebony course fur. The ropes dropped to the ground, and I stood up, exhaling a low growl in my chest. My animal instinct reacted, and I scanned through the darkness. A figure was standing in the doorway of a tent, holding a slumped-over person with his left arm. My breath caught in my throat as I recognized the long black hair flowing from a woman's slender frame.

Panting, I inhaled deep breaths and waited. As he walked closer and closer to me, a green hue started illuminating in the darkness. He released his grip, and she fell hard into the dirt. Her eyes looked up at me with a blank stare. Blood seeped from her eyes and nose as her head rocked back and forth. My heart stopped. It was her. It was Adele.

My eyes flew open, and I shot up in bed. Adele's cold eyes glaring into my heart burned in my mind. I rubbed my face and stroked my mane before looking around the room. I turned, reaching for Adele but she was missing. I pushed the covers back, and Buddy was snoring at my feet. I walked over to the entrance and let my stream cut through the wind. The sunlight twinkled against the morning frost over the mountains. Grinning, I got dressed, made our bed, and walked over to the cave ledge to look out.

My nostrils flared as I left the mountain's incline and entered the forest floor.

"Where is Adele, pup?" Buddy's head cocked to the side, and then he looked behind him. Scanning the forest, I felt a peculiar pinch in my side. Then the pain gradually grew, and I doubled over in pain. I stumbled forward a few steps and leaned against a giant oak. My eyes blurred as my head swam with uneasiness. I leaned over, panting, when the second wave of pain hit. "Del?"

Buddy barked several times, pointing to the forest. He looked back at me and grabbed my shirt, pulling me towards the forest. I dropped into the mud and called on the wolf. My lungs filled with air, and my chest was expanding as my body heated up. The pain slowly subsided, and I felt the wolf gazing through my eyes. Guiding me. I stood strong on my feet, inhaling a deep breath of the breeze blowing. Adele's scent wafted from the forest near the river.

"Come on, Buddy." My feet pounded the ground, one after another, pushing through the loose earth.

My legs burned as I pumped them harder and faster, following my instincts to find her Pain radiated down my body, and the pungent smell of meat cooking tainted the air. I flew over a huge oak lying on its side and found a giant black bear lying lifeless with smoke rising from its burned fur.

I inhaled the air and smelled Adele's scent everywhere, but it was like she'd disappeared into thin air. The bear was lying flat on its stomach with its legs sprawled out. I walked around the bear and found Buddy digging underneath it.

"Buddy! Why are you—" Then I saw her leg twitching. Adele's body was buried underneath the bear's barbequed body.

I tried to push the bear over, but it had melted into the ground, covering Adele's body. A growl rolled up from my chest as I slowly pushed the bear up, lifting it just enough to uncover her.

Adele's body was covered in dark grey ash mixed with dried blood. I pushed her body with my foot and yelled.

"Del! Del! Wake up!" Moaning, she rolled her head back and forth. I panted and pushed with everything I had, throwing the bear onto its side. Parts of its flesh dropped from its stomach, covering her body. I swiped it away and lifted her out from under the beast. Blood was seeping from the wounds on her arms and chest. A pool of blood from underneath her body had left an imprint of her in the mud.

"Del, wake up! Del, please. Don't you die on me, Del! Stay with me! Please, Del!" A lump caught in my throat as I tried to rattle her awake.

I gently carried her back to the cave. Buddy followed behind me, whimpering.

"She's going to be okay, Buddy. It's okay, pup. We've got her now."

We made it to the cave, and I laid her on the bearskin. I changed her blood-soaked clothes and wet my shirt with water to clean her wounds. Then I closed my eyes and laid my hands over her forehead and stomach. Heat boiled inside my chest, running down my limbs as I called on my power to heal her. Adele's body vibrated as I forced her wounds to close and began healing her internally.

Adele opened her eyes and mumbled, "Jake. Jake, they think I'm — " Her eyes fluttered opened and closed as she tried to talk to me.

I leaned forward, cupping her cheek. Smoke steamed from my shoulders and hands as I commenced the healing process. An odd feeling struck me to open my eyes. A glowing bright pearl light fluctuated from her body, rolling up my arms, and drifted over me. She quivered on the ground as if the electricity was also healing her wounds. Adele's eyes rolled around under her lids as her body pulsated under my hands.

"Shh. It's okay. Shh. It's okay. I've got you now."

My body relaxed as my power slowly eased her body back into a healing state. I closed my eyes, boosting the process with my gifts, and embraced the bolt of electricity.

Chapter Thirty-Two: Adele

I opened my eyes to the darkness surrounding me. Shadows bounced off the walls of the cave from the fire's peak. Blinking my eyes, my vision was muffled with a hue of gray fog. I walked over to the door, looking out. The night still had billions of stars looking over the mountains. Turning to go back to bed, I stopped in my tracks. Jake, Buddy, and I were lying in bed, sleeping. I stared down at my body and realized I was in a deep slumber. My body twitched, and I rumbled under the covers.

"What's happening?"

"You're Astral-walking."

I jumped back and turned around. Shaking my head, I couldn't believe what I was seeing. "Dad?"

"Hi, honey. It's me."

Holding up my arms, I walked right through him. "What the?" Stumbling forward, I turned around. "Why can't I hug you? I don't understand."

"You're in spirit form, Del. You can't touch or feel anything. You can only observe, and . . . well, I'm a ghost, honey."

I stood there shaking my head. "I miss you so much, Dad. It's been so, so long. I wish . . . I wish this was real."

He stepped forward and nodded. "It's as real as you make it, honey."

"Why are you here?"

"I don't know. You brought me here."

"So much has happened since you've been gone. I don't—

I don't even know where to start. Jake is back, and the house . . . is gone. I um . . . I keep having these horrible nightmares about being captured and held in a white tent. The doors flap open, taunting me when I open my eyes. A man. I think it's Victor. He knows who I am and says he's looking for Jake and me. I'm not sure what to do. I don't know . . . I don't know what to do."

"Del, you know what to do. You're strong. The man who's stalking you is just trying to scare you."

"Well, it's working. I don't know how to protect us. I don't know how to control my power. I stopped using it after you died, and now I don't know what to do."

"First of all, you need to calm down. Second, focus. Focus your power on something and then manipulate it. Train it. Control it using your mind and your heart. The power has always been there. It was just dormant. Now that you've re-activated it, you can and will get stronger. Then no one can stop you. Not even Victor. He's strong, but you're stronger. Remember that. You're stronger."

"Dad, he told me that Jake's a liar. Is that true?"

"Jake tells you what you need to know to keep you safe."

"Why does that man want him back? Why is he trying to hurt us?"

"Don't let him fool you. He wants both of you and your power."

"I'm scared, Dad. I wish you were here."

"Everything's going to be okay. You're a lot stronger than you think. A lot stronger than Jake or I ever were."

Dad's body began fading out. I reached out to stop him, but he was going fast. His voice hushed to a whisper. "You can handle this. You were born to do this."

"Dad, please don't go. Wait." I watched as his spirit form drifted away like smoke in the wind.

I walked back over to the door to look out. The night

looked different. Darker. A gray haze lingered over the ground like a mist. I left the cave and stood on the ledge, looking around. The mountains swayed, floating back and forth over the earth. The trees inhaled and exhaled long breaths, moving with the motion of the mountains. I stepped off the ledge, and my body flew, soaring over the ground like a bird in flight. I sped down the mountain and entered the forest with immense speed. I looked back to see a pearly white luminance above the ground behind me. What would normally take hours took minutes to reach the tree line where Jake and I had entered the forest. I slowed to a walk, peering through the trees. My mouth dropped. There were tents parked everywhere. White tents. Dozens of them were lined up where Dad's old cabin used to reside. Shaking my head, I knew I'd seen this before in my dreams. *This is where he is. This is where Victor is.*

I slowly walked into camp and saw the large fire burning in the middle of the campsite. Tables lined up with maps and pictures hanging up on propped-up billboards. I walked over and realized the map was of the forest. Red tacks pushed in, marking areas around White Mountain and along the river.

I walked alongside the table, scanned the photos, and stopped in front of a picture of Dad and me. Dad was standing next to the river with a fishing pole, and I was right behind him, looking back and smiling. Memories of that day flashed in my mind. Dad dragged us out to his usual fishing spot. He caught one of the biggest trout he'd ever seen, breaking his rod and reel. He was yelling curse words at the fish for breaking his line, and I fell back laughing in the sand. Jake snapped the picture and then had to go help Dad.

I continued to walk along and saw Jake's picture. He was half-dressed, shirtless, with blood staining his mouth and chest. His eyes were glowing red, and he was holding a large bowie knife covered in blood. I'd never seen Jake look like that. He looked mad with rage. Mad with blood. Dad always told Jake that he needed to learn to control the wolf. Otherwise, the wolf would control him someday. I began backing away from the table and started to turn to go back when I heard his voice.

"Hello, Adele. I've been waiting for you."

I spun around, looking up to see Victor. He towered over me like a tall, slender oak. His malicious emerald-green eyes glimmered in the darkness, taunting me. A black aura exuded the evil and darkness of his being. He reached his hand out and ran his fingers through my impalpable body. Cringing, I stepped away, shaking my head.

"Ahh, well, don't worry, I'll see you in person soon enough."

I walked backward, turned around, and ran. My feet flew over the ground as I dashed through the forest, leaving a white sheen glowing behind me. I entered the cave, and everything was just as I'd left it. I walked over to my sleeping body and lay down.

CHAPTER THIRTY-THREE: VICTOR

I sat up in my cot as I felt her presence drawing near. Even though she didn't feel me, I felt her, no matter how hard she tried to hide from me. I closed my eyes and opened my mind to see her spirit form running. A vision of glossy pearl waves parting as she sped through the forest to return home. A smile crossed my face as I blinked my eyes. I knew that Adele was coming back and would be here any moment. I stood up from my cot, walking over to the door. The tent door was flapping in the wind as cool air from the mountains breezed by. Mist and smoke exhaled from my lips as I inhaled a deep breath of my cigarette. I exited the tent, walked over to the fire, and flicked the butt.

The night was quiet, with only a few men walking the lines. They wouldn't see her coming, but I would. I always have, since she was a girl. Since before she was born. That had always been my gift or curse, however one wanted to perceive it. After all, we're . . . well, related. She took what was rightfully mine, and I'll patiently wait for her to return to take it back.

Then I just might tell her the truth about her precious father. Tell her the truth about Bill and who he really was. *Hmmm. We'll see. We'll see.*

Chapter Thirty-Four: Adele

"Del! Adele, sit up and get a drink."

I tried to open my eyes, but my vision was blurred with floating white lights. Sharp, cutting pains shot through my head and gravitated down my spine. Warm tears filled my eyes, burning my nose as Jake lifted my shoulder and head up. I blinked, trying to focus my eyes on his face. He held a cup to my lips, forcing my mouth to open. Cold liquids spewed from my throat, drizzling down my shirt.

"Drink, Del!"

I shook my head wildly as the chunks rolled up. I slapped the cup out of his hand and rolled over onto my side. Acid burned my nose as the hot liquid flowed out of me like lava. Gasping for air, I felt Jake hold my hair back. Shivering, I collapsed back into the blankets. My fingers fumbled against the wool, trying to cover myself.

"Del, please drink for me."

My eyes fluttered as I tried to pull myself back up onto my side. Jake put his hand against my back and a cup to my lips.

"Here you go, honey," he said.

The cool water slowly flowed down my throat, easing down the rest of the stomach acid.

"Jake? Jake, I keep dreaming of—"

"Shh. You can lay back now. It's okay."

My body melted back into the blanket. I stopped fighting it and let sleep come.

Blinking my eyes, all I could see was the darkness

surrounding me. Pain shot through my lower back and into my bladder as I tried to pull myself up. Jake's snores rumbled from under the mountain of blankets covering us. Jake flew up, jumping over to help me. His hair was standing up like a peacock, and his face was scrunched up on one side.

"Del? What are you doing?"

Smiling, I gritted my teeth. "I need to go to the restroom."

Stabbing pain returned to the back of my head, traveling down my spine. My hand cradled my temple as tears rolled down my face. Jake pulled me upright onto my feet. I leaned heavily into his arm, wobbling back and forth until I found my balance and walked to the door, looking out. Snowflakes pummeled down into a blanket of white. My feet sank through the cloud, slipping right into the mud.

"Del, wait. Your boots."

I shook my head, walked out into the snow, dropped my pants, and relieved my bladder. Jake stood there and shook his head, smiling.

"Better?"

I nodded, wobbled back into the cave, and went back to bed. My shoulders felt like they were carrying a heavy boulder as I walked. Jake climbed into the covers next to me, wrapping his arms around my waist. His warm breath against my neck eased my pain as I closed my eyes.

The following day, I woke up to Jake and Buddy gone. I slowly sat up to my head, feeling much less weighed down. Staggering upright, I weaved back and forth over to my bag to pull out my jeans and a long-sleeve shirt. I slipped my feet into my boots and went looking for the boys.

Jake was standing at the bottom of the mountain, walking into the forest. I carefully walked down, and he was gone. Colorful floaters blinded my vision, as my head was swimming with dizziness. I wobbled back and forth over to a tall oak to catch my breath. Buddy ran through mud, startling me, and then Jake walked up. He was carrying a couple of squirrels by their tails, smiling. Buddy sprinted through the snow, rooting his nose in and out of it, snorting. Smiling, I shook my head and looked up at Jake.

The sunlight caught Jake's complexion just right, illuminating his pale-white skin. His once jet-black hair was dulled to a peppered grey with clumps missing. He blinked his eyes, and I saw a cloud of grey hovering under his eyes. He looked completely worn down and exhausted. As I was healing and getting well, he was getting weaker. I raised my hand to cup his cheek and looked into his worn-down golden chestnut eyes. The glow had dissipated.

He forced a smile. "Well, I got us some protein."

I wobbled forward, and Jake caught my arm. He cupped his arm undermine as we walked back up the mountain. My legs were heavy, almost buckling underneath me when I entered the cave. Jake guided me to the blanket, grabbing more firewood for the fire. He sat down and started to prep the squirrels for cooking.

I leaned over. "Do you want some help? Are you going to throw them in the pot?"

"Yeah, why not. Not a lot of meat on either, so I figured just throw them in a pot with some vegetables."

Panting, I forced myself up and walked over to the buckets of water on the floor, picked one up, and carried it over to the pot.

"Del, sit down, woman. I'll get it."

"No, I want to help, Jake. Just let me help." Gasping, I walked over and dumped the water in, grabbed two vegetable cans, and sat down next to the fire. I opened the cans and added them to the pot. Jake added a little more water and threw the squirrels into the pot. Then he grabbed the other jug and handed it to me. "Drink. You need water."

I turned up the jug and handed him the rest.

He finished it off and wiped his mouth with the back of his hand. "Well, I'll have to go back to the river for water tomorrow."

Sharp pains shot behind my eyes as I shook my head. Squinting, I touched the temples of my forehead, trying to calm the pain. My cheeks were tender to the touch, burning with every slight movement.

Jake's cool hand touched my brow and ran his fingers down my cheek. "You should lie down and rest. You still have a long way to go for recovery."

Shaking my head, I grabbed his hand. "I don't want to. I wanted to talk to you. I've been down in that bed for too long now."

"Well, we can talk while you lie down. I can sit with you," Jake said.

I knew Jake was right. I needed to lie down, but I wanted to talk. I had so many questions. So many things I wanted to tell him. Jake grabbed my bag, propping my head up with it. I lay back on my side and just watched him work the squirrel skin for a little while before I finally opened my mouth to tell him what was on my mind. I turned to look outside and saw snow steadily coming in the door. The sky was a hazy gray, and the light was dimming as the ground was slowly getting covered.

Jake raised his head and inhaled a deep breath. "Smells like a snowstorm is coming. It may trap us in here for a few days."

His eyes concentrated on the squirrel. Sliding his strong hands against the skin, slowly smoothing it out. I bit my bottom lip and remembered Jake's hands sliding down my rump. I squeezed my eyes shut and looked away from him.

"Jake. I'm having a recurring dream about a man named Victor." I swallowed hard and watched Jake's expression turn from busy working to worry.

He slowed his hands and looked at me. "What?"

"Victor. How do you know him?" My body weakened. I had to inhale deeply to catch my breath. Jake's forehead furrowed as he slowly sat down the fur and looked up at me. I waited for him to say something else, but he just stared at me. He opened his mouth like he wanted to speak to me, but something stopped him. He licked his lips, closed his mouth, and looked over at the door.

"Dad warned me about him in my letter, and he's been haunting my dreams ever since I moved back into the cabin. I just . . . I want the truth, Jake. I need to know."

Jake continued peering out the entrance for a long moment. He finally looked back over at me with glossy eyes. "When I left the house. When Dad died, I was alone. I had no one. Nowhere to go. No money." He inhaled a deep breath and exhaled. "A man named Rick found me. He approached me like you did at the sandwich shop. Only he offered me a job. I thought he was like Dad, trying to help me. He offered me money and got me off the streets. He sent me for intensive training to learn how to fight and defend myself. Then he introduced me to some people that are . . . well, special like us. And then I went to work. I traveled to other countries and did jobs for him. I thought we were doing something good. I thought I was making the world a better place. That's what he led me to believe. I thought I could trust him."

Jake stood up, walked over to the entrance, and stared out.

"Rick knew exactly what I was and led me to believe that we were using our special abilities to help people."

Jake shook his head and rubbed his face. "He told me we were exterminating the bad people." He chuckled, gritted his teeth, and turned to look at me. Shaking his head, he looked outside. "Then, one evening, we were doing a job, and something wasn't right.." He inhaled a deep breath and exhaled, staring out the cave. "I headed back to our camp and lay down for the night. I couldn't sleep." He looked over at me, gazing into my eyes. "I kept thinking about you, Adele. I pulled out your picture and stared at it. I felt like I needed to find you."

He walked over to his bag and pulled out a picture, handing it to me. Smiling, I looked down at the picture for a moment and then handed it back.

"I remember that day."

"That night they ambushed us, and I . . . I barely got away. I didn't stop running until I found you at the cabin."

"I've never met Victor . . . I heard Rick talk about him a few times to other men, but I've never actually met him. I was recruited by Rick and a couple of his men. I worked closely with a few guys, and that was it."

I stared at Jake for a long moment. "I saw Victor."

"What?"

"In my dream. I walked back to my old house and saw a camp. The cabin was gone and had been replaced by dozens of white tents. A man approached me in my dream, and I think it was Victor. He had a map with our pictures pinned on it. He's been searching for us. Both of us."

Jake's gaze met mine.

His eyes flashed a fiery red for a brief moment. "I just wanted to have a normal life."

I reached my hand out, and he walked over, grabbing it. Scents of food wafted in the air as the wind picked up outside. Jake let go of my hand and walked over to the pot to stir.

Jake inhaled a deep breath and looked over at me. "I know you may not be glad that I came back into your life, but I am. I've thought of you every day from the moment I left. I just-I wanted to make sure you're okay before we go our separate ways."

Shaking my head, I stood up and walked over to him. My arms wrapped around his waist as I pushed my lips against his. "You're stuck with me now. So, you better get used to it. Okay?"

He smiled down at me. "Okay."

CHAPTER THIRTY-FIVE: ADELE

I blinked my eyes open, and darkness surrounded me. I tried to sit up, but my arms were bound behind my back. I rolled over onto my hip and scooted towards the tent door. A lantern light appeared along the side of the tent, walking down towards the door. I lay on my side, closed my eyes, and pretended to be asleep. A cold sense of dread tickled the back of my neck and flushed through the rest of my body as I heard footsteps enter the tent.

"Well, hello, Adele. You know why I'm here."

I opened my eyes and slowly sat up, staring at the tall man with glowing emerald eyes. He walked over and slammed the back of his fist into my face. My body smashed down into my bound hands, sending sharp pains into my left kidney.

"I know where you're hiding, girl, and we'll see each other soon."

My body shot up in bed, and I looked around the sun-filled room, gasping for air. My face dropped into my hands, and I rubbed my eyes. A week had passed, and my head finally didn't feel like I was carrying a boulder on my shoulders.

Jake walked in, stood at the door, and stomped his feet carrying a rabbit. He had a layer of snow blanketing the black hood of his jacket. He shook off and brushed the rest of the flakes off his shoulders.

Buddy popped his head in and ran over to me. Shaking off, he threw cold bits of snow and ice into my face. I stood up and walked over to my bag to get dressed. Jake watched me change with a crooked grin. I turned around, took off my sleeping shirt, revealing my bare back, and pulled over a long-sleeved shirt to replace it.

Jake slipped his hands under my shirt and fondled my erect nipples as I pulled down my shirt. I spun around, wrapping my arms around his neck, and pulled his lips to mine. He wrapped his hands around my waist, squeezing me against him. His bulge protruded from his pants, pressing into my abdomen.

"I have to use the restroom."

"I can't help it. We haven't been able to since . . . you know . . . you got attacked, and then you showed me your sexy back. So, yeah, I want you." Jake smiled seductively.

"I have to talk to you about something, but first, my bladder is about to burst." I walked a few feet down the mountain to relieve myself. The snow was coming down outside, and I couldn't see anything around me except a sea of white. I finished up, and a flash from my dream struck me. The hairs on the back of my neck stood on end, tingling down my spine.

His voice taunted my ears, echoing through my head as the tent doors flapped. *"I know where you're hiding, girl."*

I looked around, sensing eyes on my back. Spinning around again and again, I searched. The snow camouflaged my surroundings like a wall closing in around me. Inhaling deep breaths, I closed my eyes and squeezed. I opened my eyes and held my arms out for balance to tread through the mounds of snow as I walked back to the cave.

Panting, I leaned against the entrance. "Jake, I, um . . . I had another dream."

Jake was standing over the rabbit, skinning it. He'd already cut its head and feet off, pulling its skin back like pulling off clothes. He looked at me while working and back down at the rabbit.

"I feel like he's watching me. Like he's watching us. I don't know how, but he knows where we are. I feel him close. Waiting for the right opportunity to strike."

Jake stared at me for a moment and looked over at the entrance. He set down the rabbit and grabbed his jacket. I followed him over and watched him walk back out into the snow. His black attire stood out like a sore thumb in the sea of white. He walked down our usual path and followed it into the forest, disappearing behind trees.

Buddy tried to follow, but I held his collar. "No. Stay, pup."

After a few minutes, Jake came back, stomping in the doorway.

"I don't see or smell anyone. It's too cold, and the snow is really coming down now. So we may actually get snowed in."

Jake dropped his jacket off his shoulders and shook it towards the entrance.

He walked over to me, wrapped his arms around my waist, gazing into my eyes. "For now, we need to stay here. At least until the snow passes. Besides, you're just now doing better. You need a few more days of rest before we can go out."

Jake walked back to the rabbit and cut it up. Then he threw it into the pot, grabbed all the fixings, and poured in water. My mind wandered as I watched him prepare our food. I knew that Dad had put a protection spell around the cave to keep us safe, but something felt off. I sensed that Victor and his men would soon break through the barrier and kill us in our sleep or capture us and take our powers, as Dad warned in his letter. No matter how weak I felt, I knew our safety was at stake. I knew that we needed to move and soon.

"Jake?" He looked up at me and smiled. "I think we should leave in the morning." Jake's mouth dropped open, and I raised my hand. "I know what you'll say, but just hear me out. Victor knows where we are. I know he does. He's haunting me every night in my dreams, and he's coming for us whether we're ready or not. I think I'm well enough to travel. Hell, I have to be. We're sitting ducks here."

Jake shook his head and looked out at the snow pouring

down. He inhaled a deep breath and exhaled loudly. "Okay, but we wait till morning. Okay?"

I nodded. "In the morning."

The rabbit only took about an hour to cook. We ate quietly, listening to the snow sweeping over the mountains. Jake finished smoothing out the rabbit fur and placed it with the other blankets in the wooden bin.

I walked over to the door, looking outside. "It's freezing out there, Jake."

He walked over and wrapped his arms around my waist as we both quietly watched the snow come down, covering the mountain tops. The doorway to the cave had two feet of standing snow to push through to walk out.

I turned around, gazing into Jake's eyes. "We should lie down and get some sleep."

Jake nodded and followed me over to the bins. I pulled the covers out and laid them down. I turned around, pulled my shirt over my head, and dropped my pants on the ground, revealing my naked, light-brown figure. My black hair tickled the top of my buttock as I walked over to Jake.

I put my hands under his shirt, pushed it up, and slipped it over his head. Rows of muscles of his tight abdomen glistened from the shadow of the fire. I pushed his pants down to reveal his erect manhood pointing and ready. He ran his giant hands down my back, massaging my muscles down to my rump. He thrust his body against mine and smiled down at me before diving into my lips.

I walked backward, guiding him to our bed, and pulled away to lie down first. He admired my naked body for a moment, smiling down at me. I open my long legs to reveal my groin, pulsing and ready. I slipped my fingers down, opened my lips, and ran my finger over my clitoris.

I'd never played with myself before in front of anyone, but with Jake, I wanted to. I wanted him to watch me and yearn for my touch. I felt comfortable being myself with Jake. I wanted him to desire me as much as I craved him.

Jake's eyes glowed as he gazed down into my moist crevice. His long black hair draped into his eyes as he slowly knelt. He traced my body with his fingers, starting at my neckline and following down over my hardened nipple. His lips dove in, suckling and nibbling on my bosoms. Then, he followed down with his lips and licked my navel, tickling me. I wiggled, and he smiled as his muscular abdomen flexed down to the ground.

He ran his lips down to my groin and stopped. I continue to move my fingers up and down my crease, moistening my opening. Jake slapped my hand away playfully and licked my clitoris. He gazed up at me as he was sucking my clitoris and then pushed his finger inside me. My back arched as I exhaled loudly. My body ground against his digit, begging for more.

He grinned and licked my groin like a wolf, running his long moist tongue up and down my crease, teasing me.

His serpent-like tongue pushed inside me, flickering inside my wet tunnel. Shuddering, I tremored with pleasure, raising my hips towards his mouth. He pulled back, climbed up my body, and rubbed his member against my clitoris, begging for entry.

I moved my abdomen, guiding him inside me. He slowly pushed himself in and buried his shaft deep. He moved his hips around and finally pulled himself out. My groin shuddered with pleasure as I pushed against him for more. I squeezed his rump with my legs and pulled him back inside me. My climax rose, and I gushed my juices, squeezing his length with my groin.

Jake held his hard member inside me, slowly pulling himself out and plunging back in. My body arched with pleasure as I wrapped my legs around his waist. His eyes met mine, and the wolf peered through, hungry and wild. He picked up his speed, thrusting himself inside me. His abdomen flexed, pressing against my abdomen as he grabbed my hands and held them above my head. Gasping, my mouth dropped open, and he pressed his lips against mine, pulling my bottom lip down with his teeth. My climax rose, and I pushed against his grip over my wrists, but he squeezed harder. His lips ran up my neck and nibbled my chin.

I squeezed my legs around his waist and screamed, "Oh, Jake. Oh, you're going to make me cum again!"

He planted his knees under my thighs and propped my legs up in the air. He pounded against my rump, thrusting himself in and out of me. His organ buried deep in my crevice as I gushed juices over his hard member. My body vibrated with pleasure. He leaned over and pressed his lips to mine, panting.

His mouth grazed my ear, and he whispered,

"Ride me, baby."

My legs were weak, but I draped my leg over him and straddled his muscular abdomen. My body vibrated as I eased my groin over his girth, slowly thrusting his hard member. Jake pulled me down, wrapped his arms around my back, and cupped his mouth over my breast. I arched my back and slowly rode him, pulling his length all the way out and then easing it back in. He lay back and let me enjoy his manhood. I savored this moment with him. My gaze traced his muscular chest and met his glowing chestnut eyes. A smile brightened his face. He sat up and cupped my buttocks. His lips met mine, and I wrapped my hands around his cheeks, running my fingers through his black mane. My rhythm quickened, and I was thrusting against him. My body began to quiver, and I felt my climax rising. I didn't want to stop kissing him. I didn't want this moment to end, but the pleasure felt so good it hurt. I pulled back, opening my mouth.

I pressed my cheek against his and whispered in his ear,

"Come with me, baby."

He squeezed my rump and took control, pounding my rump against him. I surrendered to his muscular grip and was a slave to his ecstasy ride. My hands squeezed his back as my groin seized, oozing juices over his shaft. Jake stopped, filling up my insides with his juices. I finally dropped over and lay on top of him, panting.

"You okay?"

"Yeah." I got up, and he pulled me back down and kissed me, pressing his lips hard against mine. Smiling, I pulled away and walked over to wash off.

Jake wrapped his arms around my waist and fell asleep almost instantly after I lay down with him. I tossed and turned, haunted by my dream. Victor's malicious stare burned in my mind when I closed my eyes. I sat up quickly, looking over at the door. *Nothing.* The night was dark, with dim moonlight. I blinked and lay back down, staring at the cave wall. My heart raced, pounding in my chest. I knew that my dreams were a warning of what was to come. I was afraid of what that meant. I turned over to look at Jake and knew I never wanted to lose him again.

CHAPTER THIRTY-SIX: ADELE

Beams of sunlight shined into the cave, warming my face. I blinked my eyes open and stretched my legs out, yawning. Jake's snores rumbled in the blanket as I pulled out from under his arm, sitting up.

"Hello, Adele."

A hooded man towered in the entrance with glowing emerald eyes. A nefarious grin twinkled as he raised his arm up. A pistol's barrel extended from his hand, and then it clicked.

"Jake!" I screamed. Jake jumped and shot up out of bed. His body was bare as the blanket slid down his muscular build. Panting, I coughed and held my face. Acid rose into my throat, threatening to spew. Rocking back and forth, I inhaled deep breaths as I stared at the empty entrance. I knew that he was toying with me.

"What is it, Del? What happened?" He walked over to the entrance and looked out.

"Get away from there! Please!" I cried as the tears rolled down my face.

Jake walked back over, squatted down, and wrapped his arms around my shoulders. "What happened? Was it another bad dream?"

Wiping my face, I stood up and walked over to my clothes. I pulled out my pants and fell over onto the ground, pulling them up.

"Honey, let me help you." Jake pulled me up, and I finished dressing.

My voice cracked. "He's taunting me, Jake. He knows

where we are! I keep having these dreams . . . I don't know how, but he knows," I gasped, trying to push down the tears. I wiped the moisture from my face aggressively as I inhaled a deep breath. "He's coming for us. We need to go. Now."

Jake walked over and got dressed quickly. As I watched him, my eyes kept reverting to the entrance. Victor's glowing eyes and teeth inside his dark hood burned in my mind. Shaking my head, I squeezed my eyes shut. Quickly, I started packing my bag with canned foods, bowls, cups, and utensils. I walked my bag over to the cave entrance and looked out cautiously. The morning was crisp, with a heavy mist over the mountains. The snowfall had ceased during the night and left the ground with a few extra feet of white to tread.

I trudged through the snow and went to the restroom. A sea of white surrounded me, blinding my vision. My head swung back and forth, searching for any remnant of the dark visitor. I ran back to the cave and finished packing. My hands quivered as I rolled up the blankets and used a rope to tie them to my backpack.

Jake walked over to me. "Are you ready?"

"As ready as I'll ever be. Where should we go?"

"I think we should go north, deeper into the forest."

"Okay. Just anywhere but here. I know he's coming for us soon."

We exited the cave and headed down the mountain. I looked back to see a path through the snow, leading right to our cave.

"Do you think we're leaving a trail to find our cave?"

Jake looked up into the sky, staring into the treetops, and then shook his head. "No, it'll start snowing again soon."

I nodded, "Okay."

We entered the forest, carefully walking towards the river. Jake stopped and held his hand up in the air for us to pause. He reached down and grabbed Buddy's collar. "Stay, pup."

Voices were drifting towards us as we walked. Jake looked back at me, pointing with his eyes in the direction of the voices. Buddy pulled from Jake's grasp and started to run. "No, Buddy!" Buddy stopped in his tracks, sitting down.

Jake directed him to come, so Buddy ran over to him and walked alongside us.

Jake motioned for us to keep moving. "I think it's just some hunters. They smell human."

"Okay."

"Del, we need to follow the river, fill our water jugs, and try to do some fishing for food. We don't have any protein to eat except for canned food."

"Okay."

An hour passed, and Jake changed directions. He lifted his head and sniffed the breeze blowing in from the north. He looked over at me and nodded his head.

"I've never been this deep in the forest before. I'm not sure where the river is this far down."

"I've been down here before," Jake said.

"Really? When?"

He cocked his head to the side and raised his eyebrow. "The night Dad died. I fled to the forest. Wait, I may still have the map, too. I made a map on a piece of bark, so if I ever came back, I'd remember where the cave was."

"Really?"

"Yeah, Dad always said to mark it on the map. Remember?"

"I'm just surprised. A piece of bark?"

"Yeah, he said to always mark down on a map, or just anything, to find your way. Remember?"

"Yeah, I guess. I just thought Dad meant an actual map, not a piece of wood."

"What does it matter so long as it's a map, whether you created it or a printed one? Besides, when was the last time you saw a printed map? People don't usually use maps anymore. They use *Google* on their phone or computer. Not an actual paper map."

Jake dropped his bag onto the ground, digging inside it until he found what he was looking for. He pulled out an old piece of bark off a pecan tree. He ran his finger along some of the writing on the bark, mouthing something to himself. I walked over and looked at the bark, shaking my head.

"That's a map?"

"Yes, it is."

He looked up and down at the bark and then looked up again. "Okay, it's this way."

"I thought we were going to the river." I pointed in the direction we were walking in.

"We are, but the cave I have a map of is right on the water. Just come on. I'll show you. It's a little ways away, so we need to get moving."

We walked well into the afternoon before we stopped for a break. Jake sat his bag down, pulled out the water jug, and took a big swig from it. I dug through my bag, pulled out a cup, and poured some water in it for Buddy. Buddy lapped it up and sniffed the ground, walking around the trees. We both sat on a gigantic oak that lay on its side. The forest was fully awake now, with birds singing and branches crackling from the weight of the icicles hanging down. I looked up into the tunnel of trees and watched the clouds race overhead.

"Okay, come on. We should get going."

I nodded and stood back up, following Jake. Another hour went by before we finally heard the water running. Jake led the way through a clearing in the forest, and then the trees opened to a beautiful waterfall. It sprayed a cold icy mist over us as we approached it. Jake and I walked up to the water, looking down, and saw the bottom of the riverbed. Fish were swimming along the bank, eating little minnows that gathered to eat the growing moss.

Jake turned, smiling at me. "There's a cave behind that waterfall. It hides inside the rock underneath the water. We can stay there tonight and cook fish."

He pulled out a long stick from his bag and unfolded it. It looked like a collapsible fishing pole with a hook at the end.

"Wow, where did you get that pole? That's great."

"I don't know, actually. I've had it for a long time. It's been with me since after Dad died."

I nodded and smiled, watching him walk over to the mud and dig until he pulled out a long fat worm. He walked back to me, pulled the worm into pieces, and handed me the carcass.

"Gee, thanks." I laughed. Jake shrugged and turned around.

I looked up and watched the clouds move overhead. There were rows upon rows of fluff twirling through the sky. A cold breeze picked up and nipped at my ears with an icy bite. As I watched Jake, I had a sudden urge to wrap my arms around his waist. I walked over and hugged him from behind inhaling his musk. I stood on my tiptoes and pressed my cheek against his shoulder.

"What's wrong?" He clasped his giant hands over mine and squeezed.

I needed to be close to him and hold him.

"Nothing, I just . . . I don't know. I just wanted to hold you."

Jake spun around and put his lips to mine. He kissed me slowly, raising his hands to my cheeks, and caressed my skin. Tingling rushed down my body and into my loins. Buddy sped by us, startling us, and raced along the water's shore. I snapped, "Buddy!"

Buddy stopped, looking back at me.

"Come here. Stay here, Buddy."

Buddy walked over and sat down, with his tongue hanging out of his mouth to one side.

"When Dad died, I stayed in the forest for a couple of days before I headed back towards civilization . . ." Jake paused and smiled, looking into the forest as if he was greeting an old friend. "It was peaceful here."

I smiled, sat down in the sand, and watched Jake as he fished. The sun shined down and hit the water, reflecting twinkling lights off the floating chunks of ice. Jake turned back, smiling at me.

"I wish we could stay here for a little while, Jake. You're right. It's very peaceful."

I looked across the river and saw a fox on the other side fishing. He was wading in the shallow water, pulled out a little fish with his paw, and carried it in his mouth back into the forest. Smiling, I pointed. "Jake." He nodded and went back to fishing.

An hour passed, and Jake pulled out a decent-sized fish. He dropped his pole back into the water immediately and pulled another out. He laid both fish in front of me and returned one more time. He walked along the bank and moved his pole back and forth, trying to attract a fish. He pulled out his line, shaking his head.

"That's good, Jake. These two are good-sized fish."

Nodding, he collapsed his pole and shoved it into his bag. I threw the rest of the worm into the water and followed Jake to the cave.

"You have to be careful walking across to the cave. It's a hidden ledge on the cliff that the water flows over. You can't really see it from the forest. I'll go first and show you."

He walked foot to foot, sideways, with his stomach facing the wall along a tiny ledge that led to a hidden cave right behind the waterfall. He poked his head out and waved for me to come. I followed Jake's lead and carefully walked along the wall. My feet felt like they would slip a few times, but I kept moving. Buddy whimpered from the bank. He stood up on his back legs and pawed at the ledge. I turned my head back, almost falling. Gasping, I held my body against the wall. Jake came out, grabbed my hand, and led me the rest of the way.

The main part of the cave was hidden inside the waterfall. There were two openings to enter, and they exited parallel to each other. Going in one way and out the other or vice versa. The entrance we took to get into the cave had a ledge, and the other side was a drop-off onto sharp rocks on the other side of the river. A cool breeze whisked through, chilling me to the bone as I stared into the darkness. I turned around, looking behind me into the heart of the cave. It was pitch dark with no way of seeing unless we started a fire. Jake returned with Buddy across his shoulders. He put him down on the floor and went right back out again. Buddy walked over to me, shivering, with his tail between his legs.

I walked out onto the ledge and waited for Jake's return with firewood. He dropped it onto the floor and dug through his bag, pulling out flints. Once the fire started, the light revealed that the cave was a lot deeper than I expected. I looked around and saw some old drawings deep inside the hole.

"This cave is very old, and those drawings date back many years before we were even born. I don't think many people have been out this far or have discovered this cave," Jake said.

I nodded as my eyes ran along the rock's walls.

"I'm going to go find something to cook the fish on. I'll be right back."

Another cool draft ran through the cave and down my back, chilling me. Shivering, I walked over to the entrance to watch for Jake. As I stared out the opening, I noticed something peculiar. The treetops near the river swayed back and forth as if something giant was in the forest. Frozen, I stared anxiously into the trees. As soon as Jake stepped out between two large oaks, I waved. His hands were full of wood, so he nodded, smiling. He balanced up on the ledge and slowly walked across.

"Hi. I found some wood, and there are two pecan planks for the fish."

I pointed out the door to the forest, and Jake turned around to see the forest was quiet. The trees weren't moving anymore, and everything was still.

"What is it?"

I stared into the forest and then looked back, shaking my head. "Nothing."

Jake walked over to the wood and stacked the pieces against the wall. Then he walked over to the fish and laid them on the pecan pieces. "I think I'm just going to cook them whole. We can be careful and eat around the bone."

"Sounds good," I said.

"I'll get up and fish in the morning. There's good fishing in that water if you catch the fish at the right time."

"Okay."

As the fish cooked, I glanced over at the entrance to see snow coming down again. I inhaled a deep breath, pointing to the cave entrance.

"I smelled it coming in when I was searching for wood. I'm hoping it passes soon."

The fish only took a few minutes to cook before it was ready to eat. We quietly ate and listened to the waterfall pummeling down into the icy pool as the snow flurries descended. The sunlight dimmed early, and the night eased in as the snowstorm steadily picked up.

After eating, I walked over to my bag and discarded my clothes on the floor. I eyed Jake as I strolled over to the waterfall and scooped handfuls of icy water into my hands. I splashed my naked skin, letting the water run down my erect nipples and navel area. Then I splashed handfuls over my groin, drizzling water between my long legs. I glanced back at Jake as he walked up behind me.

He wrapped his arms around my waist and suckled my neck, kissing down my shoulders. His fingers slid up to my breasts and caressed my nubs, gently squeezing. A shiver rushed through my body, and I vibrated, turning my head to press my lips against his. My body heated up, and a flush of fire ran through my loins, aching for him.

Jake's manhood pushed against my lower back, begging to be stroked. He ran his fingers down my curves and found my clitoris moist and fluctuating. His finger stroked my groin, teasing his entry. I spun around, looking up at him. My hands followed his flexed six-pack down, and I grabbed his giant erection with both hands, slowly stroking.

He thrust his body against me and ran his hands down to my rump, picking me up. He smiled and pushed his groin against mine. My mouth dropped open, aching for his entry. I wrapped my legs around his abdomen, pressing my lips against his. My tongue danced inside his mouth, and I pulled back, biting his bottom lip.

Jake's eyes lit up, and he opened his mouth and revealed his fangs extended slightly. He carried me over to the blanket and laid me on my back. I moved my hips up and down, co-ercing him. He lay over me, and my lips found his in the fire's shadows. His hips moved up and down as he guided himself inside me. My lips broke from his, gasping, and I wrapped my arms around his back, squeezing him as he thrust deep inside me. My juices flooded, drowning his member.

I pushed him up. "Lay down."

I climbed on top of him and cupped my mouth over his sex. I could only take in half before he hit the back of my throat and used my hand, stroking the remainder of his shaft. Jake ran his fingers through my hair and guided my head up and down over him.

He tugged my hair back. "Ride me, baby, or I'm going to fill up your throat."

I slowly crawled back on top of him and slid his manhood deep inside me. I picked my hips up and slowly rode his hard member. A low growl escaped his chest as he grabbed my waist and took control of my rhythm, holding me down while he pounded my groin. My body vibrated as my juices exploded. Jake leaned forward with his mouth open, moaning as his juices shot deep inside me.

Exhausted, I lay over him, panting. Our hearts beat as one while we both tried to catch our breath. I turned my head, putting my lips to his as he wrapped his arms around my waist and held me. I sat up and lay down next to him. Jake put his arms around me, and we both fell asleep.

Chapter Thirty-Seven: Victor

"Alessia, where's your brother?"

I stepped behind the old oak and watched my father wrap his arm around her. Her emerald eyes glistened in the shadows of the sun setting behind the mountain. I peeked out, and her eyes darted towards me, and then she shook her head at Father.

"Victor!" he shouted.

Father stomped towards the tall pines behind the house. I turned to make a run for it but heard the leaves rustling right behind me.

"Victor!"

Sharp pains shot through my arm as he dragged me into the clearing. I glanced up at him and then gazed at the sky. A pink hue stretched across the sky as the sun was going to sleep for the night.

"Go with your sister to town and pick up Bill. I don't know why I need to always try to guess where the hell you are. You constantly have your head in the clouds and not out here helping your family. Your brother is chopping wood, your sister is preparing the candles, and where are you? Nowhere to be found, per usual. Worthless. Now, go."

He pushed me, and I collapsed into a mudhole. Rocks broke my fall, stinging my face. Heat flushed through my body, burning my cheeks, and rippled through my fingers. I looked down to see electricity sparking, going back and forth between my digits. I stared at my father's back and stood up, huffing deep breaths. I took giant steps towards him and was stopped by her. Alessia. She stepped in front of me and put her hand on my forearm. I felt her power sizzle into my chest and eliminate any fury I had toward our father. She reached down and grabbed my hand, holding it in both of hers. "It's not worth it, brother. Come, let's go to town."

I looked up into the winter sky, and it was covered in rows upon rows of gray winter clouds. A cool breeze blew from inside the trees and littered tiny icicles over the tents. I inhaled a long drag off my *Marlboro* and exhaled a wall of steam in front of me.

"Victor. Victor."

"What?"

"They're on the move again. We, um . . . we couldn't find the cave you said they were in. We looked everywhere, and there is no —"

I turned around and stepped toward Rick. Rick quickly stepped backward, bumping into the table and knocking it over. Pictures flew off and floated in the wind. Shaking my head, I inhaled another drag of my cigarette, watching Rick shudder at my mere movement.

"Clean this up, iddy-it. Do you know where they've relocated to?"

"Sir, we lost a lot of men looking near the mountain you told us they're hiding in. There were traps and —"

"And what!? I don't care. I want them found. What part of that don't you understand, hmmm?" I walked up to Rick and leaned down into his face. "I want them found, captured, and brought to me alive. Got it?"

"Yes, sir."

I inhaled another drag as I walked over to the fire, staring down at it.

Rick's footsteps echoed as he walked away. I looked up at the moon, and it was half full, peeking in and out of the snow clouds. It was staring down at me the same as it did that night. The night everything changed.

We turned down a dirt road and followed a line of trees until we came to an old cabin. The half-moon peeked through the snow clouds as I inhaled a deep breath. Snow flurries wafted through the wind, speckling icicles across my windshield. Bill looked up from his whittling and walked to the edge of his porch, smiling. The truck barely came to a halt before Alessia slammed the door and ran to him. Her arms wrapped around his neck, and their lips connected for a long moment before she rose for air, smiling.

I looked away as tears welled up in my eyes. I loved my sister and knew that eventually, she would marry Bill and leave me alone with my father. She was the only one who truly loved me. She was the only one who showed me any kindness. Tears rolled down my cheeks, burning my nose. I wiped them away quickly with the back of my arm. My heart ached, pounding in my ears. Why can't I do anything right? I wish I could make him proud of me, but he never is. I don't know what he wants from me. I wish he would just leave me alone, but I know, deep down, that he wished I was never born. My insides boiled as the dark thoughts festered, filling my heart with hatred. I looked back at Alessia and Bill walking towards the truck.

CHAPTER THIRTY-EIGHT: ADELE

I opened my eyes and sensed someone watching me. Darkness blinded my vision, causing me to blink. Creaking trees ruptured behind me, and a draft of icy snow breezed into my face. Shivering, I slowly turned back and saw a large dark shadow. I shot up in bed, spinning my head back and forth. "Hello. Hello, is anyone there?"

I looked up at the ceiling to see the morning sunlight reflecting off the waterfall. I dressed and walked to the cave entrance to see Jake with his pole in the water and Buddy sunbathing in the sand. A cool breeze nipped at my face as the snow subsided temporarily. Jake nodded, and I waved before turning around. As soon as my back was to the entrance , I froze. My mouth dropped open, and I choked on a breath caught in my throat. I was face-to-face with a giant black bear. It towered over me with a string of saliva dangling from its mouth.

Shrieking, I walked backward until a sharp part of the cave wall gouged me in the back. The bear's enormous paws stomped toward me. Trembling, I covered my face with my forearm.

"What are you doing?"

Jumping, I spun around to see Jake standing right behind me. I looked back to see the bear was gone.

"It was a-a bear," I said.

"What?" Jake said.

"I thought I saw a large black bear standing in front of me. I swear . . . it seemed so-so real."

Jake walked past me with his hands full of fish, sat them down, and looked back at me.

"You really mean it, don't you?"

He walked over to me and took my hand. Shivering, I sank into the cave wall for stability.

"What did the bear look like?"

"It was a black bear with drool hanging out of his mouth."

Jake walked over to the ledge and looked out, and then he went to the other side and did the same.

He stared out the door for a long moment and then turned around. "We may not be alone."

"What do you mean?"

Jake inhaled the air breezing through the cave as he walked back to the cave exit where he was fishing.

"I worked with a man. He's a . . . well, a shapeshifter. He was my best friend. I think he's here looking for me. He continued to work with Rick after I left. So, he's probably been tracking us, and now he's here."

The ground in the cave started to vibrate as rocks on the floor rolled down into the waterfall. I sensed a man's presence drawing closer and closer to our cave. "Jake? Someone's coming."

My breath choked in my chest as I waited for Jake's comrade to show himself. A giant black bear's head entered the cave, walking along the ledge with ease. His mouth drooped open with drool oozing from his lips. His head dipped down to enter the cave as his body began shifting in size. He slowly condensed down into a human man's body. His naked skin and hair were ebony with a slight glow to his golden-brown eyes.

"Hello, Jake," the man said. He cleared his throat, panting, as he walked into the cave.

Jake's face lit up, and he ran over and threw his arms around him. They slapped each other's backs and laughed out loud.

"Is this her? Is this Del?"

Jake looked at me, and his cheeks reddened.

"Yes."

"Been a long time, buddy. How are you doing?"

"I'm okay. I've been traveling, so I'm pretty tired."

Jake walked over, pulled some clothes out of his bag, and handed them to his friend. I stood there in shock with my mouth open. I didn't know what to say. Jake was catching up with an old friend, forgetting why he was there. I stood back and watched in awe, not wanting to remind Jake of what his friend's actual visit was about.

"So . . . are you going to introduce me, or do I have to do it?"

"Sorry, man. Del, this is Vahn. We, um . . . we worked together."

Vahn looked at Jake, then at me, sticking his hand out. I gripped his hand and felt he truly loved Jake like a brother, but he was there to do a job, as I had suspected. I pulled back my hand, staring into his eyes. A twinge of sadness slighted his smile, and I knew he didn't really want to follow through with his mission. Vahn's eyes darted towards Jake, rubbing his hands together. I sensed Vahn had many gifts, as well as being a shapeshifter. He knew my intentions when I shook his hand. He searched the room to pull his sentiments together and finally met Jake's eyes with a fake smile to subside him.

I walked past them. "I need to go to the restroom. I'll be right back."

Jake nodded and laughed, looking at Vahn. "Okay. Do you need me to come with you?"

"No." I smiled, shaking my head.

I walked into the forest and did my business. As I stood up, a sensation tingled down my spine. Someone was nearby. Someone with magical abilities lurked in the thick of the woods. I slowly turned around, peering behind me. I closed my eyes, reaching out with my mind, and a sharp pain pinged behind my right eye. A flash of him maliciously laughing flashed in my head, and then a vision of men, dozens of them, traveling our way struck.

"Oh, no!" I gasped.

I looked up at the cave and stumbled to my knees as I tried to hurry back.

When I reached the cave, Jake was holding Vahn up by his throat against the cave wall.

"Why? How could you? Why, Vahn?"

"Because that's what we do, Jake."

"No, that's what Rick and his men do. We didn't know we were killing innocent people until after it was too late. He lied to us. He lied to me!"

"How much time do we have?"

"I don't know . . . it's a guy named Victor who's looking for you. He wants you brought back alive." He looked over at me. "He wants both of you."

Jake looked over at me with glowing red eyes. I knew he was on the edge of losing control, trying to contain the wolf, but the anger and pain were seeping through his pores. His breathing sped up erratically as his gaze reverted to Vahn. I felt his anger boil as his eyes bore into him.

"Man, you knew what we were doing and never cared before."

Jake slammed Vahn's body against the rock, knocking chunks of stones out of the cave wall.

"I never knew we were hurting innocent people. I thought we were extinguishing killers, rapists, and child molesters. All this time, I thought . . . I thought . . . it doesn't matter now. Everything we did was a lie, and now I have to live with that."

Jake lowered Vahn to his feet and shook his head. A growl

rumbled from his chest, and his fangs elongated, peeking through his lips. "You were like a brother to me, and you came here to do a job. I would never have done that to you. Never." Jake shook his head and faced Vahn.

"Jake, I'm sorry, man. I thought you betrayed me. I thought you'd lost your edge and ran away like a coward. Rick said you compromised the mission, and we needed to find you. I should have asked more questions. I should have been there for you. I'm sorry, man."

"It doesn't matter now. We have to pack up and leave."

I scrambled to pack up our belongings. Jake walked away from Vahn, rubbing his face with his hands. Vahn peered out of the cave and into the forest. He lifted his head and inhaled the wind that breezed through the door.

Vahn turned to Jake. "I'm sorry, Jake. I'm sorry . . ." Vahn looked over at me with sorrow in his eyes. "I'm sorry for everything."

I walked over to the door and saw the trees rocking back and forth in the forest. Men's voices were carrying through the wind and echoed against the water. Jake walked back to the door and met my gaze.

Vahn looked over at Jake, wrapping his arms around Jake's shoulders. "I love you, brother. Take care of her and go have a family like we always talked about." He pulled back, meeting my gaze briefly with glossy eyes and slightly nodding before looking back at Jake. "Jake, whatever you do, don't stop fighting. You know you can win this war. Take out every last one of them. Don't stop until they're all dead."

Vahn let go of Jake, took his shirt off, and pushed down his pants. His body fluffed out with black hair, and his body grew in width. He stomped along the ledge, left the cave, and looked back. His nose elongated, and ears were forming as he nodded his head. He huffed, turned back around, and jumped down from the ledge, rattling the earth.

"Jake." I pointed to the other side of the cave. "We can go out the other way and drop down onto the other side of the river."

Jake kept his eyes fixed on Vahn leaving as he took a step closer to the cave entrance. "I know, Del."

I walked over to him, and we watched Vahn walk up to the tree line surrounding the forest. The night was dark, with a half-moon shining light onto the beach. It had begun snowing again, blowing cold flurries into the cave.

A dozen or more men stepped out of the darkness of the forest, holding guns. They were walking in pairs towards Vahn. Vahn paced back and forth, grunting, as the men approached him. He shifted back into his human form and talked to the men. Jake and I stepped back, hiding inside the cave, and watched. Vahn waved his arms around and then pointed towards the forest in the direction they'd just walked from. He transformed back into the bear, marching into the forest in the direction he'd indicated. Bright lights flickered through the trees like lightning as gunfire went ablaze. Vahn spun around and charged the men with his ferocious jaws extracted. His body disappeared into the darkness of the forest. Shrill screams echoed, and finally, the gunfire ceased. Everything went still.

Jake stepped forward, and I put my hand on his shoulder. "No, Jake."

Several men stood around on the riverbank, shouting at each other and waving their arms. The crowd slowly dispersed, and they started to walk toward our cave.

"Shit," Jake said. He stepped backward, pulling me back.

"Where is he, Jake?"

I tried to look around Jake for Vahn's body.

Then, I finally saw him. He was lying on the beach, shifting back into human form. His breaths were shallow and long, and then his body just stopped moving. Shaking my head, I turned around and walked into the cave. A low growl rumbled in Jake's chest as his body vibrated. He looked down at me, and his eyes were glowing blood red.

I gazed up at him, and it felt like time had slowed down. Jake's fingers sank into my arm as he was dragging me away from the cave entrance. His mouth was moving, but I didn't hear what he was saying. Walking backward, I shook my head and pulled my arm out of his grip. Jake shoved my bag into my arms and pointed to the door going out the other way.

I shook my head. "No, not without you. No, I won't leave you."

My throat tightened as I was pushed back towards the door. Tears streamed down my face, burning my nose. The sound started coming back as if the volume was slowly turned up on a radio. Lights flashed as crackling bounced off the walls of the cave. Jake wrapped his arms around me, squeezing me, and pressed his lips to mine. His mouth grazed across my cheek. "I'll be right behind you. I just want to make sure that they don't follow us. I'm going to lower you and Buddy down, and then I'll be right behind you. I promise."

He leaned in and kissed me again. I hugged his neck and bounced against his chest as the sobs came.

He pushed me back. "Now. Go."

Jake lowered me down through the cave entrance on the other side of the river. Jagged rocks awaited my drop as he gripped my hands. I walked down the wall, searching for steady ground with my feet.

"I'm going to let go, Del."

He released my hands, and I dropped.

CHAPTER THIRTY-NINE JAKE

In my heart, I didn't know if I would make it out of this cave, but I wanted to make sure that she did. I got her into this, and I'd die before I let them hurt her.

I poured water over the fire and hid in the darkness, waiting for them to come. My animal instincts allowed me to watch the first set of men slowly sneak into the room. Holding my breath, I waited in the far corner for the men to get close enough for me to jump out. My heart pounded in my ears as the first man drifted closer to my grasp.

I pounced and grabbed the man from behind, biting into his neck and ripping out his throat. Lights flashed as his semi-automatic rifle went off, exploding bullets into the walls. He dropped to the ground, and his body vibrated as he slowly died. His finger steadily held down the trigger, and he continued to shoot his rifle. I slid down on the ground with him, held up his arm, aiming his gun at the men who followed him in. Three more men got hit and dropped to the ground. Once the gun emptied, a metal grinding metal sounded through the cave. I dropped his arm, and silence filled the room. I stayed on the ground, waiting for the next set of men to show their faces.

After a few minutes, pebbles from the walkway rattled as they rolled down the walls of the cave. I inhaled a deep breath and slowly exhaled as I waited for the next victim. More men walked in, stopping at the door. A peculiar ding hit the floor, and then a can landed right next to my paw. A pungent cloud rose from the can, filling the room.

I jumped up and ran towards the men, claws first. I sliced the first man's face with one swipe, knocking him back as the second one opened fire. Dropping to the ground, I bit into his thigh, ripping out a chunk of flesh. The second man shot the first man in the back, and he fell back on his rump, holding his leg, screaming. I lay over him, ripping his throat out with one bite, and spat it into the water. I looked out of the cave to see two more men standing next to the river.

A monstrous growl escaped my lips as I jumped out of the cave. The two men spun around and ran into the forest. One of them tripped, falling face-first. I lunged onto his back and twisted his neck until it popped. The second man turned around and shot at me, waving his semi-automatic weapon back and forth through the forest. Grunting, I ran towards him, leaped into the air, and landed on top of him. I knocked him down, grabbed the gun, and snapped it in half. I sliced his neck and then opened his chest with my claws. The man shuddered as blood squirted out of his open neck. A growl vibrated in my chest as I stood back and watched him die.

I ran back to the cave, drug out all the bodies, and threw them into the forest several feet away.

I entered the cave, grabbed my bag, and jumped out of the other side. I raised my snout, inhaling the cool breeze whispering through the air. I knew I needed to find Del before they did.

CHAPTER FORTY: ADELE

Pointy rocks were gouging into my hands and legs after Jake dropped me from the cave. My body was numb as I stumbled around in blood-soaked clothes. Buddy fell between two rocks, whimpering. I struggled, dragging my bag and staff as I walked over to pull him out. Lights flashed above me, and shrill screams echoed, jolting me to move faster. Buddy's nails clicked, sliding down each rock as he tried to follow me. I moved as fast as I could, leaving the cave behind me with glossy eyes. The trauma I'd escaped began to die down, so I peeked over my shoulder to see the flickering lights come to a halt. Silence hummed in my ears, echoing like a heavy drum as my heart pounded in my chest.

Squeezing my eyes shut, I pictured Jake's face in my mind, his arms wrapped around me as he'd said *I'll be right behind you. Right behind you.* I chanted in my mind. I looked back again, and the cave was still quiet. Anger burned inside me as I aggressively wiped away runaway tears.

The water hissed in the darkness, thrashing violently against the jagged rocks. Finally, my foot stepped down off the rocks and sank into snow and mud. I helped Buddy step down, and we picked up our speed. I glanced back, hoping to see Jake, but I only saw a mirage of what could have been our cave.

A violent gust of wind whipped through the trees, and a crackling noise echoed in the forest. Buddy's head swung around, and a low growl erupted from his chest. "I know, pup, I hear it too." I peered through the trees but only saw darkness in the forest. I picked up my speed, following the moonlit river.

Another loud crackle rattled off in the distance, stunning my steps. I stopped, spun around, and held my breath, listening. Nothing. As soon as I took another step, another crackle sounded, but this time it was right behind me. Whipping around, I looked again. The forest was eerily silent, with thick sheets of snow pouring down, blinding my vision. A tingling sensation ran down the back of my neck and trickled down my spine. I sensed someone was approaching, and it wasn't Jake.

I squeezed my bo staff in both hands, held my breath, and listened. My heart was pounding in my ears as steam exhaled from my lips. Buddy took two steps forward, cocking his head from side to side as the hair on his hide stood up. A rumbling growled in his chest, and he bounced, barking at something in the darkness. Footsteps echoed through the trees and then started pounding in the snow closer and closer to us. I stepped backward, turned around, and started running.

"Buddy! Come!"

Buddy ran ahead of me, and I looked back to see a man right on my tail. I had to do something quickly, so I dropped to my knees. He plowed into me, falling over onto the ground. I pulled the knife out of my boot, plunged it into his leg, and stabbed him in the chest. Buddy ran over and bit his arm. The man lay back, coughing, and waved his arm to get Buddy off. I reached over his body, pulled out my knife, and stabbed him in the chest again. He turned and slapped me across the face, knocking me back. Cold, wet snow frosted my cheek as I rolled over, panting.

The man howled, gritting his teeth as he extracted the knife. I slowly pushed myself up, slamming my bo staff across his chest, knocking him back. He rolled over, groaning, and pushed his rump up first. His legs wobbled, and he fell onto his side, lying still.

I was panting, and my arms dropped as I relaxed. Exhaling, I went to turn around when something wrapped around my neck. Buddy lunged at the guy, biting down and pulling his leg. The man kicked Buddy hard, knocking him off. Buddy ran around to the other side, biting the other leg. The man kicked and stomped toward Buddy, trying to throw him off. My fingers scratched, trying to get a grip over whatever was constricting around my neck. My rump thrust backward, and I tried to knock him back. He stood firm with his legs planted apart. Gasping for air, I dangled, with my feet barely touching the ground. My face was burning, and drool oozed from my lips as I gasped to inhale a breath. Blinking my eyes, I felt myself fading away. My feet kicked back and forth, struggling in the air.

I closed my eyes and felt my power fluctuating inside my chest, calling me to not give up. A voice spoke to me from the darkness.

Open your eyes, Adele, and fight. Open. Now!

Electricity flashed under my lids, forcing my eyes open. Power rushed through my veins, pulsating from my toes, through my limbs, and into my fingers. I reached my hands back toward the man's body, letting go. His screams echoed through the forest as he released his tight grip from around my neck. I dropped to the ground and spewed streams of bright red blood, staining the snow on the ground in front of me. The man stood back up and kicked me in the side. I flew over and landed on my stomach, sinking into a blanket of snow. I gasped for air, blood oozing out of my mouth. I rolled over onto my back, holding up my hand to shield my face.

He stomped his foot at me, and I raised my fingers, unleashing my power again. A bright white stream of light flowed from my fingers, shooting into the man's legs. His body convulsed as he dropped to his knees, vibrating down until he was lying on the ground. His body seized, bulging his eyes wide and melting the skin off his bones. Blood soaked the ground underneath him, outlining his body in the snow. I slumped over, sinking down into a blanket of white. I gazed up at the flurries drizzling down into my face, kissing my cheeks as my eyes grew heavy. Inhaling deep breaths, I closed my eyes.

"Del. Adele, wake up."

My eyes fluttered open as I looked up at Jake standing over me. He was nude and had his hand over my face, caressing my cheek. He looked like a god as his eyes glowed and his skin glistened from the snow trickling down his muscular body. My heart swelled with relief. Tears filled my eyes, and a lump formed in my throat.

"Hi," Jake said. Jake reached down, picked me up, and carried me.

"Hi," I whispered in a hoarse voice. I put my hand on his cheek and gazed into his eyes. "I'm so glad you're okay."

My eyes were begging to close as my body swayed in Jake's arms.

"I'm so tired, Jake. So very tired." My head dropped back, and I closed my eyes.

CHAPTER FORTY-ONE: VICTOR

"Victor. Victor."

I turned around, and Rick was standing there with his arms crossed. A few of his men walked out from behind him with bruised faces and blood splattering over their bodies. I peered around him to see the camp was empty.

"What?"

"Sir, the men found them deep in the forest, staying in a hidden cave next to a waterfall. It was a day's walk from the original area you said they were hiding."

I pulled a cigarette from my pocket and put it in my mouth. Turning around, I walked over to the fire and pulled out my match. I plucked it, holding up the flame to stare at it.

"Victor. Victor, come over here with us."

I was staring into the flames of the bonfire, mesmerized by its power.

Alessia waved at me with a big smile on her face. Smiling, I walked over to her.

"Here, I got you a glass. I want you to drink with us."

She handed me a mug, pouring something inside that smelled like rubbing alcohol. Nodding, she smiled. "Go on."

The cool drink warmed my throat, tingling all the way down to my belly. Nodding, I grinned.

Bill raised his glass, knocking it against mine. "We want you to be the first to know of our news."

"What news?"

Alessia burst with excitement, giggling and shaking in her boots.

Bill looked over at her and then back at me. "We're getting married."

My heart sank the minute I heard the words leave his lips. My smile diminished, and I stood still, trying to piece together what he'd just said. I turned up the mug and gulped several drinks of ale, emptying the cup. Swaggering back and forth, I almost dropped the glass.

Alessia's smile faded quickly. She knew I wasn't happy about her news. I didn't want to hurt her, so I faked a smile. "Congratulations! When are you planning to get married."

Alessia looked over at Bill and then at me. "In a month. You see, the thing is, Victor, I'm pregnant." She paused and looked over at Bill again and then back at me. "Please, don't tell Father. I don't want him to get angry."

I shook my head. "Of course not. I would never tell him anything. I hate him."

My words were slurred, and dizziness twirled in my mind. I held my arms out and tried to control my balance and stop swaying back and forth.

"Victor, are you okay?"

Blinking, I looked over at Alessia and smiled. Her beautiful emerald eyes glowed against the night sky.

"Of course, sister. What a great day this has turned out to be."

"Victor. Victor. What do you want to do?"

The moon was hiding behind rows upon rows of snow clouds in the sky. Snow flurries drizzled down slowly, threatening to cover the ground with another sheet of white. The fire crackled, popping a large piece of wood in half. I inhaled a deep drag of my cigarette and held it in for a moment before releasing it.

Father walked over to us as I stepped backward, almost falling over. Alessia stepped in front of him with her hand up. "Father, we have good news to share with you."

He smiled down at her. "Yes, dear. What is it?"

Bill walked over, wrapping his arms around Alessia's waist as she looked up at him, smiling. "Bill has asked me to marry him, and I said yes."

Father glared down at her and looked over at Bill for a long moment. "No." Father's expression was dry, and his voice was calm as he spoke.

"What . . . what, Father?"

"No. I didn't give you permission to get married."

He walked over, grabbed Alessia's arm, and pulled her behind him.

Father stopped in mid-step and whipped around. "You're with child? You stupid little whore!"

Alessia started slapping against his grip as tears rolled down her face. "Father, please. Stop, you're hurting me."

"Shut up, whore!"

He slapped her across the face, knocking her to the ground. Bill ran over to Alessia, dropping on the ground next to her. Anger flashed through me, burning my insides. I threw my mug down, stomping over to Father.

I walked right up to him, and he threw his head back, laughing out loud. "Oh, what are you going to do?" He stepped forward, growling in my face. "You're weak and a coward. You couldn't hurt anyone even if you tried."

Father turned around and started walking away when I raised my hand and aimed it at him. The anger grew inside me, manifesting into something dark I'd kept hidden away for many years. Quivering, I held my breath as the pain shot from inside my chest, traveled down my arm, and raced through my veins. My hand was seizing as the electricity sparked between my digits. Out of the corner of my eye, I saw a bright white light bulldozing toward me. A giant man, glowing a pearl white, stepped in front of me and shoved me back. My body thrust through the air, wind fanning my hair, and then I dropped down into a pile of logs next to the fire.

"No!"

My eyes blinked open, and I saw a blinding white light flowing into Bill. Pain rushed through my body, radiating down my spine. A stream of electricity bolted from the sky, and a cloud swirled around Bill, absorbing into his flesh. I opened my mouth to scream over hushed lips. My lids fluttered, and I finally closed my eyes.

"Victor? What do you want to do now? Jake killed all of our men except for a few. It's freezing, and I can't send for more men until the morning." Rick shifted his weight looking back at his men and then at me. "Are you even listening? Victor?"

I turned around and was on him before he could say another thing. "All I heard is that you're all worthless and can't seem to do anything right. Don't patronize me, boy. In the morning, send for more men to come immediately, and then we'll head into the forest. Got it! Are you listening? Can you hear me now?"

"Yes . . . yes, sir. Okay."

He turned around and walked to one of the tents. I inhaled another drag of my cigarette and flicked it into the fire.

CHAPTER FORTY-TWO: ADELE

I opened my eyes and heard the tent door flapping in the wind. I lifted my head and looked up to see his green eyes blinking in the darkness.

"Where is he?"

"I don't know."

He lunged towards me, putting his face into mine. "Where is he?"

Flinching, I turned away and closed my eyes.

His sharp claws wrapped around my chin and squeezed. "You think he really loves you! He doesn't love anyone. He's a killer! What did he tell you? He didn't know he was killing innocent people!" He laughed and shook his head. "He's using you, and when he's done, he'll leave. That's what he does. You, of all people, should know that."

I opened my eyes to blankets weighing over my face. Jake's arms hugged my shoulders as I tried to pull them back.

"Jake, you're squishing me." I shoved his arm back, but he squeezed tighter. Jake moved around and kicked his feet, sitting up. His hair was sticking up on one side and slicked down on the other. Giggling, I pushed my arms out, patting his hair down. It popped right back up, standing straight up.

"What?"

"Nothing." Yawning, I smiled and turned over. Jake pulled the covers back and sat up.

"Are you naked again?"

"You're like an oven, girl. I was cooking in there with you."

His manhood greeted me, awake and ready. Smiling, I looked away as my face heated up.

He smiled at me seductively with his eyebrow arched. "What? I can't help it. You turn me on in the morning with your crazy hair."

"My crazy hair! Your hair's slicked up like a peacock on one side." I laughed, trying to push his hair down again.

Jake lifted the covers and poked his head under. He ripped my pants down and crawled up between my legs. His soft skin pressed against my midsection, sending tingles through my groin. Jake pressed his manhood against my clitoris, rubbing it until my crevice was moist. His lips engulfed mine as I pushed against his chest with my palms, shaking my head.

"What are you doing? We're being chased by people who want to kill us, sleeping in blankets on the ground."

"I don't care. I want inside you."

Jake tongued down my neck and thrust my shirt up, suckling my nipples. My eyes darted around us, and I lifted my head to check the forest.

Jake's hands cupped my face. "We're alone."

His lips pressed hard against mine as he pushed his manhood inside me. Gasping, I wrapped my legs around his bare buttocks. My climax rose, and I shivered as I flushed warm juices over his erection. He slowly pulled his member completely out and thrust back in, pushing himself deep inside my crevice. My lips broke from his, and I erupted, showering him with my juices again. His body hardened, and he pressed his lips against my cheeks, exhaling loudly as he thrust one last time. His body trembled as he filled my insides with his climax.

He rolled off me and lay there panting for a long moment. I pulled up my pants, climbed out, and walked over to the nearest tree, squatting down to relieve myself. Something black peeked out of the corner of my eye. I looked up, and the words caught in my throat. Frozen, I mouthed Jake's name, but my lips were trembling.

Inhaling a deep breath, I screamed his name. "Jake!"

Jake catapulted out of the blankets as he was changing into the wolf. A man was running toward me as I pulled up my pants. He plowed into me, knocking me on my back. His weight crushed my body, pushing my face deep into the snow. He leaned forward, gritting his sharp teeth, and his hands wrapped around my throat. Flashes of red burned through his eyes as he choked me. I torqued my body sideways, throwing both legs over him, and pushed him into the snow.

I jumped on his back, lifting his head and twisting his neck until it popped. Panting, I spun around and looked for Jake. A surge of men and bullets flooded from all directions. I hid behind an old oak, looking around it. Shots fired a line up to the tree, blowing off the loose bark around my head. Bobbing my head out, I scanned for the culprit.

A few feet away, a sniper had a scope waiting for his chance. Looking down, I saw a couple of large pieces of wood on the ground. I picked them up and darted out in front of the shooter. Zig-zagging, I made it close enough and hurled the sticks at him. He dropped the gun and started running away.

My feet pounded the ground, and I leaped through the air, landing on the back of his legs. He dragged my body briefly before turning around and punching me in the nose, knocking me back. Blood drained down my cheeks, gagging my throat. I leaned over and spewed red all over the snow. He lunged at me, pummeling my face as I held my hands up, trying to block his hits.

"Don't move! He wants to speak with you."

"Who?"

"I do." A familiar voice rang from behind me.

Wide-eyed, I slowly turned around, blinking. It was him,

the man from my dreams. He walked in front of me, smiling his mischievous grin. Inhaling a long drag of his cigarette, he exhaled a wall of smoke and flicked the butt with his thumb, ashing it.

The man eyed me up and down, sizing me up, and squatted down in front of me. He inhaled another drag, exhaling a cloud before he spoke. "You look like her. The shape of your face is like . . ." He reached his hand out as if he was going to touch me.

I slapped his hand away. "What! You crazy piece of shit!"

He stood back up, looking around the forest. "Where is he?"

I shook my head, looking back at the man with the gun and then at him.

This didn't feel right. This isn't what I dreamed about.

I shook my head. "Where's who?"

"Don't lie to me, girl! You know who!"

I glanced up and saw him looking away, so I slammed my fists into his knees, knocking him back. He stumbled back, grunting. A blast to my cheek sent me flying into the air. I dropped down, and my face planted right next to some blood in the snow. Pain exploded through my eye, and tears welled up, burning and streaming down my face.

He stomped over to me, leaning down into my face. "I'm only going to say this one last time, girl! Where is he?"

The sniper kicked my stomach. "Look up when he's talking to you!"

"Where is he?"

I looked up and saw Jake's paws walking up in the corner of my eye. I smiled up at the man, cackling.

I threw my head back and paused. "Fuck you!"

Jake walked behind him, claws erect, and slit Victor's throat. At first, Victor's mouth dropped open as he stumbled back and forth. Blood poured out from the corner of his mouth, streaming down his chin. Victor stumbled again, almost falling over, and reached up, grabbing his throat. He clawed at it, dropping to his knees. He looked around, and his gaze stopped on mine. His eyes briefly shifted from his emerald green to a deep blue before he fell face-first into the snow.

I stared at his body and watched it sink into the sea of white. His chest twitched, and he stopped moving.

Jake walked over, pulled me up, and nodded.

"I'm okay," I said. I turned to see the ground was littered with blood and dead bodies.

Buddy was lying on his side, panting heavily. Jake walked over to him, dropping to his knees. His breathing picked up, and he huffed full breaths as his body transformed back down into a human man. Blood and cuts covered his bare flesh. Buddy's panting subsided as his eyes blinked open. He sat up slowly, looking around, and rolled over onto his belly to stand up. He excitedly ran into a pile of snow with a blanket covering his back. His whole body started shaking the icicles from his limbs as his tongue hung out to one side.

Jake sat down on his rump, exhaling loudly as he rubbed his face. "We can't leave the bodies everywhere. I guess we should build a fire and burn them. Especially Victor's body."

I nodded. "Yeah, you're right."

Jake walked over to our blankets to get dressed.

"Let's drag all the bodies into a pile over here, and then I'll start the fire. Pull off all knives, weapons, and clothes we can use later."

I followed Jake's directions and started dragging bodies over. Jake squatted down next to the fire and got the flames going. I stood over the fire and watched the bodies burn. Walking around, I ensured we had all of them in the burn pile when I realized that Victor's body was nowhere to be found Cocking my head to the side, I opened my mouth to tell Jake when Buddy started yipping.

"What is it, pup?" I looked up to see hunters off in the

distance. Jake met my eyes, nodded, and walked toward the hunters. His hands were waving back and forth, pointing them away from our fire and back toward the river. The men shook Jake's hand and followed his directions. Buddy met him halfway as he walked back over.

"It's already getting late. We need to start thinking about where we want to sleep tonight," Jake said.

I smiled, walked over to Jake, put my arms around him, and squeezed. He put his lips to mine, pulling me close. "Will this ever be over, Jake?"

"He's dead now. Technically, we're free now."

Nodding, I stared at the fire. *We're free now.* The words echoed in my head. *Free.* I looked up at Jake and opened my mouth. I wanted to tell him that I didn't see Victor's body in the fire, but something stopped me. *I must have missed him. I must have covered him up with another body.* I watched Jake kill him, but something inside me told me this wasn't over. That he wasn't actually gone. As odd as it sounded, I still felt him nearby.

"I'm hungry. We should try to find something to eat before the sun goes down. Maybe we can fish?"

Nodding, Jake looked back toward the direction of the river. "Maybe. We'll have to walk down and get back to the river and hope it's not full of ice."

"Yeah." Nodding, I stared at the fire.

"Come on, pup." Jake whistled. "Let's go."

CHAPTER FORTY-THREE: ADELE

We walked back to the river and followed the riverbank for a while before stopping. Jake was staring out over the water, scanning for a place to fish. I crunched down into ice that had molded along the bank and looked out to see little chunks floating in the water. I exhaled as steam blew from my mouth. The sun was already settling in the west and hiding behind the tips of the oaks protecting the forest.

"Del, I don't know how much luck I'll have catching anything, but I'll try." Jake attempted a half smile.

Buddy was ahead of both of us, running along the icy bank. Jake whistled a quick tweet to stop him from running further out. Buddy stopped and halted where he was. Jake dropped his bag, pulled out his pole, and extended it.

"I need bait."

Nodding, I watched Jake start digging into the dirt along the forest line until he stopped and pulled out a fat grub. He squeezed it in half, putting a piece on the hook. He handed me the unhooked half of the grub, and I walked over, sitting down near the forest line, and watched him fish.

Jake dropped his line into the water and walked along the bank with a taut string, trying to catch a fish's attention. He looked back at me, shrugging his shoulders.

After an hour, Jake walked his line out with a little white perch flopping on the bank. He walked over to it, dropping his shoulders as he frowned down at it. Standing up, I pulled out my pocket-knife and cut its head off. A small piece of meat was on my knife, so I tilted my head back and dropped it into my mouth. Jake's eyes widened as he stared at me, dropping his mouth open in shock. Coughing, I almost spit the meat in his face as laughter rolled out of my chest.

"Ew, is that good?"

Shaking my head, I laughed. "No. It's terrible."

"Well, okay, then." Jake laughed.

I finally stopped laughing and caught my breath. Jake cut some fish meat off and popped it into his mouth.

"Not bad." He gagged, frowning.

Nodding, I cut another bite of fish and popped it into my mouth. I called Buddy over and fed him a couple pieces of fish, too. We picked out all the meat around the bone of the fish and threw the remaining carcass into the water. The sun was going to bed for the night, quickly settling behind the mountains. We picked up, heading back into the forest. It was almost completely dark, so we followed the tree line along the river for some light. Jake seemed to know where he was going, pulling me along. He raised his head up every few minutes, sniffing the air and looking around. The wind shifted, blowing cold icicles from the treetops, and showered my face.

"Jake . . . Jake."

He turned around. "What?"

"Where are we going?"

"I don't know, honey. I'm trying to find us a safe place to sleep. We'll probably sleep on the ground again, but I was trying to find something more hidden."

"Okay."

We continued walking well into the night. The sun had completely set, and the moon was drifting up into the sky when I decided to stop. I walked over to the river and looked up at the quarter moon shining down.

"I'm going to rinse off really quick. This may be the last chance I have to wash off for a while." I turned to face Jake, kicking off my boots in the sand. "Do you want to join me?"

"Nope. The water's probably freezing."

My shirt came off first, revealing my nipples peaking in the cool breeze, and then I dropped my pants to my ankles. Jake grinned ear to ear as he stared at my bare body. My long black hair tickled the top of my buttocks as it whirled through the wind breezing across the river. I stepped into the water, and my teeth started chattering. The icy shards were piercing against my skin as the current ran through my legs. I splashed water over my flesh, washing off my limbs first.

"Are you freezing?" A playful grin arched Jake's lips.

His eyes glazed over me with desire, licking his lips and trailing down to my groin area.

"No, It's fine." I lied, but it aroused me to watch him get excited as I teased him.

Shivering, I wiped down my body one last time and then stepped out. Jake walked over, wrapped his arms around me, and hugged me tight . I pursed my lips up, embracing his kiss. My tongue stroked his, and I pulled back, biting his bottom lip. Jake ran his hands down my waist, groping my rump. He pulled my rump up, wrapping my legs around his waist. He broke his lips from mine, panting as he whispered in my ear. "I want you now."

"We need to find somewhere to sleep."

He put me down. "You're mean."

Laughing, I put my clothes back on and led Jake by the hand into the forest. We walked a few hundred feet before I stopped to pull out our blankets and lay them on the ground. I pushed my boots off and laid them next to us, and then I grabbed Jake's pants, pulling them down to reveal his excited manhood.

I put my lips on his shaft and thrust it as deep as I could take him. He grabbed my head, driving his erection inside my mouth. I pulled away, looking up at him. He gazed at me with wild eyes, panting with a deep wanting. Laying down, I pushed my pants down and opened my legs.

He crawled on top of me and pushed his manhood deep inside me before I could wrap my legs around him.

Our mouths collided, breathing deeply as he hammered inside me. My crevice spasmed, and fluids dripped down my legs and rump. Jake pulled back, gazing into my eyes as he thrust deep inside me again and again. A low growl escaped his chest, and he dove into my mouth. My body vibrated, seizing underneath him. Pulling back, he thrust harder and faster.

He sat up, propping my legs over my head. His fingers pushed behind my knees, and he unleashed, pounding me into the ground. My hands shoved against his chest, and he slapped them away, holding me there as he pummeled me. My body shuddered, and I cried out. He cupped his hand over my mouth, let go of my knees, and lay over me, pushing his lips to mine. His tongue trailed down my chin, and he suckled my neck. My legs began to tremble, and my body vibrated as my climax skyrocketed again. He pushed my hands over my head, holding me down and sank his fangs into my neck. A surge of electricity flashed inside me, shooting into him from my groin to his. The combination of pleasure and pain shuddered my body to the core. His body seized, and his manhood hardened, filling me up. Our bodies breathed as one, trembling together. Panting, Jake twitched as his organ ejaculated inside me.

"You okay?"

"Oh, yeah. That was exciting. I've never felt that way before. You sent a surge through me that pushed me deep inside you. I didn't want to stop, but you forced me to cum, and it felt so good." He panted. "Are you okay?"

"Yes, I'm okay. Just . . . just tired." I panted.

Jake climbed off of me, laying down beside me. Turning over, I lay across his masculine chest. A cool breeze whisked through, brushing snow flurries over our blanket. Fluffing it out, I pulled it up around my neck and kissed Jake's chin, running my lips down his neck. Jake wrapped his arms around me and held me against his heart.

We both closed our eyes and let the sleep come.

Chapter Forty-Four: Adele

Lifting my head, I opened my eyes. A cool breeze wafted through the tent door, reflecting a dim light from outside. My head dropped back down, burying my face into the dirt. Throbbing pain shuddered through my wrists and ankles as I tried to move. I forced my body over onto my side, pushing myself up slowly. Another gust of icy wind blew through the door and rattled my bones, sending chills down my spine. I scooted on my rump, trying to get closer to the tent door. I almost reached the door when light filled the room. Black shoes walked up to me. Looking up, I saw him. Victor.

"Adele! Wake up, Del!"

Cold winter wind nipped at my bare breasts as I bolted up. The sun's beams shined into my eyes, blinding my vision. Shaking my head, I rubbed my eyes.

"Are you okay?"

I quickly nodded as I turned to look around us. His face was burning in my mind as I blinked.

"I-I'm fine . . . just a bad dream."

I reached into the covers, pulled out my clothes, and got dressed. Wind gusts blew a cloud of snowflakes into my face. I wiped them away aggressively as I walked over to the large oak to use the restroom.

Jake gathered up our blankets, eyeing me as I walked back over.

"Are you sure you're okay?"

I opened my mouth, wanting to tell him about my dream, but something stopped me. I nodded, grabbing my bag and throwing it over my shoulder.

"I'm famished. You wore me out last night, girl. Let's go find something to eat." He leaned down, grabbed my waist, and pulled me into him, pushing his lips against mine.

I scanned the forest when Jake pulled away. He smiled down at me and held his hand out for me to take. I forced a smile and accepted his hand as we walked together.

After about an hour, Jake stopped and opened his bag, pulling out a compass. He held it up, and we continued to walk until the sounds of water greeted us. We walked up to the bank, and Jake pulled out his pole. He found some bait rather quickly and threw his line into the water. I saw a large rock sitting next to the tree line, walked over, and basked in the sun. Buddy followed me over, plopping down next to my feet.

Not long after Jake dropped his line in, he pulled out his first fish, then his second — one right after the other. He looked back at me, smiling and nodding as he held up his fish. He walked them over to me, laying them on the ground like trophies. The fish were two good-size trout. Jake dropped his line in again, catching two more. He nodded as he pulled in his line, folded his pole, and put it back into his bag. Proudly grinning, he walked over to me.

"Can we make a fire? Will it be safe?"

"Should be okay."

"Does that mean we can head back to Dad's house? Or, I guess, the land that's left?"

He looked into the forest and then back at me. "Yeah, it does, actually. I just thought we should give the stragglers a couple of days to clear out before going back there. What do you think?"

"Yeah."

Chills shivered down my back. A sensation ran through my spine, warning me that someone was nearby. Someone with abilities. My head spun around, checking the forest. I couldn't see through the wall of oaks, so I got up and walked over, looking through. A doe with her fawns looked up at me as she sniffed the air. She was walking through the forest and stopped to graze. Rubbing my face, I trudged back over to Jake. He was sitting on the ground, cleaning the fish, and throwing the bones into the water.

"I think we should walk further into the forest before we have a fire."

Jake looked up at me with his brow furrowed, studying my face. After a few minutes, he nodded, reached into his bag, and pulled out a piece of cloth, wrapping the fish. He shoved the fish down into his bag and stood up.

"Ready?"

"Yep, let's go." I forced a smile.

Jake knew I was up to something, but he didn't force the conversation. I looked away, reached down, and scratched behind Buddy's ears, trying not to make eye contact with him. Jake pulled out his compass and nodded, leading the way.

"Maybe we can make it back to the cave with the waterfall before the sun goes down," Jake said.

"Yeah," I said.

I didn't want to tell Jake about my dream. I had this unsettling feeling that Victor wasn't gone. He was lurking in the darkness and waiting for the right time to attack us. I know I saw Jake kill him, but somehow, I felt he was still alive and was waiting for the right time to come out again.

We walked for an hour before Jake turned around to stop me. "I'm starved. Let's just stop here and eat. If we hurry and eat, I think we'll still have time to make it back to the cave."

"Okay."

Jake looked at me for a minute and watched my expression. I felt him watching me and trying to read my body language. Turning around, I walked over and picked up limbs and branches lying on the ground.

I acted as if everything was okay. I didn't want to mention anything until I knew for sure he was still alive. Jake followed my lead, gathering twigs and damp leaves. He walked over, dropped them in a pile, and then cleared out a space to build a fire.

I walked out to the forest and looked around, checking the area. A cool breeze blew remnants of damp snow through the trees. I grabbed more pieces of wood lying in a pile next to an abandoned stump and walked back over to Jake.

Jake was knocking the flint together, trying to get a spark. "I hope the ground and limbs aren't too wet."

Jake stared down at the flame, waiting for it to catch. I sat on the ground next to him and watched him work. A tree limb snapped behind me, causing me to jump to my feet and spin around. The wind picked up and blew my hair into my face, sending cold chills down my spine. Twitching, I checked back and forth, in front, and behind me.

"You're awfully jumpy," Jake said.

I looked back to see Jake had the fire started. He was sitting there watching me.

"Oh, I uh . . . I just heard something and was checking."

Jake got up, walked over, and wrapped his arms around me. "It's okay. He's gone, and we don't have to run anymore. We can head back home and start living now."

Smiling, I looked up at him and nodded. He gently kissed me for a long moment. I wanted to start a life with Jake more than anything. I wanted to get back to work, settle down, and put all of this behind me, but I felt that this wasn't over yet.

"I'm starving, girl. We need to go find some bark or something to cook this fish on."

"Okay." Nodding, I walked back out into the forest and found a couple of pecan trees. I pulled three large pieces of bark off and turned around to go back when something caught my eye. A bright, almost fluorescent white was glowing a few hundred yards away. I cocked my head to the side, slowly walking towards it. It looked tiny because of the distance away, but I couldn't make out what it was. It was bobbing back and forth, in and out of trees, and then dropped onto the ground. I turned back to Jake, and he was still working on finding wood for the fire.

I softly called his name. "Jake. Jake." He looked up and started walking toward me.

"What?"

"Something white is over there. Look." I pointed between two large oaks off in the distance.

Jake looked, shaking his head. "I don't see anything, honey."

I looked again, and it was gone.

"I guess I'm seeing things. Never mind." Shaking my head, I rubbed my eyes and handed Jake the pecan pieces.

The fish didn't take long to cook. Jake split up the food in three ways, giving us each a good portion of fish to eat. We sat for a few minutes in silence, listening to the birds singing as we let our food settle.

We set off again, looking up at the sun that was glaring down through the pines and oaks swaying in the afternoon wind. Buddy stopped, turned around, and made a weird whining noise, running back toward us.

"What is it, Bud?"

A branch crackled on the path right behind us. We both spun around to see something white glowing behind us. I sauntered over to the bush to hear a low, muffled whimper crying in the bush.

"What the?"

Jake walked over, reaching his hand under the bush, and pulled a puppy out by the scruff. It cried and growled, kicking its feet. Jake held it up, and it was a little white female wolf.

"Wow, she's beautiful, Jake."

I reached out and started petting her head gently. Jake pressed her against his chest, and she started licking his fingers. Buddy ran over and tripped right as he reached us, running his nose into the mud. He snorted and hacked, trying to paw off the snowy mud covering his snout. Shaking his head, he stood up on his hind legs and attempted another sniff. She snapped, and a growl rolled from deep in her chest.

"She's so skinny," I said.

"Yes, she is. I can fish more when we get back to the cave, and hopefully, I can catch enough for everyone."

"Buddy! Calm down!" Buddy started bouncing up and down, utterly excited about our new family member. Squatting down, I held the pup so that Buddy could sniff her. She snapped at him, warning him to leave her alone.

"Okay, okay. That's enough, Buddy. You have plenty of time to sniff her rump later." I stood up, coddling the white pup as we walked. "Maybe we should go ahead and go fish again. She probably hasn't eaten in a while."

"Yeah, you're probably right."

We turned and started walking towards the river. It didn't take long before we heard the river's strong current rushing downstream. Jake walked out into the open first, and then we followed. I sat the little pup down, and Buddy started acting silly. He dropped onto his belly, rolling over onto his back, and kicked his feet in the air with his tongue hanging out to one side. Poking Jake's shoulder, I pointed at him. We both laughed for a good minute and I helped him find more worms.

CHAPTER FORTY-FIVE: ADELE

The afternoon sun felt warm and inviting as I sat in the sand. I wrapped my arms around my knees and watched the water rush over the river's rocks, angrily pushing down the current. Jake pulled out a couple of small trout and then threw his line back in, waiting. A deep orange painted the sky as it settled behind the trees. The wind blew hard, whipping my hair over my head and into my eyes. I looked behind me, and there he was, staring at me from the forest. I flew up from where I was sitting and stared at him.

Jake yelled, "Ugh! I think I got a big one."

I ambled towards the forest, not breaking my glare at the figure.

"Jake," I said.

I felt a sharp pain in my shin and looked down to see Buddy pawing my leg. My head shot back up, and the figure was gone. I rushed to where the forest met the beach, searching. I felt eyes eerily watching as the light in the forest slowly diminished. Chills ran up my spine, tickling the back of my neck. I looked back at Jake, and he was holding a massive fish that he had to grip with both hands. He looked up at me, grinning from ear to ear. Nodding, I smiled at Jake.

"We should get going. Do you think we'll make it back to the cave?" I wasn't sure if going back to the cave was a good idea.

What if he's waiting there for us with his men?

Jake looked down at the fish, smiling. He laid the fish in the sand, held it down with his foot, pulled out his pocketknife, and sawed off its head. He cleaned it up quickly and wrapped it in the cloth we used to carry the meat.

"Yeah, if we hurry—"

"No! What if we run out of daylight? Or what about all those dead bodies lying around?"

"Del, I cleaned up before I left, and it's a good cave. What's going on?" Jake stared at me with his brows furrowed. He knew something was up.

I looked down and then towards the sun setting behind the trees. Our sunlight was recessing rapidly, and we needed to get going. I didn't want to tell him that I kept seeing Victor in the forest. I honestly didn't know what or who I saw. It felt so real.

"Del!"

"No, you're right. Let's go."

I walked past him and started heading back the way we came.

"Del!"

I ignored him, continuing to walk.

"Come on, pup," I said.

Jake ran up to me, looking over at me as we walked. Buddy ran ahead of us, leading the way along the river.

The wind picked up again, blowing moisture through the air. Reaching back, I pulled up my hood over my head. The newest edition to our family was whimpering from behind. I turned around to see her stumble and trip over her own feet. I walked back, picked her up, and started carrying her. She licked my face, trying to climb up my shoulder.

"Shh. Little one."

An hour went by, and I could see the pointy rocks reflecting off the water. The sounds of the waterfall grew louder, spraying a cold mist into the air.

Jake stopped and put his hand on my forearm. "Wait."

I held my breath, listening as I held the little pup tight. All I could hear was the sound of rushing water over the rocks. Jake raised his head, inhaling the air. A low growl escaped his chest as he began trudging towards the cave. Buddy was a few steps behind Jake, following him with his snout to the ground.

"Let me go first. I'll be right back."

"Okay." My breath steamed in front of me as I watched Jake disappear into the darkness. The moon barely rose in the sky and was hidden behind rows of snow clouds.

After a few minutes of Jake leaving, I started walking toward the cave again when I heard a peculiar sound echoing off the trees. It sounded like an animal calling off in the distance.

Tingling raced down the back of my neck and into my spine, alerting me that someone with abilities was close. His evil intentions were radiating through me, shuddering my body. I swallowed hard and spun my head back and forth, searching the darkness for any movement.

Another sound erupted, but this time it was right behind me, toying with me. A growl rose from the little pup's chest as she stared into the darkness, quivering in my arms. Quick footsteps started stomping toward me. My heart was pounding in my chest as my blinded eyes blinked in the darkness, spinning around and searching. I dropped my bag from my shoulder, dragging it in the snow and exhaling clouds of steam.

My arms ached, squeezing little pup against my chest with one hand and my bo staff with the other. The crackling footsteps came to a halt a few feet away and went silent. A bark erupted from the little pup's snout, and then something emerged from the darkness. A large black wolf walked out slowly and held up his paw, cocking his head to the side. He slightly resembled Jake, but something felt wrong. The little pup growled, snapping at his paw. I pulled her back.

"Jake?"

A cloud of steam blew from my mouth, and moisture started drizzling through the air. The wolf took steps forward as I looked into his eyes. His eyes were black as night, reflecting a hollow stare.

Dropping the little pup behind me, I gripped my staff with both hands. The wolf took another step forward, so I threw a punch and went for his face. He leaned backward, dodging the hit. A loud growl came from deep within his chest, erupting like a ferocious lion. He flipped through the air backward and dropped onto all fours as his body vibrated. Shaking, he transformed and shrunk down into a black panther. His midnight fur glistened in the moonlight, glowing a deep blue. Whipping his head back and forth, he prowled around me. Stalking. I followed him with my eyes as he moved with ease.

My knees bent as I gripped my staff, inhaling deep breaths. I focused on my power. Forcing my power to surge through my body like a current of electricity. My skin began to glow a pearly white as it flowed up and down my limbs and into my staff. I knew I was ready. I knew I could fight this beast and win.

Smiling, I stopped and stood up. "What are you waiting for?" I held my staff up with both hands. The drizzling turned into a hard rain, rolling down my face and soaking my clothes. The panther stopped, cocking its head to the side. I took a step forward, and the cat jumped back in surprise. "What? Are you a scared kitty?"

The panther roared, taking two more steps, and lunged at me. I raised my staff, striking the beast. A white bolt of lightning shot from the bo staff, and into the panther, like a fireball. The panther collapsed, screaming in agony. Red and white flames were swirling around his body in waves. He pawed at his snout and rolled around on the ground, trying to put out the fire. Stepping back, I stumbled over the little pup. I picked her up and held her as we watched the panther burn. His black fur faded away, and a man with bare white skin appeared.

A hand touched my shoulder, startling me. I swung around, and my body ignited a bright white light. Jake gazed behind me at the man whose remains were melting into the earth. His mouth dropped open as his body slowly drifted back down into human form.

"Are you okay?" Jake asked.

Dropping to my knees, I slumped over. My body convulsed as my power was flickering off like a light bulb.

"I'm so tired, Jake," I said. I was worn down, and my head started pounding. I stood back up, trying to walk toward the cave, and stumbled. Jake wrapped his arm around my waist and walked with me.

The jagged rocks greeted us as we entered the path back to the cave. Inhaling a deep breath, I gazed up at the dark hole in the rock. The climb was treacherous, rising above our heads at least twelve feet.

"I'll go first, and then I'll pull you and the pups up."

I squatted down and felt my body dropping between the rocks. My limbs were weakening, and I needed sustenance and sleep to recover. I nodded and watched Jake take two steps forward, effortlessly leaping up into the hole .

He turned around and looked down at me. "Are you ready?"

Pawing at my leg, Buddy whimpered behind me.

"I know, Buddy. In just a minute."

Jake reached down, and I handed him the little pup first. Then I walked over, grabbed Buddy, and pushed him up. Lastly, I threw my bag and bo staff up to Jake, waiting for him to come back for me. He reached down and pulled me up with ease. I felt light as a feather as he pulled me in. Walking to the back of the cave, I made up our bed and sat down to rest.

"I'll go get firewood," Jake said.

Jake returned with his arms full of wood and leaves. The rain started pouring against the waterfall, hissing inside the cave opening. Jake started the fire, adding wood.

"I tried to gather as much dry wood that I could, but it started pouring again."

I walked over and sat next to Jake, staring into the fire. Jake stood up, walked over to the entrance, and stared out for a long moment before speaking.

"How long have you known that he was still alive?"

I stared at Jake's back and didn't answer. I didn't know what to say. I suspected he was still alive, but I had no actual proof.

"I don't know if he *is* still alive, Jake. I just ... I ..." Rubbing my face, I panted. "I don't know what I think anymore."

Jake spun around, gazing into my eyes. "Why didn't you tell me you suspected he wasn't dead? Do you not trust me? I trust you, Adele. I always have. I never doubted for a moment that I couldn't trust you. Why can't you trust me?"

Shaking my head, I opened my mouth.

Jake cut me off. "You saw him, didn't you, back at the river. That's why you acted so strangely. You saw him, and you didn't tell me. Why?"

Jake's eyes glowed a golden chestnut brown with a hue of red around the cornea of his eyes. His nostrils flared, and his musk grew stronger as he grew angrier.

"I wanted to, but I wasn't sure if he was real. I thought maybe I was seeing things. I just ... I didn't know what I was seeing."

"Damnit, Adele. You could've gotten killed. I don't know what I would've done if anything had happened to you."

He turned around, looking out into the rain again. I stood up, walked over to him, and stood behind him for a long moment. Then I wrapped my arms around his waist and hugged him, laying my head against his muscular back.

"I'm sorry, Jake. I won't keep anything from you again. I still don't know if he's still alive. I haven't actually seen him except in my dreams. It's like he's taunting me to scare me. He's trying to make me feel trapped."

Jake wrapped his arms over mine and held me for a long time. The rain soothed my heart, and I wanted to treasure this moment for as long as possible.

"No more lies," Jake said.

"Okay."

"I mean it, Del. We have to be able to trust each other."

"Okay."

"Let's make dinner."

"Okay."

Jake turned around, looking into my eyes. He leaned forward and kissed me gently. Electricity streamed through me, rushing to my heart and pounding in my chest. Smiling, I pulled back, gazing into his eyes. I turned around, and Jake slapped my rump hard. I shot a dirty look back at him, and he smiled, enticing me to come back over. I winked, giving my rump a little shake, and walked over to pull out the fish. I laid them out on the fillets, handing them to Jake to put over the fire.

We both sat in silence as we watched the fish sizzle over the fire. The pups lay together next to the fire, snuggling. I smiled, watching them, and then looked back at Jake. Nodding, he smiled back at me. He reached over, pulling the fish off, and we all ate. The little pup gobbled down her food, so I gave her half of mine. Thunder rolled through the forest, echoing off the walls of the cave. After cleaning up, we walked over to the bed and lay down. Closing my eyes, I draped my body across Jake's chest. He held me tight, wrapping his arms around me.

CHAPTER FORTY-SIX: JAKE

A cool breeze blew the hair across my face, waking me from my slumber. Blinking, I tried to sit up, but sharp pains shot through my arms, burning down to my wrists. I looked down to see the silver glimmering in the moonlight.

I shifted my legs, and smoke whisked through the air, discharging from my ankles' bounds. My throat constricted as I tried to swallow back the severe reaction to the metal binding me. I looked up to see a wall of white tents. The door of one of the tents was ominously flapping in the wind. A shrill scream reverberated through the tents, and then a pool of blood splattered across the wall of the tent directly in front of me.

Jake! She was screaming my name. Her voice was echoing through my mind. My body drew into itself from crippling pain. Gritting my teeth, I closed my eyes and forced my limbs to move. Leaning forward, I squeezed my paw under the metal that bound my ankles and pulled with everything I had. Steam rose from my paw, and then blood drizzled into the dirt. The chain dropped from my ankles, and I ripped the chain around my wrists apart, shattering them into pieces. Stumbling forward, I pushed myself up and ran over to the tent. I threw the flap open to see her lying on the ground. Blood was oozing from her eyes, nose, and mouth. I dropped to my knees, scooping her lifeless body into my arms, and howled.

"Ha, ha, ha! Stupid wolf. Did you really think you could hide from me?"

I turned around, and his body was shimmering an emerald green in the darkness. A monstrous growl rumbled up from my chest, escaping my lips. I lay her down and leaped up, galloping towards him.

"Ha, ha, ha. Is that all you have, stupid wolf? I would have ex-pected you to be more clever than that."

My body fell forward as Victor disappeared. His voice was taunt-ing me from behind as a glimmer of light glowed in the darkness. I spun around to see his contemptuous smile. He stood there with his arms crossed, awaiting my attempt. Victor looked down at Del and then back up at me. My heart was aching, and my eyes reverted down to her body. Smoke rose in the air as her body disintegrated, dissolving into a gray matter and melting into the ground. I dropped to the ground, crawling over to her body as my body slowly trans-formed back into human form. I approached her. My face fell over her ashes as I let the tears flow. I didn't care anymore. I was too late. I couldn't help her.

"Why? What do you want from me?"

"Oh, I never actually wanted anything from you. It was always her. I've been looking for her for many years, and you led me right to her. You see, I'll let you in on a little secret. Bill took something from me many years ago, and when I killed him, I realized that he hid it from me. He gave it to her, and now I'm here to collect."

My eyes flew open, and I shot up in bed. Light from the waterfall was shadowing the walls of the cave. The fire glowed an orange hue of light inside a pile of ash. I dropped my head into my palms, rubbing my eyes. Shifting her body, Del exhaled a deep breath into the covers.

It was only a dream. It was only a dream.

I sighed and lay back on the bed, closing my eyes.

CHAPTER FORTY-SEVEN: ADELE

The next morning, I woke up to screaming echoing through the forest. My heart pounded in my chest as I jumped out of bed and ran to the door. Jake looked up from fishing and waved. Nodding, I flashed my hand up into the air. I turned around and walked back over to the bed, dropping down.

Jake walked into the doorway with his hands full of headless fish. "Are you okay?"

"Yeah. Why were you screaming?"

"Screaming? I was fishing with the pups."

Shaking my head, I rubbed my eyes. "Okay, it must have been a bad dream. I just . . . I don't know anymore. I, um . . . let's pack up and go after we eat. Okay?"

Jake nodded, turned around, and went back down to get the pups.

He stopped at the door, looking back. "Oh, hey. I named little pup. What do you think about Gaia?"

"I love it."

We quietly ate and then packed up to head home. Minutes turned into hours as the day slowly went by. I looked up through the trees, wiping my forehead. The sun was slowly settling west as the mid-afternoon turned into the early evening. Jake turned back and checked to make sure I was keeping up. Smiling, I nodded.

As we continued into the evening, I thought about how I would pay a visit to my agent and try to get my life back on track. I wasn't sure what I could say had happened, except maybe I was on a trip and didn't know my house had blown up.

Visions of my house exploding flashed in my mind. Squeezing my eyes shut, I shook my head and picked up speed. Jake reached back and pulled me up to walk alongside him, smiling as he cupped his hand over mine. Before we knew it, the sun was hiding behind the trees, darkening the forest quickly. The temperature started to drop drastically as a steady rain began drizzling overhead.

"Do you think we are almost there?"

"Yes, we're very close now."

Jake raised his nose into the air, sniffing the cool breeze that blew through the leaves. A peculiar look grazed his face as he looked around.

"What is it?"

Shaking his head, he raised his hand to wait. He walked ahead, entering the darkness of the forest. Buddy ran on with Jake, and I squatted down and held back Gaia, petting her mane.

Jake walked back over to me quietly. "Okay, let's go."

"What was it?"

"Nothing. I thought I smelled something."

Jake reached his hand out for me, and I grabbed it, following him to the mountain.

"We are almost there now," he said.

We walked to the familiar path of the mountain's foot and stopped. The smell greeted us first, and then flies landed on my arm, flying from a dark hole in the earth. Then it dawned on me—the traps. Jake's glowing eyes looked over at me through the darkness. His musk slightly changed, and I knew he was using his gift to guide us through the traps we'd set before leaving. The ground began inclining as we were climbing up now. Jake and Buddy led the way, and I picked up Gaia, carefully carrying her up the mountain.

We slowly entered the cave, and it was pitch dark. I felt

along the wall with my hand, waiting for Jake to light the fire. I heard the stones as he struck the flints. A dim light bounced shadows against the wall, lighting up the abandoned space. Jake began stirring the ash under the big pot. He walked over to the logs, grabbed a couple, and gently placed them next to the flame. I was gazing around the room and saw that everything was as we had left it. Tidy and untouched.

Jake dug around in his bag, replacing the few uneaten cans into the bin, and brought one over to the fire with a fork.

"Well, it's better than nothing for tonight." He shrugged, holding up a can.

I nodded as he handed me the fork. "Yum, green beans." I took a couple of bites and spooned a few for each dog. Buddy dropped the bean on the floor, pushing it around with his paw.

"Really, spoiled pup."

Gaia scooped up Buddy's bean and cocked her head to the side when he pawed her.

"See, that's what you get for not eating."

We finished the can, and I walked over to make our bed for the night. Jake grabbed two more logs, putting them on the fire. Buddy and Gaia snuggled up together and were already snoozing for the night. When I turned around, my eyes met Jakes as he stood up from the fire. A warm sensation rushed through my loins, craving his body against mine.

A provocative smile brightened his face. "What?"

I prowled over to him like a lioness, pulling my shirt over my head, and then dropped my pants on the ground. He wrapped his arms around my waist, pulled me close, and pushed his lips against mine. The heat from his lips sent shivers down my spine. He leaned down, cupping his mouth over my breast, and nibbled on my nipple. My fingers slipped under his shirt, running along his six-pack abs. Jake jolted back, smiling as he held my arms.

"Did that tickle?" I laughed.

"No! I'm not ticklish."

"Oh, whatever." I laughed.

Jake pulled his shirt over his broad shoulders, flexing his rock-hard arms and fluffing his hair up. Smiling, I gazed up at him. My heart began aching because I knew no matter what happened between us, I would always love him. I couldn't deny it anymore. I wanted to be with him and no one else. Always and forever.

His smile faded, and he started shaking his head. "What Is it?"

"It's nothing. I, um . . . I just . . . I love you, Jake."

Smiling, Jake's face brightened. "I love you, too."

I reached up, pressing my lips against his as I wrapped my arms around him. Pulling my mouth away, I suckled his neck and followed down to his chest. His smile withered into desire as he looked at my body, slowly devouring my bare flesh. I dove into his lips again as my fingers found their way down to his pants, stroking his erection.

"Lay down," I said.

I dropped to my knees and crawled over his hips, straddling his manhood. My hips moved up and down, rubbing my moist clitoris over with his hard shaft. Shivering, I was dripping with moisture as I excitedly lay over his chest, pressing my breasts against him, and lifted my hips up, guiding his length inside me. Heat rushed through my body as he slid deep inside my crevice. I cradled his member, slowly moving my hips back and forth. My juices dripped down the sides of his shaft as I quivered with excitement.

Jake pressed his lips against my neck, nibbling up to my ear.

His lips grazed my cheek, breathing hot air over my skin. "Fuck me, baby."

I shook my head, and his chest rumbled. He wrapped his

arms around my waist and slithered his fingers over my rump, holding me down. My eyes darted to his as the wolf glared back at me. His member thrust deep inside me, bouncing my body on top of him and pounding inside me. I pushed against his chest, but he held me against him until my climax erupted. Jake slowed his rhythm and released his grip, running his fingers up and down my back, caressing my skin. His lips were hot and traced down my cheek to find my lips. His broad arms folded over my shoulders and held me as his motion sped up again. Our bodies were dancing, folding in and out of each other as one. My climax climbed, and I vibrated as it grew closer.

"Not yet, baby. Oh, I'm going to fill you up."

His head tilted back, and his member hardened as I bounced on top of him. His body jolted, flexing every muscle as his juices shot inside me. Panting, my back arched as I howled, erupting over his rigid member. My body relaxed as I melted into him.

After a few minutes, I finally lifted my head to kiss his lips gently. He wrapped his arms around me and held me tight. A flash of lightning lit the night, trickling shadows along the walls. We both turned our heads, looking outside. A growl from deep in the earth followed, echoing through the mountains. I lay down next to Jake on my side, and he wrapped his arms around me, kissing between my shoulder blades.

"That was some good lovens," he said.

Another rumble rolled through the mountains, quaking the ground underneath us. Jake and I both jumped and looked at the door.

"I guess a big storm is coming in."

Jake walked over to the water jug and poured water over his body, washing off.

A woman's voice echoed, calling my name from the storm outside. "Adele. Adele." Rain poured, seeping inside the cave entrance. "Adele. Come to me, Adele." The woman's voice was crying from afar in the darkness. My body was drawn to her calling. Her voice was controlling me and forcing me to obey her. I stood up, sauntering over to the door, and showered in the rain. Water trickled down my face, plastering my hair against my naked body. Lightning flashed, and a woman stood on the mountain across from me. Her naked body glowed a pearl white with lightning bolts fluctuating throughout her body. Tingling flushed through me, drawing my hair and limbs towards her. My breasts peaked, and my skin was covered in goosebumps.

A burning sensation rose from my toes and crawled through my flesh slowly. Lightning flashed again, and the woman motioned her hands, calling me to her. A burst of white light exploded from the earth and traveled up into the sky, skipping across the clouds. My body reacted to the electricity, igniting with white and red luminous bolts.

"Adele. Adele, don't be afraid. Embrace your power and let the electricity guide you. Let it in. Let . . . it . . . in . . ."

The electricity from the storm was calling me. I yearned for its power. My hands rose into the air in front of me as if I were being pulled towards it.

"Adele! Adele! Del! What are you doing?!"

Jake was standing behind me.

I turned around to look at him. He took a step backward. "You're glowing. Are you okay?"

"Yes, I feel . . . I feel alive."

Panting, I turned my head around, opened my mouth, and exhaled loudly. I stepped out into the rain, standing on the ledge of the entrance, and raised my arms up into the air. My body was numb to the cold water rolling down my skin. I swayed back and forth with the wind — teeter-tottering on the edge of the mountain.

"Del! Please come back inside. Please!" Jake stepped onto

the ledge, wrapping his arms around me, and pulled. "Del! Stop this and come inside. Please!"

My eyes were fluttering and then I heard a monstrous explosion crackle in the sky. I looked up to see the woman's eyes burning into my soul. A bolt of lightning shot up into the sky, bouncing back and forth between the clouds, and then shot back down towards me. I flailed my arms back and threw Jake into the cave just as the lightning struck me, entering my chest. My screams echoed through the mountains as I absorbed the red electricity bolts into my body. It felt like a thousand knives cutting into my flesh as I absorbed the power. My body began to lift into the air, and I floated up over the ledge of the cave. I was hovering over the ground as the power rolled through my body. I opened my eyes and dropped to the ground, hanging from the ledge.

"Del!"

Jake's voice was screaming my name, but my eyes only saw darkness. Blinking, I tried to keep them open, but the darkness was pulling me in. Rain pummeled against my skin, soothing the fire inside me. I was lifted in the air and floated out of the rain.

CHAPTER FORTY-EIGHT: VICTOR

I closed my eyes, concentrating. Her presence was drawing closer and closer to home. I knew it was just a matter of time for her to come looking for me. She was being drawn in, the power forcing her to reunite with me even if she didn't want to face her destiny.

"Victor? Victor, it's morning, sir."

Turning around, I looked out the tent door. Smoke mixed with steam was exhaling from my lips. I nodded and stood up, pulling over my hood. The morning sun blinded me as I stepped out into the daylight. The ground was covered in blocks of ice and moisture from the morning dew. Looking over at the trees, I followed an already-paved path into the forest. Wildlife fled into hiding, and the sounds of morning happiness diminished into a whisper as our group entered the forest. My mind wandered, and the memories of my sister lingered in my cold heart. Alessia's smiling face burned in my mind as I stepped through the trees.

I awoke and saw the bonfire remnants from the night before. My eyes fluttered as I looked up into the sky and saw buzzards circling above me. A sharp pain vibrated through me, paralyzing my limbs as I tried to move. I held my breath, grinding my teeth together. I climbed out of the pile of logs and sat on my knees, looking around. Stumbling, I stood up and started walking towards the house when I saw him. The buzzards weren't circling me. They were circling what was left of him. Father.

Shaking my head, I limped over to the house that was once my home. I pushed the door open to see clothes and garbage strung across the floor. I was abandoned and left to become food for the vultures. She'd left me behind and didn't look back.

"Victor. Victor!" Rick's voice echoed in my ears.

I turned around and saw his rosy cheeks glistening in the sunlight. Steam clouded in front of him as he huffed. He pointed behind me, and I saw a couple hiking the trails in front of us. The woman was watching us, running her finger along the line of men walking with us. Her husband was holding his rifle, cocked and ready. I looked over at Rick, and he nodded back just before he walked away from our group with two men. Our men were dressed in all black, hoods covering their faces, and carrying semi-automatic rifles. Rick spoke with the couple, nodded, and then pointed to us.

A bright smile and nodding consisted of what we knew was a false story to divert the woman. Shaking her head, she turned to her mate and started to stomp away when Rick raised his handgun and walked behind the man, aiming at his skull. Blood splattered, covering the man's jacket, and skirted across the woman's face. A shrill scream echoed through the woods, and then Rick was done. The two hikers were being dragged off somewhere not as noticeable. I turned and started whistling as we continued on.

Chapter Forty-Nine: Jake

I ran over to Del, lying in the cave's entrance, and saw a woman floating over the mountain. She watched me pull Del into the cave and nodded. I nodded back and carried her over to our bed. I walked back over to the door and looked out to see that the woman had disappeared.

I ran back over to Del, shaking her. Her body was burning hot to the touch. I put my hand over her forehead, and an electrical charge tickled my fingers, running down my arm. The hairs on my head lifted and were pulled toward Del's body.

"Del. Adele?" I whispered her name, but her eyes fluttered briefly before she closed them again. The storm gurgled a slight rumble, slowing down outside.

I sat back and watched her sleep until the storm had completely passed.

The next morning, I got out of bed to look outside. It was early morning, and the dew was still hovering over the mountain. I scanned the rock for the mysterious woman from the night before, but there was no sign of her. Rubbing my face, I yawned and walked out to relieve myself.

When I walked back inside, I noticed a burn spot covering the ground of the doorway. Del rolled over onto her side, moaning. I walked over to check on her, touching her new silver mane that streaked the front of her hair. Exhaling, I walked over to the fire and squatted to blow on it to reignite it.

"Hello, Jake."

Spinning around, I saw that there was no one there. The pups were both lying next to the fire asleep. I grabbed my bo staff and knife and walked over to the cave entrance. My heart was pounding in my chest as I trudged down the mountain a few feet. I raised my nose, inhaling a deep breath of the wind blowing from the north. Shaking my head, I walked back up to the cave and sat next to Del.

A cool breeze whistled in the doorway, wafting up to my ear. *Jake.* My head spun around as I searched the cave. I sensed his presence was near and knew he was toying with me. I stood up, squeezing my staff between my fingers.

I will kill him this time and make sure his body burns.

Chapter Fifty: Adele

M y eyes fluttered open, and I heard crackling from the fire. My nose crinkled as I inhaled a deep breath from the smell of burning flesh. Raising up, I felt a sharp pain rip through my chest. I looked down, lifted up my shirt, and saw my skin was branded with a tattoo lightning bolt stamped across my chest. My finger gently skimmed over it, feeling the ruff exterior of my flesh.

Jake sat up and put his hand on my arm. "Hi. How are you feeling?"

I looked around the room, and something seemed out of place. I stood up and walked around, searching.

Shaking my head. "Something's not right. I don't re-mem . . . something feels off."

Jake stood up, walking over to me. "Maybe you should come to lie back down. You've been through a lot the last few days."

"Last few days? I've been sleeping for days?"

A deep growl from thunder rumbled against the mountains.

"Yes, you've been asleep ever since that thing happened. Do you feel okay?"

I nodded, looked around the room, and headed back to the entrance.

Jake ran over and grabbed my hand. "Um, maybe you should stay in tonight. Please?"

My eyes were drawn to the cave entrance. I waited for the flash outside before turning around and heading back to bed.

My eyes blinked, and a flash of lightning bursting through me flooded my mind. I dropped to my knees as a sharp pain shot behind my eye, burning inside my head. Cupping my hands over my face, I inhaled deep breaths.

A glimpse of a woman staring at me from the mountain flashed in my mind. Her eyes glimmered through the darkness, staring into my soul. My body seized as another sharp pain shot behind my eye again, and her voice rang in my head.

Adele, I am the Goddess of the Mountains. You were chosen to rule these mountains as a protector. A dark entity lurks in the darkness waiting for the right moment to strike. Use the power I have given you to stop him. You will know what to do when the time comes, my child.

Jake wrapped his arms around my shoulders, helping me back to bed. I melted back into bed, rolling over and pulling the covers up to my chin. Smiling, Jake put his lips to my forehead.

After a long silence, Jake raised his hand , petting my face. "You scared me. You passed out and didn't wake up. I shook you the next morning, and you just slept."

Shaking my head, I just smiled at him. "I'm okay, just sore, and my head hurts."

"I didn't even go hunt today. I didn't want to leave you alone."

"I'll be okay now. Let's sleep, and tomorrow will be better."

The next morning, I woke up early and got dressed. My feet were sloshing through the mud as I exited the mountain and walked into the forest. I gazed up into the trees, watching the birds singing their morning songs as I did my business. As soon as I finished, another sharp pain started shooting behind my eye, and then a flash of a red-bright light entered my body. I gagged, my breath catching in my throat as tears flooded my cheeks. A breath escaped, and my lungs were heaving. I was coughing as air filled my lungs.

Quivering, I sat upright and opened my eyes. A tingling sensation ran down the back of my neck, alerting me that someone with abilities was nearby. Spinning around, I saw a man watching me. He stood completely still and cocked his head to the side, burning a hole right through me.

"Hello, Adele."

Jolting forward, I turned around to see Jake standing there with a half-smile, watching me. Buddy ran over and flopped down onto his stomach, dragging his back feet behind him until he reached me. He pushed his head up against my shin, grunting. Gaia ran over and sat on one of my boots, yawning. I looked back toward where the man was standing, and he was gone. Jake turned his head and looked, too.

"Why didn't you wake me? What is it? Did you see something?"

"I thought I saw him again." I didn't want to say his name. I swallowed hard, listening to the throbbing pain drum through my head. He was standing there staring at me. I don't know. I . . . um. My head really hurts, Jake."

Squeezing my eyes shut, I cupped my hands over my brow.

"You probably need to eat, honey. Let's try to fish. We can go to the river. Are you up to going?"

"Is it safe to go with him still out there?"

"We need to eat. After that, we will figure out what to do," Jake said.

Nodding, I looked back over to where the man was standing. I squeezed my eyes shut, listening to my heart pounding as a dull pain knocked on the back of my head. Exhaling, I opened my eyes and swallowed hard. Jake was watching me, so I forced a smile and bent down to scratch behind both pups' ears. Jake nodded and led the way back to the river.

An hour had passed, and I heard the water roaring down the river. Jake held his hand up for us to stop and whistled for the dogs to stop. Buddy ran over to me, and Gaia followed, sitting down on my feet. Jake walked out into the opening of the river, looking around. He walked down a few feet and then turned around, waving us to come out.

"I think we can just fish here."

"Okay."

"Are you okay, Del?"

"I'm fine."

Jake set up his pole and threw his line into the water. I walked down the river a little further, dipping my hands into the water, and splashed my face. I went in for a second splash and opened my eyes. Startled, I fell back onto my rump, wiping the water from my face. I slowly crawled back over to the water and looked at my reflection. I'd changed. My eyes glowed an emerald green, and my hair had grown a silver streak out the front of my hairline. I shook my head, my mouth dropping open as I fingered the hair draping my face.

Water ran down my face, dampening my chest as I squeezed my eyes shut and opened them again. As I gazed in the water, a shadow crept up behind my head and opened dark holes where its eyes belonged. Emerald green began glowing through its orifices. I shot up, spinning around to see nothing behind me.

I looked over at Jake, and Jake was casting his line into the water. The pups were sunbathing a few feet behind him. My head whipped back around to see nothing was there.

My eyes look like his eyes. Why? Why is he doing this to me? I don't understand what's happening.

"Del? Will you hand me the water jug?"

I nodded, stumbled over to my bag, pulled it out, and handed it to Jake. He gulped several drinks before handing it back.

"Hey, will you fill it up?"

"Jake?"

"Yeah."

"Jake, my hair. It's . . . and my eyes . . . they're green."

Jake slowly turned to me. "Yes, when everything happened, you changed." His eyes widened as he nodded. I knew he was forcing a smile because he didn't know what else to say. "I still think you're beautiful, so it makes no difference to me."

A single tear rolled down my cheek as my bottom lip started quivering. I nodded, walked over to the water, and looked down to see my reflection stare back at me. I dropped the water jug in, filling it up. I half expected to see him creeping behind me again, but he never reappeared.

After I put up the water jugs, I stared into the forest. The Goddess of the Mountains had warned me of his intentions. I knew he was lurking in there, waiting for us to turn our backs, and then he would pounce.

Jake pulled out a large catfish, dropping it into the sand.

"Del, will you cut his head off? Careful, he's a cat."

I nodded and did as he asked. My eyes darted to the forest several times before settling down in the sand with my arms folded over my knees.

Jake said, "What are you doing?"

"Nothing, just watching you."

Smiling, Jake nodded.

The afternoon was drifting into the evening when Jake decided to give up. He caught two large catfish and lost one with part of his line. He rolled up what he had left of the line and then wrapped up the fish. I stood up and was starting to walk over to him when I dropped to my knees.

Severe sharp pains rattled through my head, stabbing behind my eye. I squeezed my eyes shut and saw him. His back was facing me, and then he slowly turned around. His eyes bore a hole into my soul that was burning through my heart.

I shook my head, but his malevolent smile sent chills down my spine.

I see you, Adele, and I will be meeting you soon enough. You can't run from me. We are . . . connected.

His voice echoed through my head, deepening as his lips hung on the last word he spoke. I dropped into the sand, and my body seized, shivering as he had a hold of me. My eyes blinked open as I tried to focus on Jake's face. He was hovering over me, trying to hold my body still.

A few minutes felt like an hour as my body finally came to a halt, relaxing in the sand. Jake picked me up, hugging me against him. We quickly walked back to the cave, and Jake laid me down in our bed while he cooked the fish. I blinked over at him, watching him sear the fish over the fire.

"How are you feeling?"

"I'm okay, Jake. I'm okay."

He nodded, but I knew he was terrified that I was very sick. I sat up, and we ate our food in silence. Jake cleaned up and threw a couple more logs onto the fire before lying down to sleep.

"I love you, Jake," I said.

He squeezed my waist and put his lips to my ear. "I love you, too, Deli smelly."

Smiling, I squeezed my hands around his and let the sleep come.

Chapter Fifty-One: Adele

I opened my eyes, and the darkness surrounded me. The tent door was flapping, opening, and closing ferociously in the wind. Sharp pains shot through my wrists as I scooted on my rump to the door. A strong gust of wind blew, teasing my freedom as I stared out into the darkness. Oakwood burning wafted in the air, crackling in the hot coals.

The camp appeared empty until I heard his footsteps stomping toward me. Shadows danced along the tent walls making minutes seem like hours as I waited for his debut. I pushed myself back to where I started, and the footsteps approaching my tent stopped. I lay down on my side, closing my eyes.

"Del, wake up!"

I shot up in bed and looked around the room to see Jake snoring next to me. Rubbing my face, I sauntered over to the water jug and raised it. Water ran down my cheeks, dampening my shirt. Wiping my mouth, I walked over to the door and looked out. The sky was clear, with the dismal moon shining through the mountain peaks. My bladder was full, so I walked out and squatted. Once I finished, I walked back up with my arms wrapped around my shoulders, gazing over the mountains.

"Beautiful night."

My head whipped around, and he was standing there staring. Squeezing my eyes shut, I opened them after a few moments. A cool breeze was wisping over the place he was standing. Shivering, I quickly went back into the cave to see

Jake squirming in bed as he exhaled a deep breath under the covers. I grabbed two logs and sat down next to the fire. Inhaling a deep breath, I swallowed back a lump in my throat as I stirred the glowing coals. I swiped away runaway tears, looking at the door and then over at Jake.

He was toying with me, and all I wanted to do was just go home and have a normal life again. I was tired of his games. I was tired of being afraid.

I got dressed, sat down next to the fire, and waited for the sun to rise. Once the sun peeked through the mountains, I grabbed my bo staff and shoved a knife into my boot. I turned, staring at Jake and my pups for a long moment. I knew it could be the last time I would ever see them again. A warm tear rolled down and stung my bottom lip. Nodding, I inhaled a deep breath and exited the cave, following the path down the mountain and entering the forest.

The morning was cool as I walked through the remaining dew settled over the ground. Birds were just waking up from their nightly slumber. I held my bo staff close to my chest, following the long walk back to where Dad's cabin used to reside. Jake's smiling face was flashing through my mind as I walked further away from the cave we had grown to learn to survive in. After all this time of him being out of my life, I finally had a chance to get to know him again.

I'll make this right and have the life I always dreamed of having with Jake.

Shaking my head, I knew that this was something I had to do alone. I knew that I could beat Victor and free our lives of his horror. My mind was racing with what-if's when I sensed something nearby.

Tingling raised the hairs on the back of my head and ran down my neck and spine. I slowly looked around and spotted a man standing there, glaring at me. I gripped my staff with both hands, staring back at him when I realized I recognized him. His ghostly white hair and glowing crystal-blue eyes stood out like a sore thumb in the forest. His skin seemed almost translucent against the towering oaks surrounding him. A mischievous smile revealed sharp fangs with bright red gums. He was the man who had watched me through my kitchen window.

I took a step toward him, and before I knew what was happening, I was knocked off my feet and landed on my rump. Coughing, I rolled over, gasping for air. The man stood in front of me with a malicious grin.

"Aw, what's wrong, stupid girl. Did you fall down?"

I rolled over onto my stomach, pushing myself up, and clutched my bo staff again. I stepped forward, swinging at his head. He disappeared from my sight, came up behind me, and slammed his fist into my face.

Raising my bo staff up, I swung and missed. He disappeared again, and then he reappeared in front of me. He headbutted me, and I flew back, landing hard on my rump again. My face burned as I choked, trying to catch my breath. I sat up, and warm liquid was pouring from my nose. Anger rushed through my body, flowing up my spine and into my arms. My bo staff glistened with white light, glowing with readiness and will.

I focused my power and saw the man running towards me in slow motion. His legs pounded down, one after another, with immense speed. His hands glowed a pearl white color, and his face was transforming into a demonic being as he ran.

Aiming my staff, I let go. A fireball shot out of my staff and side-swiped him. His run slowed, and he stumbled, dropping to the ground. I walked over to him, aiming my staff at his temple. He appeared to be knocked out. His glowing hands calmed down and faded back into normal hands. His eyes remained closed, and his body was still. I slowly walked closer to him, holding my staff up. His chest moved as he took long deep breaths. I stepped back and was turning around when I felt a sharp pain in the back of my head. My legs buckled, and I started collapsing into the ground. My head pounded as I tried to open my eyes. I raised my staff up, and it was jerked from my fingers. My hands reached in the air as a hard blow hit me again, blasting a sharp pain in my eye. I tried to blink my eyes open, but one of my eyes was sealed shut.

"Jake, Jake."

My body was lifted up into the air, and I floated over the path home. I closed my eyes and let the darkness come.

Chapter Fifty-Two: Adele

I opened my eyes and looked over to see a tent door flapping ferociously in the wind. Shaking my head, I realized the nightmare taunting me, night after night, had come true. Tears rolled down my face and pooled in the dirt against my lips. Dried blood and salty residue burned my tongue. Inhaling a deep breath, I gritted my teeth and tried to move my bound hands and ankles. Pain vibrated my body as I rolled over onto my back, sitting up on my rump. Blinking, I tried to focus, but my vision was distorted. As I slowly started scooting on my backside toward the door, I heard men's voices echoing through the flap.

"Sir, I've alerted him that she's here. He's on his way back."

"Keep an eye on her."

"Yes, sir."

I peeked outside and saw two men walking away from my tent in different directions. The table with pictures remained standing, along with a great bonfire in the middle of the camp.

Where is he? Where could Victor be? I thought he was here and waiting for me to come. I need to get out of these ropes and be ready when he returns.

I scooted back to the middle of the tent, looking around the room. It was empty except for a few boxes. I started scooting over to the boxes when I heard a car pull up into the camp. *It's him.* I sensed his presence. I felt him pulsating through me.

He can feel me, too. How? How can he feel me? It doesn't make any sense. I don't know what's happening. I don't understand.

I inhaled a deep breath and tried swallowing back the

tears. Victor was inside my head. He could feel my emotions. He could see my fears.

No. No. No. What's happening? How's this possible? I don't understand.

I inhaled another breath, trying to calm my breathing.

Concentrate Adele. Focus. Push him out. Clear your mind. Get out. Get out. Get out.

Car doors slammed, and my heart was pounding in my chest.

He's coming. He's walking towards me now. Focus, focus, focus.

I turned, waiting for him to enter the tent. His footsteps walked along the side, stomping down into the dirt. A hand reached in, holding the tent door open. A tall man with a black hood covering his head entered the tent. He walked to the back of the tent and grabbed a wooden stool, pulled it over in front of me, and sat down on it.

He pushed back his hood, revealing his midnight blue hair, gazing at me with glowing emerald eyes. A smile turned up his lips, revealing a sharp set of fangs overhanging the bottom of his lip. He pulled out a cigarette pack from his pocket and put one in his mouth. He offered me one, and I sat still, staring back at him. He nodded, lighting his butt, and exhaled a long breath of smoke.

"Hello, Adele. I've been waiting for you to come and visit me. How have you been?"

I shook my head, blinking. Sharp pains shot through the top of my skull, racing down my neck and back. I knew what he was doing, and I was fighting it. I slowly closed my eyes and opened them again, forcing a wall up and barricading my mind from his evil. I felt his dark intentions chipping away, trying to force his way in to control me.

"I know who you are. What do you want, Victor?"

"Ah, so you know my name. Hmm. If you know so much, girl, you should already know what I want. Tell me what you think you know, and we can compare notes." Chuckling, he rocked back as he exhaled a long breath.

"You don't scare me, Victor." I adjusted myself, rolling over onto my knees, and looked straight ahead at him. My focus darted to the tent door, and I saw two men standing outside. I looked back over at Victor, studying him. His gaze never left mine as he inhaled another long drag of his cigarette.

"Well, I'm waiting, girl. Tell me what you think you know."

"I know that you're following us because you want Jake back. You want to capture him to use as a weapon. You want to use me as bait so that he'll come back to you willingly." I inhaled a deep breath, looking down at the ground. My eyes slowly glided back up at him as I smiled. "You don't know what I am capable of, and when this is over, I will kill you once and for all."

Victor broke from my stare and held up his cigarette butt, staring at it as he rolled it around between his thumb and first finger. He flicked his ashes in the air and took one last long drag before dropping it into the dirt and squishing it with his boot. He looked at me and broke out into laughter, cackling hysterically.

I stared at him, forcing my power to awaken. The fire inside me flowed like a river, violently racing through my veins and begging to be unleashed. I dropped my head, looking down to see my body begin to glow. White shards of electricity ran up and down my limbs like waves of water.

I closed my eyes, focusing on the binds around my arms and legs. The power inside me ignited and burned through the ropes, sizzling against my skin. The ropes dropped onto the ground, smoking as I stood up and stared into Victor's eyes.

He glared at me with a malevolent smile, cocking his head to the side.

Raising my hands, I forced my magic to create a fireball and fired it at Victor's head. He lifted one hand, and with a flick of his wrist, he boomeranged the fireball back toward me. I dropped to the floor, barely dodging the hit. Hovering in the dirt, I looked back and saw a smoking ring ignited in the tent wall.

I slowly turned back to face Victor, panting. I stood back up, and he raised his hand into the air, making a fist. My throat constricted, and I felt like something was squeezing around it, strangling me. Gagging, I ran my fingers over my neck, searching for relief. Victor's knuckles turned white from the force he put behind his fist. His eyes were glistening in the darkness as he squeezed harder and harder.

My body rose into the air, dangling my legs and fighting to breathe as I was gasping for one last bit of air. My eyes bulged open, and I raised my hands into the air, beckoning my power. I let go of the pain and pushed my fury through my fingertips, shooting another fireball at Victor. He raised his other arm, only this time, it sideswiped his wrist, scalding him. His hand dropped, and I collapsed into the dirt.

Coughing, vomit spewed out of me and puddled in front of my face as I shook, inhaling deep breaths of air. I looked up, and Victor's arm was glowing a green hue. He trudged over to me, glaring down. I rolled over and looked up at him, forcing a smile through my gritted teeth.

He lunged forward, kicking me in the face. Blood oozed from my nose, pooling in the dirt in front of me. I rolled over onto my stomach, inhaling a deep breath before pushing myself back up. Victor walked back over to his stool, sat down, and popped another cigarette in his mouth.

"I'll let you in on a little secret, Adele, before I end everything." He puffed on his cigarette and then let out a long breath of smoke before speaking. "I knew your parents. We were close."

"Ha! Liar! My parents would never befriend a person like you. They were good people. My dad was a great man, and he helped people. He would never be friends with a killer like you. Try again, asshole!"

I slowly wobbled, pushing myself to my feet. My power fluctuated as it was building back up. I looked up at Victor, raising both hands in the air. My palms quivered as I inhaled a deep breath, letting go. Fireballs shot out of my hands, blasting against Victor. He raised his hand, swiping them away as if he was swatting a fly. Vibrating, I tightened my stance, placing my feet firmly down, and fired again. I used everything I had and watched him react as if nothing was happening. He continued to rattle on, talking and talking.

"Bill was just like me. Only he hid it better." Victor stood up and started walking toward me.

I slid my feet backward, trying to move away from him, but I grew weaker. He stopped in front of me and looked into my eyes. My power extinguished, and I dropped my hands to my sides, panting. A drop of blood flowed from my nose, running down into my mouth. The metallic taste burned my tongue, turning my stomach.

"You see, I was never here for Jake. I was looking for you. When you returned to Bill's cabin and absorbed his powers, I knew it was time for me to make my move." Inhaling a deep breath, Victor's fangs protruded as a mischievous smile arched his brow. "We are connected because we are related. Your mother, Alessia, was my sister. Your father, Bill, killed my father and took his power. The power I was supposed to inherit when he died. I'm here to take back what's rightfully mine." His face started to transform into something demonic as he placed his hand on my forehead, closing his eyes.

My strength failed, and I was frozen—a prisoner to Victor's grip. Stabbing pain cut through my head like a razor, shattering what little of me that was left. My body started convulsing when he poked a hole into my wall and started absorbing my power. My eyes rolled in the back of my head, and I knew that my body was dying. I felt myself drifting away.

"Adele. Adele."

Blinking my eyes open, I saw a flash of lightning appear. The Goddess of the Mountains appeared in the tent behind Victor.

I could hear her voice speaking in my head. *You can do this, Adele. Don't give up. Fight! Fight back, and you'll win!*

I gazed into Victor's eyes and saw his face glistening a deep emerald green that fluctuated with black shards of electricity throughout his body. I closed my eyes and put my hands against his chest, letting go.

"No!"

Electricity shot out of me, piercing into him. Victor's body folded into itself as he dropped to the ground, quivering. I stepped towards him, and a hard blow hit me in the chest. My body drifted through the air and fell hard, landing on my back. Coughing, I gasped for a breath as the wind was knocked out of me. I rolled over onto my side, and another hard blow smashed against the back of my head. My eyes closed.

Chapter Fifty-Three: Adele

"Del, wake up. Adele, please wake up."

I opened my eyes and saw darkness surrounding me. Swallowing, I tasted mud and dried blood on my lips. I tried to sit up and realized I was lying on the ground face down. Grunting, I rolled over onto my back. My eye was swollen shut, and all I could hear was the tent door flapping in the wind.

"Del, it's me, Jake."

Muffled sounds were echoing through my head. My eye fluttered open and closed as I tried to turn my head. I winced in pain from a hard tug pulling on my arm.

"It's okay. It's me, honey." Jake put his face up to mine. "I'm so sorry. Let's get out of here before he comes back."

Jake turned me over and started cutting the rope around my wrists and ankles. My limbs dropped, and I shuddered as the pain was rumbling through my body. Jake put his arm around my waist, draped my arm over his shoulders, and pulled me up. Gritting my teeth, I felt warm tears rolling down my cheeks. Jake walked me over to the side of the tent and sat me on the ground. He opened a slit cut along the tent, poking his head out.

"Okay, you go first. Just wait for me on the other side. I'll push Buddy after you, and then we will move together. Okay?"

"Wait, where's . . . where's Gaia?"

"She wouldn't leave the forest. I'm sure she's just waiting for us."

I nodded, and Jake opened the hole, so I could crawl through. We were in a row of tents that lined up, and on the other side was another row of tents parallel to ours. I could smell the fire burning close by and food being cooked. Jake crawled on all fours, looking both ways. A walkway went between the rows of tents, leading straight to the big fire.

"There's a path going straight to the fire that's cooking food. Several men are standing around the fire holding guns. I'm going to check behind the tent and see if there's a safer path to take."

Jake walked behind the tent, disappearing. He came back around, waving for me to follow him. I took his hand, and he led the way along the tent. He stopped and pointed at the forest that was straight ahead. He continued forward and stopped with his finger over his lips. He pointed to the right and then the left, nodding his head. Voices of men approaching echoed through the tents as they walked back and forth guarding the territory.

Jake looked back at me and toward the voices again. Shaking his head, he turned to me, gazing into my eyes for a long moment before he wrapped his arms around my shoulders. His heart was pounding against my cheek as I lay against his muscular chest. He pulled back and kissed me, holding me tight. Shaking my head, I sensed the words beating from his heart before he spoke.

"I love you, Adele. I've always loved you. When we were kids, you gave me that sandwich . . . It was love at first sight. I always wanted to be a part of your life, but I was scared I'd get you hurt or killed." He put his hands on my cheeks and kissed me slowly. "I should have dealt with him long ago. I need to end this now. He'll never leave us alone if I don't." Shaking his head, he exhaled a long breath. "I want a life with you. I want a real start, and the only way we can do that is if I fight him. I have to take care of this. Victor has to be stopped."

I shook my head. "No, Jake. No, it's not what you think. Please stay with me. Don't go. Please!" I wanted to tell him everything, but there was no time. Men were everywhere, and I was in no condition to fight. My heart pounded, drumming in my ears.

"It'll be okay, I promise." He kissed me and hugged me again.

"Please, Jake. It's not what you think. Please wait!" Jake let me go, and his body began changing as he turned away from me.

His voice was deepening, and a low growl escaped his chest. "Run now!"

Turning around, I limped out into the view of all the men. My legs pumped on the ground as tears rolled down my cheeks, blinding my vision and burning my nostrils.

I entered the forest and hid behind an old oak tree, peering into the camp.

A loud crackle behind me caused me to look back and see a man coming up behind me. A sharp pain pierced between my eyes, and a brutal hit in the back knocked me off my feet. I open my eyes to see my dog's body lying motionless on his side, with blood dripping from his mouth. "No, Buddy. No!"

It's over, and we're all going to die. My dog's gone. Jake's gone. There's nothing left now.

My hair was pulled up over my head, guiding me to stand up.

"Shut up, bitch!"

I was punching and kicking at the man, but he reached around and slapped my face.

"Stop it! Grab her and shut her up!"

A sharp pain blasted the back of my head, and I closed my eyes.

CHAPTER FIFTY-FOUR: JAKE

I heard Vahn's voice in my head. *Fight, Jake. Fight.* His voice echoed in my mind. *Fight.* I watched Del hobble to the trees before I turned around and stepped out into the view of men walking up from the middle of the tents. I called on the beast as I headed straight for the enemy.

Growling vibrated through me as my body towered in height. My legs pounded down, running towards the enemy at full speed. Gunshots fired, whisking past me as I stormed the camp. Screams echoed, shuddering through my canine ears. I sliced through the men with my claws, one after another, stopping anyone who attempted to get in my way. I set my sight on him, and I wasn't stopping until he was dead.

Victor stepped out with a butt burning in his mouth, watching me drive towards him. He inhaled a deep drag, blowing out a gray cloud of smoke. A smile crossed his face as I drew closer and closer. Stopping, I stared at him, a hundred feet away, face-to-face. Grinning, he lifted his gun and shot. I kept moving swiftly back and forth, missing every bullet intended for me. Victor shook his head, dropped his weapon, and turned to run into one of the tents.

I followed him, throwing the tent door open. As soon as I crossed the entrance, Victor disappeared, and I felt a heavy blast slam across my chest. My hair blew in the wind as my body glided through the air. I dropped down into the dirt, landing hard on my back. Gasping, I turned over and coughed as I tried to inhale a breath. Victor walked over, holding a large piece of wood.

He threw it down and turned to walk out of the tent. "Just stay down, wolf."

I leaped off the ground, trying to jump on his back. My body stopped in mid-air, floating as if I was being held up by someone or something.

Victor slowly turned around with his hand extended in the air, quivering. His face was maimed with a blackened char across his neck that stretched over his eye. He blinked, looking up at me with one emerald eye and one silver eye.

His hand lowered, and I dropped hard into the dirt. The men standing next to him walked over to me and bound my wrists together. The pain slowly started burning my wrists and paralyzing my fingers. I looked down to see a small cloud of smoke billow up from where the binds were wrapped around me.

A glimmer of silver reflected off the bit of light flapping in the tent. Heat wrapped around my limbs, rushing down my veins and stunting my use. My arms seized first, and then my legs began quivering. My body began dwindling down into my human form, rupturing the wolf and his existence. They pulled me to my feet, dragging me out of the tent naked. Victor's face lit up with a malevolent smile as he watched me being taken away.

It was a trap. Victor had planned to trick me the whole time by using her as bait. The men threw me down into the dirt in front of the fire. A man walked around in front of me and stood there. I looked up to see Rick. He was shaking his head. I fought through the pain, kicking my feet out, and tried to hit him. My skin sizzled as the shackles were burning welts into my bare flesh. Gritting my teeth, I grumbled in my chest.

"All this time and you never wondered why we looked for you out of all other people. *Stupid.* You are just a big dumb wolf, aren't you?" He threw his head back, cackling.

He turned to walk away, and I stretched my leg out and

tripped Rick, knocking him down in front of me. I wrapped my legs around his neck on the ground, choking him. His body vibrated as he slapped my legs. Two soldiers walked up, pointing their guns at me. I challenged them with my gaze as I looked up.

"Let him go." Victor's voice rang from behind me.

I squeezed harder, and Rick's body finally went limp. I released my legs and let his lifeless body drop to the ground. Blood flowed from his mouth, pooling into the dirt. Rick deserved to die. He was my friend, or so I thought, and he betrayed me like everyone else. The two soldiers pulled his body away, and Victor walked out in front of me, inhaling his cigarette.

"What do you want from me, Victor? I'm here. Let's end this. Here and now. Me and you!"

Victor exhaled a long drag off his cigarette and started laughing. "Do you honestly think after all this time that I was after you? I told you who I wanted, and as I said before, you led me right to her." Victor turned around and stepped over to the side. "Look. There she is now."

My heart pounded in my chest when I saw her. The dream I had before flashed before my eyes as I watched the events unfold and come true.

I looked up to see Del being carried back from the forest. Her body hung lifeless in someone's arms.

"Just a matter of time, wolf."

Chapter Fifty-Five: Adele

I opened my eyes and heard the tent door flapping in the wind.

"No, no, no. This can't be happening. This can't be happening." Tears rolled down my face as I peered through the darkness.

I pushed myself up onto my rump and looked down to see rope binding my wrists but not my ankles. I inhaled a deep breath, working my feet towards the tent door. The day had turned into night as the moon had risen to the occasion. I peeked outside and saw Jake sitting by the fire. His head was hanging down into his lap with his eyes closed. He was in human form with bloody gashes on his chest and legs.

"Jake. Jake," I said.

Jake looked over at me, and his mouth dropped open. I nodded, tears rolling down my cheeks. He nodded back and then looked around the campsite. I scooted back into the tent, looking around in the darkness. My heart thumped in my chest as the tent flapped ferociously in the wind, anxiously warning me of what was to come. I knew Jake wouldn't be giving up, nor would I.

I needed a plan. First, I needed to free myself from the rope. I scooted back toward where I'd started, closing my eyes. The electricity flowed through me like a current. I envisioned the bounds around my wrists and began burning a hole through its side. The pungent smell was drifting through the wind and out into the camp. The rope dropped onto the ground, and I stood up and ran over to the tent door again.

Jake was gone, and his shackles were lying next to the fire. A round of gunshots began ringing through the camp, and a group of men sprinted past my tent door. Screams followed, with more rounds of gunshots echoing through the darkness. I stepped back, looking over at the rope. I ran over and threw it off to the side.

I stopped and looked over at the door. I felt him drawing near. *Victor*. He was headed towards my tent. Anger radiated through him, driving him to me.

I heard him growling in his mind. "I'm finishing this. I'll kill them all if I have to."

I ran around in a circle. I didn't know what to do. I sensed Victor drawing closer and closer. I quickly dropped onto my rump, flopping over onto my side with my hands clasped behind me. Victor stormed into the tent, dragging his leg and holding a gun. He limped over to me, grabbed my shoulder, and pulled me up. I gripped my fists together tightly behind my back, pretending to be tied up. A trail of blood followed him as he walked.

He jerked my arm, gritting his teeth. "Stand up, girl! This is ending now!"

His scowl glistened in the darkness as he glared down at me. I realized I'd maimed his face and blinded one of his eyes. A smirk arched my lips and lit up my face. His malicious smile hardened, and he slapped me across the cheek with the back of one of his hands.

"You won't be smiling for long, girl. I'm about to end you and your stupid wolf."

Victor stepped in front of me, cupping his hands over my shoulders, and glared into my eyes. Nodding, he closed his eyes and began whispering something under his breath. The heat from his fingers rushed down my shoulders, burning my flesh.

"No, stop. Stop!"

He opened his eyes, and they were black as night. He was chanting something over and over again. I closed my eyes and tried to fight him off, but a mist-like substance enclosed my body like a barrier, preventing me from moving or using my power. My vision blurred as tears rolled down my cheeks, burning my flesh as my lips quivered.

"Please, stop. Please." I could only beg for mercy. I was at his will and had no power over my body.

Victor opened his eyes, staring down at me with a demonic gaze. "Now, let's go lure out your wolf."

He dragged me out of the tent, walking me over to the front of the fire. The full moon beamed bright with millions of crystals shining in the sky. Steam was blowing through my lips as I limped beside him. I scanned the area, looking for Jake. The camp was eerily quiet and littered with bloody bodies.

"Jake!" Victor shoved the gun into my side as he screamed. "Jake, come out, or I will end her life here and make you watch!"

I saw Jake step through the trees from inside the forest. He was in wolf form, somehow holding a gun.

"That's it," Victor said.

Time slowed down as I watched Jake emerging from the trees. Victor's finger lingered over the trigger as he was slowly lifting his arm. Frozen, I felt my lips quiver as I tried to take back control of my body. Closing my eyes, I inhaled a deep breath and exhaled slowly. My power teeter-tottered up and down inside me, wanting to awaken. Fighting to emerge. The electricity inside me burned, hammering against the barrier. Throbbing pounded inside my head as warm blood streamed down my face.

"Del, open your eyes and focus."

I opened my eyes to see Dad stepping out from behind a tent and nodding at me. His lips didn't move, but I heard his whispers in my heart.

"You're strong and can beat him. Focus. You can do this!"

A cool sensation started trickling down my neck and spine. I listened to my body, letting the electricity ignite and flood my veins. Pulsating, alive, and ready for a fight. I was awakened. I embraced the pain and used it to grow stronger. I wasn't afraid anymore. I could control my power. I released my grip, turning to face Victor.

"No." I inhaled a deep breath and screamed. "No!" My voice shuddered through the camp, echoing into the trees of the forest.

I broke through the barrier, banishing the smokey mist around me. I reached my hands up to Victor's face, cupping his cheeks. The magic flowed like a volcano erupting through my fingers. My body was glowing a bright white light, and bolts of electricity charged into him. All of my rage, sorrow, and pain were imploding into him. I wanted him to suffer. I wanted him to pay for everything he took from me — my family, my home, and my life. I wasn't going to let him take any more. I wanted him to die and never come back. My mouth widened as the screams flowed over my lips. Drumming in my ears pulsated through my body as my power was fully awake.

Victor's body started seizing as he collapsed to the ground. His skin boiled, and his flesh started melting off his bones and seeping into the dirt. My hands broke free, and I collapsed next to him, trembling.

Jake walked up in wolf form and watched Victor's body disintegrate into the earth.

Victor's flesh bubbled, and steam hissed as the last remnant of his being folded onto itself.

Jake knelt down, wrapping his arms around me as his body transformed back into his human self.

Tears began streaming down my cheeks. "I'm so glad you're okay."

Jake stood up, pulled me to my feet, and held me tight. "The sun will be up soon."

"Yeah."

A sizzling sound screeched through the ground, and a gray smoke-like mist rose from the earth where Victor was lying. The mist hovered in the air above him and began circling me, and then started flowing into my body like a cyclone. My body seized and started shimmering with a bright white light. A sharp pain shot through me and heat rose from my head, cascading down the rest of my body. I rose into the air as the power immersed itself inside me. A lightning bolt shot up from deep inside the earth and slowly lowered my body to the ground. Jake reached out, touched my face, and ran his fingers down my hair. Electricity fluctuated over my flesh like static, shocking him. As he pulled back, I turned to look at him.

"Your hair. It . . . it turned completely silver, and your eyes are glowing a deep emerald green."

I brushed my fingers through my hair as it was transforming into a luminous silver. Tingling rushed down the back of my head as I blinked and realized my vision was evolving.

The trees guarding the forest exhaled a long breath and fluttered in the sky as if waving to me for the first time. Animals that scurried deep into the woods stopped and sensed that I had embraced my power as one of the most powerful magical beings.

I realized, at that moment, not only could wildlife feel me, but also everyone else with magic inside them.

Jake watched me as I scanned the area around us. My body vibrated with white shards of electricity that flowed through my limbs. Closing my eyes, I listened to the different species of magical creatures. Whispers wafted through the wind and gradually turned into screams. Tremendous pain shattered through my head, and red shards filtered through me.

Shaking my head, I opened my eyes. "I want to go home."

Jake nodded as he walked over and grabbed clothes off one of the dead men lying on the ground. He helped me stand up, and we walked back to the forest, where little Gaia greeted us. She was lying next to Buddy, panting in the grass.

Jake squatted down, putting his hand over Buddy's midsection. "I can help him, but there's something I have to do first. Wait here."

Shaking my head, I raise my hand up to stop him. "Don't go back there."

"Just one last time."

I watched Jake walk back over to the camp, searching for something. He stopped next to one of the jeeps and grabbed something from the back. A red canister. He walked over to the far end of the camp and started pouring. He repeated the process for each end of the campsite, then finally walked over to Victor's ashes. He stood over him for a long moment before finishing off the can. Jake walked back to me, shaking his head and patting his pockets. I nodded, lifting my hand up, and a white bolt of electricity flowed from my fingertips and struck the ground of the campsite. Flames began to ignite in the middle of the tents and proceeded to follow the paths of gasoline. We stood and watched as fire engulfed the entire camp. Jake's fingers intertwined with mine as he looked over at me, smiling.

"Let's go home."

"Okay."

The End

ABOUT THE AUTHOR

I live on a beautiful lakefront property in Texas. I enjoy gardening, fishing, and being outdoors. When I am not spending time with my family and pack of rescued four-leggers, I am sitting on the porch with a cup of coffee and my laptop.